My Daughter's Lies

BOOKS BY JULIA ROBERTS

My Mother's Secret

The Woman on the Beach

The Dilemma

THE LIBERTY SANDS TRILOGY

Life's a Beach and Then...

If He Really Loved Me...

It's Never Too Late to Say...

Christmas at Carol's

Carol's Singing

Alice in Theatreland

Time for a Short Story

One Hundred Lengths of the Pool

As J.G. Roberts

THE DETECTIVE RACHEL HART SERIES

1. *Little Girl Missing*
2. *What He Did*
3. *Why She Died*

My Daughter's Lies

JULIA ROBERTS

bookouture

Published by Bookouture in 2024

An imprint of Storyfire Ltd.
Carmelite House
50 Victoria Embankment
London EC4Y 0DZ

www.bookouture.com

ISBN: 978-1-83525-382-3
eBook ISBN: 978-1-83525-381-6

In memory of Sadie Walsh.
27th January 1925 – 14th January 2024

ONE

MELISSA

23 June 2023

The function room is warm, filled to capacity with high-spirited teenagers on a balmy early-summer evening, but I'm pretty sure that's not the cause of the beads of perspiration forming on my top lip.

Nor is it because I'm about to deliver the speech that my husband, Steve, was going to give up until a few minutes ago. He's been unusually quiet since we took our places at the top table. Come to think of it, he has been unusually quiet since yesterday evening when my best friend, Sadie, who has flown over from New York especially for our daughter Ruby's eighteenth birthday party, came to our house for dinner. Maybe his nerves were already starting to build at the thought of presenting to a room full of teenagers who would be at Ruby's party to drink, dance and have fun. They wouldn't be there to listen to a fifty-something wax lyrical about his perfect daughter.

He seized his opportunity to bow out of delivering the speech I've painstakingly crafted over the past couple of weeks with hopefully the right blend of humour and pride when I reached for his hand under the table to give it a reassuring squeeze. He leaned towards me for what I thought was going to be a peck on the cheek but instead whispered in my ear, 'You do it. You're so much better at this sort of stuff than me.'

I'm not so sure about 'better', but there's no denying I'm more experienced at communicating with people than Steve is, although it's usually while sitting behind a giant microphone from the safety of a soundproofed studio.

I saw the look in his eyes as I turned to question his plea. It was somewhere between fear and panic.

'Are you sure?' I mouthed silently to him.

Turning eighteen is a big moment in our daughter's life and I wanted him to give the speech after the part he'd played in getting Ruby to agree to a party. But it's out of his comfort zone and I didn't want to force him.

He nodded, visibly relaxing when I mouthed, 'Okay.'

I could do without the onset of a hot flush as I'm about to get up from the table and take my place on stage. The beads of perspiration on my top lip have now joined together to form a salty moustache and a rivulet of moisture is trickling down my spine.

Reaching for my napkin, I surreptitiously dab at my top lip just as Sadie taps her dessert spoon against the side of her glass to gain everyone's attention. The volume of noise doesn't diminish, so she pushes her chair back from the table for greater impact exactly as I'm doing the same thing. For what can only be a millisecond, we stand facing each other on opposite sides of a round table strewn with party poppers and shiny table confetti. I'm not sure what I read in her expression before her eyes flick onto Steve's face, then back to mine, her eyebrows raised. I give an almost apologetic shrug. She'll have to wait for an explanation about the last-minute change of plan.

One of the teenagers shouts out, 'Speech,' and the rest of

the room turns it into a good-natured chant. 'Speech, speech, speech, speech!' echoes around the room as cutlery is banged on the tabletops.

Ruby buries her head in her hands. She asked to see what I had written to check it wouldn't be too embarrassing to sit through in a room filled with her friends, but I refused, promising her that a) I would keep it short, b) her dad would be delivering it, and c) Auntie Sadie would have final approval. That seemed to satisfy her at the time, so, like Sadie, she must be wondering why it's me getting to my feet rather than her dad.

Considering Sadie moved to New York before Ruby was born, they have a surprisingly close bond. Ruby insisted on coming to Heathrow with me to collect Sadie despite it being in the middle of revising for her A level exams.

'I've put in all the work already, Mum,' she said by way of explanation. 'If I don't know the answers by now, a couple of hours of revision isn't going to make any difference.'

Our daughter has always been pragmatic, but maybe that's because she has been blessed with so much. Not only is she predicted three A stars in her recently completed A levels, but she is also the star pupil at Milsom Radcliffe, the dance academy she has attended since she was five years old. And, if all that isn't enough, she is far and away the most beautiful girl in the room, and that's not me wearing the rose-tinted glasses that many mothers do – at least, I don't think it is.

Unlike me, she has blonde waist-length hair, blue eyes bordering on violet, and a size-ten hourglass figure. It could be argued that I also have an hourglass figure, it's just that my hourglass is more filled with the sands of time. It's a few years since I've seen a size ten, or even a size twelve to be honest, but I'm more comfortable in my own skin now than I've ever been.

I'm conscious of everyone's eyes on me, including Ruby's best friend, Megan, who is sat at her side. She's gazing at me from under her long brown lashes coated with mascara, with a mildly surprised expression on her face. All of our close group knew it should have been Steve about to take his place behind the lectern, so they must all be wondering why he is not.

Sadie retakes her seat, but I feel her eyes following me as I make my way on to the stage. I'm not going to lie, it's slightly unnerving. I hope she doesn't think that I've convinced Steve to let me give the speech. We discussed it at length during our online party-planning sessions and agreed that it would be nice for Ruby's dad to take centre stage for a change. I want to tell Sadie that it wasn't my choice, but that will have to wait as there are now a hundred pairs of eyes focused on me, waiting for me to start and, more importantly, finish so that the party bit of the evening can properly begin.

'Firstly, before we talk about Ruby,' I say, shooting my daughter a glance, 'I want to thank you all for coming and getting into the spirit of things with your amazing costumes.'

I'm not just saying it. I've been truly impressed by the effort most of Ruby's friends have made to come in fancy dress. My daughter looks almost ethereal as Elsa from *Frozen*, with her long blonde hair caught back off her face in a thick braid which is falling over her left shoulder. My mum, Linda, dusted off her sewing machine and did an incredible job in following her granddaughter's meticulous instructions. The off-the-shoulder bodice fits snugly with sheer sleeves attached and a flowing train in the same blue fabric which almost matches my daughter's eyes.

At her side, Megan is dressed as Anna from *Frozen* – an obvious choice once Ruby had decided on Elsa. Over the years, the two have been more like sisters than friends. Megan's hair is a coppery brown rather than red, not dissimilar to Sadie's, although I'm pretty sure hers will be courtesy of trips to the hairdresser if my own grey roots are anything to go by. Otherwise, Megan's costume is very authentic. Mum said it was easier to make as the fabric wasn't so tricky to work with, but she would have been happy to oblige no matter what Megan had chosen. She's also an only child, but her parents are very different from Steve and me. I wouldn't exactly say they are disinterested in her, but it has always been down to us to take both girls to dancing competitions and have the sleepovers at our house. We haven't minded at all. I was an only child, so I'm fully aware of how lonely it can be. We didn't want that for Ruby, or Megan for that matter.

Some of the boys have been a little less imaginative than the girls, but Troy Hanson from Ruby's class at school would probably win the best costume prize if there was one. He's quite a chunky lad and tall with it and has fully embraced the brief and come as Shrek, complete with sticky-out ears stitched on to the green skullcap covering his hair. I can't help wondering if he's given any thought as to how he'll remove the green make-up on his face, neck and hands. If not, he'll spend the next few days looking as though he's about to throw up.

As I raise the speech aloft, I notice a slip of paper fall out from between the sheets and spiral down towards the floor.

'One minute,' I say, bending to retrieve whatever has fallen, a smile still playing at the corners of my mouth at the thought of a green-tinged Troy going about his day. The smile instantly disappears and I'm glad of the temporary protection of the lectern when I see what is written on the slip of paper in block capitals and red ink:

SHE'S NOT WHO YOU THINK SHE IS

My pulse is racing as I take hold of the paper and screw it into a small ball, which I conceal in the palm of my hand. Slowly I get back to a standing position, gripping the sides of the lectern for support. Everyone is waiting for me to launch into a speech proclaiming how wonderful my daughter is.

Everyone, that is, except the person who put the slip of

paper in my notes. They must be in this room. I checked the speech papers were in order moments before we all took our places for dinner, and I haven't noticed anyone leaving, or any spare seats. I'm just surprised that I didn't see anyone approach the lectern and fiddle with the pages of the speech, and yet someone must have. How else could the note have got there?

Gazing out on the sea of expectant faces, I try to compose myself. Someone is gazing back at me knowing that I have read their words, but who? And, more importantly, what could they possibly mean?

TWO

MELISSA

23 June 2023

Enthusiastic applause fills the room, accompanied by wolf whistles and more banging of cutlery on tables at the end of my speech about Ruby. I suspect it is more to do with the subject matter than my delivery, which fell a long way short of my own exacting standards. It had been difficult to remain focused on the words I had so carefully crafted while glancing around the room searching for anyone with a guilty expression on their face.

I make a beeline for the bar and order myself a large gin and tonic rather than retaking my place at our table. I am just wondering if I've got away with my underwhelming performance when Sadie touches my arm.

'Are you okay, Mel?' she asks. 'Far be it for me to criticise, because you did a much better job than I could ever do, and I'm sure nobody else will have noticed, but you seemed a little less...' She pauses momentarily. 'A little less fluent than usual.'

To stop my hand from shaking, I cup the oversized glass of gin and tonic and take a huge sip to buy myself a couple of moments to collect my thoughts, feeling the warmth of the alcohol spreading across my chest.

The entire time I was speaking to the room filled with friends and family, recalling favourite moments from Ruby's childhood, the same question kept running through my mind. Who slipped that note between the sheets of paper and what did their words mean?

No one in our close group of family and friends expected me to be giving the speech, so it must have been intended for Steve's eyes. I can't help wondering what he would have done had it actually been him standing up there. Would he have stopped mid-flow and demanded to know the meaning of the note? He's usually quite laid-back about things, but not always where our daughter is concerned.

There was an incident at a dance festival when she was thirteen. An adjudicator marked Ruby down in every dance, to the amazement of not only her dancing teacher, Grace, but most of the other parents. My normally mild-mannered husband had been so incensed on his daughter's behalf that he had confronted the adjudicator at the end of the festival to ask the reason for the poor marks, to which she had apparently replied, 'She's a good dancer, but she'll never make it in the profession with her physique. I'm saving her from future disappointment; managing her expectations, you might say.'

Ruby was only carrying a little puppy fat before an inevitable growth spurt, and I was appalled when Steve told me.

Against my advice, he'd eventually been honest with Ruby when she'd persisted with her questions regarding what Doreen Starling had said to him. I was fearful that it could start an unhealthy relationship with food at a vulnerable age.

'So basically, she called me fat,' Ruby had concluded.

Some less confident thirteen-year-olds might have starved themselves, spiralled down into the depths of anorexia or forced themselves to be sick after eating. Fortunately, Ruby did neither but instead kept a keen eye on what she was eating and drinking and a record of her weight and measurements. She didn't diet as such, nor was she fanatical about it, but that was thanks to her sensible approach to life after a thoughtless and ill-conceived remark from a dinosaur adjudicator who belonged to an era where all professional dancers had to be skinny.

I never let on to either Ruby or Steve that I'd complained to the governing body of the dance organisation. Ms Starling was struck off the list of adjudicators before she could do lasting damage to someone less self-assured than our daughter.

It had fleetingly crossed my mind to demand who had slipped the note into the speech, but I was determined not to ruin Ruby's special night, especially if that was the intention of the person who wrote those words.

But what if the assumption had been that I would be making the speech? I'd often been asked to host school events because of my background in media and my job on the radio. Maybe the note did get to the intended recipient after all? Perhaps someone is genuinely trying to warn me that Ruby is struggling to be as perfect as Steve and I think she is and that we should cut her some slack. Or is the motivation jealousy?

Right now, I'm confused, not to mention angry and upset in equal measure. Why would someone deliberately want to sabotage the first party that Ruby has had since she turned six? Whatever the meaning and possible truth behind the words, it was cruel and vindictive. She's well-liked amongst her friends from school and dance class – at least I've always believed that to be the case. Could there possibly be any truth in the words? What if our daughter is not who Steve and I believe her to be?

I take another long sip of my drink and risk a look in Ruby's direction. She's on her feet at our table, surrounded by friends giving her hugs. She looks happy and relaxed now the speech is done and the rest of the night will be devoted to partying. The band are due to finish playing songs from the musicals in around fifteen minutes and then the DJ will take over with dance music.

Tearing my eyes away from her smiling face, I direct my attention back to Sadie. I should have realised that my best friend would be aware that something wasn't quite right, but now is not the time or the place to have a conversation about it.

'I'm fine,' I finally respond, setting my glass back down on the bar. 'I was just on the back foot a bit, trying to remember if I'd written anything that was more personal to Steve's memories of Ruby's childhood than mine. It came across okay, didn't it?'

I'm not sure that she believes me. Sadie and I have been friends since we were in the first year of grammar school together after her family moved to East Sussex from Harrogate. Some of the others teased her about her accent, but I loved the way she pronounced things differently from the rest of us. She's long since lost most of her Yorkshire twang, but thankfully she hasn't picked up an American drawl.

Once we became friends, I discovered that Sadie lived on the next road from me. She would wait on the corner of her road so that we could walk to school together in the mornings. We would stand on that same corner in the afternoons chatting for half an hour or more before I reluctantly left her to head home. Neither of our families was well-off in financial terms, but at least she had a happy home life, which was more than can be said of mine. Although my mum never actually used the words 'You ruined my life', she might as well have. She made me feel that way every single day.

'Like I said, no one but me would have noticed anything,' Sadie is saying, 'but we know each other inside out and I just sensed something was off.' She stops speaking, possibly waiting for more of an explanation. When it's not forthcoming, she continues. 'Maybe it was just a bit overwhelming for you. Goodness knows, I felt emotional hearing all the lovely things you were saying and they're not even my memories, so I can only imagine how you must have been feeling. I don't know where all those years have gone,' she adds, shaking her head.

'I know,' I agree.

'Sometimes it doesn't seem like two minutes since you and I stood on the corner of my road putting the world to rights and giggling over our latest crush,' she says. 'But at others it seems like a lifetime ago.'

How funny that Sadie should be transported back to our teenage chats just as I had been a few moments earlier. She's right. There's been a lot of water under the bridge since then and so many secrets shared between us. We tell each other everything... Well, almost everything. I will mention the note to her, but not right now.

'It's several lifetimes ago if we're talking about the average age of the people in this room,' I say, making a deliberate effort to move the conversation away from the speech. 'I honestly wasn't sure about the whole musicals theme that you and Ruby came up with for tonight, but pretty much everyone got on board with it – even us,' I remark, sweeping my hand over the velvet bodice of the dress Mum made for me to wear in my guise as Eliza Hamilton, wife of Alexander Hamilton, the American president who never was.

Ruby had been delighted when I'd finally managed to get tickets to see *Hamilton* after the show had been a sell-out sensation for the first few months of its run in London's West End. We both knew most of the songs from the many times we'd listened to the soundtrack on the school run or the longer journeys to dance competitions, but it had been a much more immersive experience watching the drama play out from our seats in the dark auditorium. The first half of the show was spectacular and attention-grabbing with some slick choreography and plenty of humour from the actor playing King George. But it was after the interval that my emotions truly kicked in.

I'm pretty sure that every mother in the theatre was close to tears, if not actually crying like a baby, as I was after the first dual when Eliza lost her precious boy. Her strength of character and what she went on to achieve in her life was the main reason I wanted to be her for a few short hours tonight.

I wasn't sure whether Ruby had been as affected by the show as me until we were sat in Piccolo's afterwards, waiting for our food to arrive.

'What would you have done, Mum?' she'd asked.

At first, I'd thought she was referring to the scene that had so upset me because she must have been aware of me dabbing my eyes.

I'd started to respond, but she held her hand up to stop me.

'No, not that bit. I meant what would you do if you found out that Dad had cheated on you like Hamilton did to his wife?'

I can still remember the sensation of my blood turning to ice. I'd started to shiver uncontrollably despite the warmth created by the crush of post-show diners in such a confined space. I'd blinked rapidly as though unable to process the thought before I recovered myself sufficiently to speak. 'Thankfully, that's not a situation I'm ever likely to find myself in. Your dad and I found our soulmates when we found each other.'

Ruby had seemed about to say something else, but our food had arrived, and the moment was gone, much to my relief.

'Eliza Hamilton was a good choice for you,' Sadie says now, nodding her head in agreement with her own statement. 'I was toying with the idea of one of Henry the Eighth's wives from *Six*, but I haven't got the legs for that type of costume anymore.'

Sadie must be fishing for a compliment because she most definitely does still have not only the legs but also the body of someone twenty years her junior. Maybe it's living the single lifestyle in the city that never sleeps, or perhaps she's succumbed to the surgeon's knife for a little nip and tuck. Whichever, she is still a stunning woman without needing to add the caveat 'for her age'. Rather than commenting, I merely shake my head with a wry smile on my face.

'Then I considered Elphaba from *Wicked*,' she continues with a mischievous glint in her eye, 'but the thought of the green make-up put me off. Goodness knows how that lad is going to clean his Shrek make-up off,' she laughs, nodding in the direction of Troy Hanson.

'I know. I've been thinking that too. I hope his mum's got a good biological washing powder 'cos something tells me it's going to be all over his bed sheets.' We both laugh, before I ask, 'What made you decide on Fantine?'

'She had a tragic end after a good start in life. A bit like me.' She obviously sees the look of concern on my face because she continues, 'Joke! *Les Misérables* is my favourite musical and I fancied blacking out a few of my teeth and wearing a skullcap with a few random tufts of my hair pulled through. There's no competing with these gorgeous young girls, so I went completely the other way. It's earned me a few comments.' She adds, winking, 'And probably a bit of speculation.'

She recovers herself well, but there's something about Sadie's glib remark that has set alarm bells ringing in my head. I'll have to pry a bit when just the two of us have dinner tomorrow night before she heads back to New York.

'There you are,' Steve says from behind me. 'I wondered where you'd run off to after delivering my speech so eloquently. I'm sorry if I threw you under the bus, Mel, but in the end, I just couldn't face all those people looking at me.'

Sadie rolls her eyes in exasperation. From the moment Steve had agreed to stand up and speak at Ruby's birthday bash, she questioned whether he would actually be able to carry it off. She doesn't dislike Steve, but she's always viewed him as the weaker partner in our marriage. Maybe it's because she's not married herself that she doesn't understand that being the supportive wind beneath someone's wings is a sign of strength, not weakness.

'I know, I know,' Steve continues, holding his hands up in a submissive gesture. 'I'm a complete wimp and I'll probably regret it tomorrow. But I didn't want to ruin Ruby's big night. Am I forgiven?'

It's funny that Steve should use the exact phrase about ruining Ruby's night that has prompted me to stay silent about the note. I'm still concealing it in the palm of my hand because my evening bag is slung over the back of my chair at the table, and I have no pockets in my costume so there was nowhere else to put it. I want to have a proper look at it when I get home, both to check that I read it properly and to see if I recognise anything familiar in the handwriting. It was only the briefest of glances earlier, but I'm pretty sure it was handwritten capital letters, rather than printed from a computer.

'Of course you're forgiven,' I say, fixing Sadie with a look and shaking my head to prevent her from making a derisory comment. It's annoying that she has been proved right about the speech, but at least Steve has been truthful about his decision. Honesty is one of the things I've always loved about my husband. 'It's our night too. We're celebrating eighteen years of being parents to our beautiful daughter,' I affirm, planting a kiss squarely on his lips.

Steve really is the best dad a child could wish for. And to think fatherhood was almost denied him. Unbidden memories of the numerous unsuccessful rounds of IVF treatment threaten to crowd my mind, but I suppress them. They're not for tonight; tonight is a joyous occasion, and I won't let anything tarnish it. Not even the note.

'You two have done an amazing job on the room,' Steve says, glancing around.

'Thanks, Steve. It's quite a transformation,' Sadie replies, accepting the compliment.

She's right. When we arrived at Foxwood Golf Club nine hours ago, it was a bland wood-panelled room, bearing little resemblance to the riot of character and colour that currently surrounds us. Sadie's background in theatre design before her change in career not long after her move to New York was the main reason for enlisting her help. Following her meticulous plans, the two of us, along with our army of helpers, have created a fantasy land.

I sometimes wonder if Sadie misses the excitement of opening night on Broadway. My guess is that she gets the same kind of adrenaline rush from the fabulous parties that her interior design clients hold to reveal the refurbishment of their homes. Her client list reads like a 'Who's Who' of the New York elite. No wonder she is reluctant to leave a city that has adopted her as one of its own. I'm so proud of what she has achieved.

'Thank you,' I say, squeezing my best friend's arm in gratitude. 'When Ruby suggested the theme for her special night, I would never have imagined we could create anything quite like this. It's spectacular, or in Ruby speak, "awesome".' I make speech marks with my fingers.

We both laugh. I'm sure there was a favoured word that we both overused to describe something amazing when we were teenagers growing up, but if there was, I can't remember, and it will have long been consigned to the history books.

'It won't look anything like this when I come in for a quick beer at the nineteenth hole after my round in the morning,' Steve adds.

'Let's hope not,' Sadie says, laughing. 'And Ruby should take some of the credit too for coming up with the musicals theme in the first place,' she adds, raising her glass in Ruby's direction. 'It gave us a huge amount of scope to be creative. Who's the Freddie Mercury character she's talking to? Her boyfriend?'

'Ruby doesn't have time for boyfriends,' I say, following

Sadie's eyeline to where Ruby is in animated conversation with a boy whose back is to us, before returning my gaze to her. 'With revision for her A levels and dance practice for the World Dance Festival a couple of weeks ago, she barely had time to eat and sleep.'

Sadie raises her eyebrows, a half-smile on her face. 'Well, maybe now the pressure of all that is off, she'll be allowed to have a social life. She certainly looks pretty into him.'

I try to make eye contact with Steve, wondering if he noticed the veiled criticism, but he's in the middle of ordering a drink from the bartender so probably didn't hear the remark.

'No one's ever said she can't have a social life – or a boyfriend for that matter,' I say, a hint of irritation in my voice. 'She's just never shown any interest in anything outside of studying and dancing. Her choice,' I add, as if to underline the point.

Sadie's comment has rattled me. She's right; even from this distance Ruby's body language while she's talking to the young man dressed as the former frontman of the rock band Queen seems somehow intimate, as though there is no one else in the world but the two of them. I'm now curious to know which of Ruby's school friends has so captured her attention. I feel a prickle of apprehension. Could that be the meaning of the note? Has Ruby got a boyfriend that she's chosen to keep from her dad and me? Why on earth would she do that though? It doesn't make any sense.

As though she's aware that I'm watching her, Ruby glances over in my direction and raises her hand. Freddie Mercury turns momentarily. It's difficult to be sure from this distance, especially with the addition of the distinctive moustache, but I think it might be the brother of one of Ruby's dancing school friends. I've seen him a few times when he's been waiting outside in his car to drive Sasha home after class. He appears to say something to Ruby before turning away to join a new group of people while she heads over towards us. The sparkle in her eyes is clear to see as she approaches the bar.

'This is just the best night ever,' she says, reaching her arms around me and squeezing me so tightly that I'm struggling to breathe. 'Thank you, Mum,' she whispers into my hair, holding me for a fraction of a second longer before releasing her grip, 'and you, Dad,' she adds, flinging her arms around his neck.

Steve looks vaguely embarrassed at the open display of affection. In my world, hugs and air kisses are the norm, but not so much in the building trade. Sadie comes to his rescue.

'Do I get a hug too?' she asks, reaching her arms out towards Ruby, who immediately obliges.

'Everyone says they're having an awesome time,' Ruby says, and Sadie and I exchange a look at the use of her favourite word. 'The speech wasn't as embarrassing as I thought it might be and we've still got the DJ and dancing to come. In my wildest dreams, I never imagined my party could be this good.'

My heart is full to bursting. The success of tonight more than compensates for the drama we had in getting Ruby to agree to having a party. She looks the happiest and most relaxed I've seen her in months.

'Who's Freddie?' Sadie asks.

'Freddie?' Ruby says, looking puzzled.

'You know, the Freddie Mercury chap you were just chatting with. You seemed to be getting along well,' Sadie says, clearly hoping for some kind of revelation from Ruby.

'Oh, you mean Kyle,' Ruby replies. 'He's Sasha from dance class's older brother. Mum said it was okay to invite him to look out for her,' she adds, briefly flashing me a look. 'Sasha's a bit shy and might not have come otherwise.'

It's a plausible enough explanation, but Sadie doesn't let it lie.

'Right,' she says, a hint of amusement in her voice. 'He's a good-looking boy. Are you sure there's nothing you want to tell us?' she probes with a twinkle in her eye.

'I suppose he is. I hadn't really noticed,' Ruby says, shrugging her shoulders, but the flush on her cheeks suggests otherwise.

Could Sadie be right? Is there something going on between the two of them?

'I'd love to stay and chat, but the DJ's about to start,' Ruby says. 'Promise me you won't be doing your dad dancing, Dad,' she adds over her shoulder as she heads off to join a group of girls already on the dance floor.

'Cheek,' Steve mutters. 'I was quite a mover in my time.'

'Weren't we all,' Sadie agrees, 'but those days are long gone.'

She delivers her comment with a hint of humour that belies her wistful expression. Maybe I'm overthinking it, but I'm not so sure it's just the recognition that the three of us are ageing. Knowing Sadie, though, she'll soon let her hair down – what little there is of it on show through the slits she's cleverly cut into the Fantine skullcap – when I drag her onto the dance floor. Past my prime or not, there's no way I'll miss the opportunity to have a couple or more dances to pass the time until last orders at 1 a.m.

I can only hope it will take my mind off worrying about the meaning of the note.

THREE

MELISSA

24 June 2023 – the day after the party

The house is quiet this morning, which, in my current fragile state, is just as well. I have a sore head despite only having drunk a couple of glasses of champagne and the large post-speech gin and tonic at the bar. The remainder of the evening, I stuck to water and soft drinks as I'd promised the function room staff that we would take all the decorations down so the cleaners could get the clubhouse back to its normal pristine state before the Saturday morning golfers wanted lunch or, like Steve, a post-round drink.

Considering we didn't get into bed until 3.30 a.m., I'm amazed that Steve was up and out by 7.30 for his early tee-off time. Goodness knows what possessed him to book it so early the morning after Ruby's party. I noticed the time when the cup rattled against the saucer as he placed a tea on my bedside table before giving me a peck on the forehead and telling me he'd be back for a late lunch. That same cup of tea is now on the draining board waiting for me to load it into the dishwasher, contents cold but still intact, apart from the small amount that slopped into the saucer while I was carrying it back downstairs.

I went straight back to sleep after Steve left, only to be woken a couple of hours later by a tap on the door. Ruby, also looking remarkably fresh after the partying and the lateness of getting to bed the previous evening, announced that she'd had her breakfast and was taking Baxter out for a long walk to blow the cobwebs away.

I rolled onto my back and stared up at the ceiling for a couple of minutes before throwing the summer duvet off and sitting up. That's when I realised that I wasn't just tired. The inside of my head felt like a thousand miniature miners were working at a coalface with their pickaxes. I was grateful for the paracetamol that I kept in my bedside drawer and that I'd had the foresight to bring a glass of water up to bed with me. The thought of taking the tablets with cold milky tea turned my stomach.

Although my head is still fragile, I'm beginning to feel a bit more human now that I've had a slice of toast and a coffee, and the tablets are starting to kick in. I want to be firing on all cylinders when Mum comes down or she'll have a go at me for drinking too much, even though I didn't.

I was quite surprised when she agreed to stay the night at ours. She has probably only visited our current house half a dozen times in the eleven years we've lived here.

'What do you need a great big house like that for?' she'd said when I'd pulled up on the driveway a week after we moved in. 'There's only the three of you and you're too old to have any more children, so why do you need five bedrooms?'

Not 'what a lovely house' or 'it's a great neighbourhood to raise Ruby in'.

'Why must you always show off about how much money you and Steve have?' she'd added.

It's funny how people, my mother included, think that

everyone who works in the media earns a fortune. That certainly isn't the case for presenters on local radio – at least not in my experience.

My move into radio from print journalism the year after Ruby was born had enabled me to get back into working without sacrificing precious time with my long-awaited child. Given a choice, I would have preferred to wait until Ruby was of school age before picking up the reins on my career, but that ceased to be an option after the company that Steve did most of his work for went into liquidation, owing him over eighty thousand pounds.

I'd been incredulous when Steve had told me the sums involved and we'd had one of our infrequent arguments when I'd demanded to know why he'd allowed the debt to grow to that extent. We'd soon realised that arguing about a situation over which neither of us had any control was pointless. We needed a way of making our mortgage payment each month to keep a roof over our heads while paying off the money Steve owed to his suppliers. He could have chosen the easy route and declared himself bankrupt, which to all intents and purposes we were, but Steve was too proud to do that. So, the only other option was for me to cut my maternity leave short and go back to work earlier than planned.

The opportunity to join the team at Wavelength Radio as the weekend early breakfast presenter came up at just the right moment. The pay was similar to my senior reporter's role on the paper, but I was only required to work two mornings, and they were both days when Steve could look after Ruby. It meant there were no extortionate childcare costs eating into our income, especially as Mum had made it very clear that she was not going to be an unpaid babysitter and Steve's parents lived three hundred miles away.

It took a while, but by the time Ruby started primary school, we were back on an even keel financially, after a lot of scrimping and saving and going without luxuries like foreign holidays. We instead opted for the cooler climes of the Scottish Borders and the hospitality of my in-laws. It's so sad that neither of them lived long enough to see their only grandchild reach her eighteenth birthday. It's one of the drawbacks of having children later in life, which was their choice with Steve but something that had been thrust upon us.

My move from early-morning weekends to the weekday morning slot from 10 a.m. through until 1 p.m. coincided with Ruby starting school. The times fitted in perfectly with the school day, meaning I was always there to pick her up and hear about her day.

So, my mum's comment about us showing off our wealth by buying a big house had not only been inaccurate regarding our wealth but also hurtful. We'd stretched ourselves to buy a property that would have plenty of equity in it if we ever found ourselves in a similar situation and needed to sell to stay afloat. Fortunately, we haven't been in that position, although we'd come close during the pandemic lockdowns when Steve was unable to work.

I'm in the process of loading the breakfast things into the dishwasher when I become aware of my mum standing at the kitchen door watching me.

'Morning, Mum,' I say, tipping away the cold tea and giving my cup a quick rinse under the tap in the hope that it will help remove the ring that is currently staining it. 'Did you sleep okay?'

'Like a baby,' she replies. 'Although I'm not sure about that mattress. I gave up trying to turn over before I dropped off to sleep and I've just woken up in exactly the same position. Can't be that good for your back, I wouldn't have thought,' she grumbles.

My mum is talking about the memory foam mattress on the bed in the spare room and for once I have to agree with her. It had originally been on our bed and Steve loved the way the latex moulded around him, but I found it claustrophobic. Exactly as Mum just described, the effort of turning from sleeping on one side to the other was huge. It lasted two weeks on our bed before I ordered a new pocket-sprung mattress and the stupidly expensive foam one got relegated to the spare room. Steve still gets to sleep on it occasionally if he's snoring a lot and I throw him out of the matrimonial bed because I have an early start the next day.

'I'm with you on that, Mum,' I say, rinsing the toast crumbs from the plates, having moved on to loading the lower rack of the dishwasher.

'You are?' she says, surprise evident in her voice.

Mum and I don't have a bad relationship, but I wouldn't describe it as particularly close either. My birth when she was only eighteen prevented both her and my dad from going to university – at least that's how she tells it. I'm sure they would have been able to sort out a creche facility if they'd really wanted to continue with their higher education. It's easy to be judgemental, but it's always felt like they used becoming parents as an excuse for not going to university. They spent most of the time they were together, before my dad died, complaining and arguing about it. Some of my earliest memories, when I could only have been around two or three, are of lying in my bed and listening to their raised voices. I don't remember any actual words, just the feeling that if it wasn't for me their lives would have been very different.

It made it even more difficult for me to accept my own inability to conceive. I was desperate to have children and lavish on them all the love and attention that I felt had been so sadly lacking in my childhood, but it just wouldn't happen for me and Steve, and goodness knows we tried. Once it became clear that we might have trouble conceiving, we went down the route of IVF, but that too was unproductive. It's no wonder that both

Steve and I view Ruby as something of a miracle. After all the medical intervention, she was eventually conceived naturally. I can feel heat starting to creep up my neck and into my face, so I keep my back to Mum, even though I've finished loading the dishwasher.

I reach for a sponge to wipe the draining board and say, by way of explanation about the bed, 'I like to be able to thrash around a bit in my sleep and that mattress is like sleeping in a coffin. We'd get rid of it, but it cost quite a bit and it's not slept on very often, so it would seem like a waste of money.'

I'm making the point about not throwing away a perfectly good mattress to prove to Mum that I can be careful with money. She's already expressed her disapproval about the amount of money we've spent on Ruby for her eighteenth birthday. It's not just the party. I heartily regret telling Mum that we're going to buy Ruby a second-hand car to encourage her to have driving lessons, having shown no interest so far. It's not a completely selfless gesture. Driving her to and from dancing classes three times a week and having to hang around in the car for an hour is incredibly time-consuming.

'At last, you're starting to appreciate the value of money,' my mum says.

I resist the urge to defend myself.

Instead, I turn to face her with a steady gaze and change the subject. 'Can I get you some toast and coffee?' I ask. 'Or do you fancy an egg, or some cereal maybe?'

'Toast is fine,' she says, 'but I'm perfectly capable of getting it myself.'

'Of course you are, Mum, but I'm standing right next to the bread bin and the toaster, so it's easier if I do it.'

We lock eyes for a moment, and I think she's going to argue, so I choose to defuse the situation by saying, 'Besides, it's the least I can do after all the work you put in on our costumes for the party.'

That seems to placate her, and she pulls out one of the kitchen chairs, the legs scraping against the tiled floor, before settling heavily into it. Mum hasn't been quite so mobile since she had an operation a couple of years ago and has put on some weight as a result, a situation she moans about a lot and yet is unwilling to do anything to rectify. I've suggested maybe taking up yoga or going swimming as an alternative to running, which she can no longer do because of her hip, but all she does is make excuses. Yoga classes and swimming cost money, whereas going for a run was free is the one she uses most often – although during the winter, she also moaned that it was too cold for swimming. She has a point about the cost of fitness activities, but she flatly refused my offer to pay for an annual gym membership, even when I suggested it could be a birthday or Christmas gift.

'She's too proud to accept what she sees as charity,' was Steve's response when I told him about it.

'People made a lot of effort with their costumes last night,' my mum comments while I busy myself filling the kettle with water and putting it on to boil.

'Yes, they did. Granary or white toast?' I ask as I reach into the bread bin.

'Whichever,' she replies with a slight shrug of her shoulders. 'You know me, I'm easily pleased.'

It's a good job I have my back to her again so she can't see the smile I'm working hard to suppress. My mum could be described as a lot of things, but easily pleased is not one of them.

I select two slices from the thick-cut farmhouse white loaf and drop them in the toaster slots. I have a vague recollection of her moaning that the seeds from a sandwich I'd made for her using granary bread had cracked a filling that had cost her a small fortune to have replaced. I don't want a repeat performance of that, particularly as she seems to be in good humour this morning.

'Thank you for getting into the spirit of it too. I know Ruby was pleased after you said you weren't going to bother,' I add, spooning granules of coffee into a mug. I've tried Mum with 'pod' coffee previously, but she claims it tastes too bitter because she drinks it black and without sugar. Gold Blend is her preferred choice, so I had to go out and buy a jar after she accepted the invitation to stay over.

For the party, Mum made herself a nun's habit similar to the ones worn in *Sister Act*. At least it wasn't as sacrilegious as it would have been a few years ago when she was still drinking to excess. Watching her knocking back a bottle of wine with her dinner and several colourful cocktails afterwards would have been standard before she gave up drinking alcohol. She still enjoyed herself though, especially with all the praise heaped on her when Ruby explained to anyone who'd listen that her nana had made all our costumes.

I say all, but Steve's was the exception. He'd played it safe by hiring his *The Greatest Showman* ringmaster costume.

'That was before I realised how seriously everyone was taking it,' my mum says, accepting the mug of instant coffee I'm handing her. 'You must have spent a fortune on all the different fabrics you bought for Ruby's and Megan's outfits. And yours and Sadie's.'

Maybe I'm overly sensitive to my mum's criticisms, but I get the sense that she thinks the costumes should only have been for the teenage guests. That had been my initial thought, but Ruby and Sadie had outvoted me, insisting that everyone apart from the staff should get into the spirit of the themed night. To be honest, I enjoyed dressing up, as I suspect did Mum, although she would never admit it. And she's right about the cost of all the different fabrics. Gone are the days where making your own clothes is the more affordable option. I think we could have hired all four outfits for what it cost to buy the fabric, let alone the patterns and all the extras like buttons and trims.

We struggled to find material with a sparkling snowflake pattern for Ruby's Elsa costume, so we made our own, laboriously applying individual diamanté stones with the aid of a matchstick and glue. It took many hours, but the result was worth it. And then there was all the man, or should I say woman, hours my mum put into it. She'd refused to accept any money, saying it could be her contribution towards her granddaughter's 'coming of age' as she couldn't afford to help with the actual cost of the party. And the costumes are ours to keep as a tangible reminder of a lovely evening.

Lovely, apart from the note, of course.

My stomach twists as I relive the moment of discovery. Was it any wonder that my delivery had been less polished than I would have liked when I was concealing those accusatory words in the palm of my left hand?

I was too tired to get into a discussion with Steve about it when we eventually got into bed last night, and besides, I wanted to give myself a bit of time to think about who it might be from, what they meant and why they had chosen to try to disrupt Ruby's night rather than approaching Steve and me in private.

Our daughter has never given us any cause for concern. She works hard at school and has no attendance or behavioural issues. Her free time is split between dancing class, visiting her nana and, since we got him during lockdown, walking Baxter. I've never noticed the aroma of tobacco on her clothes as I've put them in to wash and we've had sensible discussions about vaping and alcohol misuse. So, what did the writer of the note mean? Unless there was some truth in Sadie's suggestion that Ruby has got herself a boyfriend. But if that is the case, why wouldn't she just tell us? It's not really that big a deal.

'Did you hear me, Melissa?'

For a moment, I panic. I was so lost in my own thoughts that I totally tuned out of the conversation with Mum.

At my blank expression, she says in a voice that's a little too loud and leaving short gaps between each of her words, 'I said, I hope Ruby appreciates all the effort everyone went to.'

'Of course she does, Mum,' I say, recovering my composure and handing over her plate of hot buttered toast. 'She said as much when she came over to us at the bar last night while you were enjoying all the praise for your clever seamstress work. I'm surprised you didn't take a few orders for clothes.'

'You know, that's not a bad idea,' she replies, sinking her teeth into the crunchy toast. A dribble of melted butter escapes the corner of her mouth which she catches with her tongue, a thoughtful expression on her face. 'I could certainly do with a few extra pounds to help ends meet with this spiralling inflation. Maybe I should put an advert in the post office window,' she adds, going in for another bite.

I can't help but smile. My mum hasn't embraced the age of technology when it comes to social media. I have now got her using WhatsApp, which is a minor miracle, although she insists on calling it What's Up despite the multiple corrections from me and Ruby.

'Maybe the dry cleaners would be a better option,' I suggest. 'They do repairs and stuff on site, so advertising dressmaking services there would make more sense. Or I'm sure Ruby wouldn't mind setting up an Instagram account for you. You could post pictures of your creations and take orders.'

Mum takes a sip of coffee, seemingly oblivious to how hot it must be without the addition of milk to cool it. 'I'll give it some thought,' she says.

I know she won't. Lack of ambition and belief in herself has played a large part in the life she has led. It's a shame, because she is undoubtedly a talented seamstress. When I was young and money was tight, Mum made all my clothes and her own too, but she refused to do it for other people. Even after my dad died and she was really struggling just to keep the roof over our heads and food on the table, she declined, saying she didn't need people's charity.

'Where is Ruby, anyway?' Mum continues. 'I was hoping to see her before I head off. Don't tell me she's still in bed?' she adds, giving a disapproving shake of her head.

'No,' I reply. 'She was up before me this morning. She stuck her head round my bedroom door at half past nine to say she was taking Baxter out for a walk. Mind you,' I say, glancing up at the kitchen clock, 'I would have thought she would have been back by now.'

'Maybe she met up with someone and they stopped off for a coffee somewhere,' she suggests.

'Megan's working this morning.'

'Who said I was talking about Megan?'

The comment is innocent enough, but there's something about the way Mum says it that suggests otherwise.

'Do you know something I don't?' I ask and then am immediately annoyed with myself for rising to Mum's provocation. She does stuff like this sometimes because she and Ruby are close, and she likes me to think that my daughter confides in her more than she does in me.

'It depends what you know,' she counters, tipping her head back slightly to finish her coffee before placing her mug on her plate and pushing her chair back to get to her feet. 'Shall I load these into the dishwasher, or shall I just leave them on the draining board for you to deal with like everyone else does?'

It's another dig at the way I run around doing stuff for my family. I hadn't realised she'd noticed I was stacking more than my own dirty dishes when she stood watching me from the doorway earlier. I've long since learned not to rise to every comment and criticism aimed at me by my mum, and besides, I have more pressing things to worry about.

Mum has a self-satisfied expression on her face, which has me wondering if she actually does know something about Ruby that I don't. If so, could she have been the one to leave the cryptic note between the pages of the speech last night? And if she did, was it out of concern for Ruby or yet further disapproval of the way Steve and I parent our daughter?

'I've got it,' I say, reaching across the table for her crockery with a forced smile on my face.

'Fine,' she responds. 'Is it okay if I have a shower before I head home? That immersion heater of mine costs a fortune to heat the tank of water.'

'Of course. Have a bath if you prefer, it's all the same to me. I've left a bath towel on the dresser in your en suite bathroom.'

She grunts her thanks and turns towards the door.

'Oh, and Mum,' I say, taking a deep breath to psych myself up for the question I feel compelled to ask, 'you would tell me if there was something important about Ruby that I needed to know?'

She turns back towards me, her eyes searching mine. She's not wearing the expression she does when she wants me to believe that she's got the better of me in a disagreement. 'The only thing you need to start accepting is that Ruby's eighteen.' There is a gentleness to her tone that I'm not used to, which is a little unnerving. 'She's not a child anymore. You and Steve need to stop treating her like one. You've always viewed her through rose-tinted spectacles, and although she's a good girl, she's not perfect. Nobody's perfect,' she adds, turning away from me.

I stand, numbly, watching Mum climb the stairs, unsure what to make of her words. Her comment may have been well-intentioned but, if anything, it has heightened my concerns that my daughter is keeping secrets from me.

I think of the note stashed in my evening bag. I need to have a closer look at it.

FOUR
RUBY

January – five months before the party

The applause is deafening. Ruby sinks into a deep curtsey and holds it a fraction of a second longer than she normally would to allow herself to drink in the appreciation of the spectators in the audience, most of whom are her fellow competitors or their friends and family. She knows she's given an outstanding performance as Eponine, her favourite character from *Les Misérables*. Deep in her heart, she'd felt every word of the lyrics as they left her lips and lived every extension and contraction of her limbs in the exquisite choreography of the dance.

When Grace, her dancing teacher at the Milsom Radcliffe Academy, had come up with a list of routines she wanted her girls to perform at the National Dance Championships, several of them had put their names down against 'On My Own', including Ruby's best friend, Megan. There were some disappointed faces when it was announced that Ruby would be given the song and dance to perform, but Megan was the first to put her personal goals aside and was quick to congratulate her friend. The aim was for the dancing school to do well and most agreed that, with Ruby performing it, first place in that category of the competition was almost assured, just as it was in all the other categories in which she was entered. There were fewer than usual this year as Ruby had had the additional pressure of revising for her mock A levels, which she had sat over the previous two weeks, but she would still be adding considerably to the Academy's overall points total.

As the volume of applause begins to wane, Ruby leaves the stage. She's long since learned that it's better to leave an audience wanting more rather than to overstay your welcome. Her grandmother, Linda, who never attends the competitions but always wants a blow-by-blow account over a cup of tea the following day, told her it's an important lesson in life too. When Ruby questioned what she meant, she simply replied, 'You'll find out soon enough.'

She's barely reached the wings at the side of the stage when Megan bursts through the door from the auditorium.

'That was incredible,' she says, rushing towards Ruby and throwing her arms around her. 'There's not a dry eye in the house.'

Ruby can't resist a smile at her friend's use of language. Although they're a similar age, Megan sometimes sounds as though she's eighty rather than eighteen. It can probably be attributed to the History of Theatre course she's studying at college along with her A levels, rather than her parents' influence. They are younger than Ruby's parents in age and choose not to socialise with any of the other parents from the Milsom Radcliffe Academy. They stopped taking their daughter to dancing class because Melissa was happy to pick her up and drop her off. They also stopped going to watch their daughter compete in dancing festivals when it became clear to them that she was never going to be the winner while Ruby was around. They have high expectations which Megan struggles to live up to. With every small failure, the relationship with her parents has become more fragile. It's little wonder that Megan prefers spending her free time with Ruby's family, and the more she does, the greater her parents' lack of interest in her.

'I'm glad I haven't got to follow that,' Megan adds, inclining her head towards the girl who is waiting nervously in the wings before taking her place on the stage. 'You literally blew that out of the water.'

Ruby shrugs nonchalantly. To an observer, the action may appear arrogant, however it's anything but. There's no denying Ruby's natural ability. She has a beautiful voice with a lovely quality about it, but she's worked hard with her vocal coach to understand the light and shade required to optimise a performance and the difference timing makes.

It's less about ability and hard work with her dancing though. Some students have all the same attributes as Ruby, flexibility and learned technique, but she has something else. Call it star quality or the X factor. Whatever you call it, Ruby possesses it in abundance. When she takes to the stage, whether solo or amongst others in a group performance, eyes are drawn to her every move. The principal of the Milsom Radcliffe Academy has high hopes that Ruby will make it in the incredibly competitive world of showbusiness if she chooses it as her career.

Big decisions are around the corner for her though, because she's also very bright academically and her dad wants a university education for her. Her mum is more willing to listen to what Ruby wants for her future and she's tried to tell Steve that university isn't necessarily the right thing for everyone, even someone as academically gifted as Ruby, particularly if the other thing you excel at has a shorter shelf life. It's an ongoing conversation. University choices had needed to be made if Ruby wanted to have a place, subject to achieving the right grades, but Melissa was determined that no one would be forcing Ruby to do anything against her will. She persuaded

Steve to allow their daughter to also apply to the prestigious Laine Theatre Arts in Epsom for their three-year diploma course, after a conversation she and Ruby had had on the way back from a very successful World Dancing Competition the previous year. At the time, Ruby had felt confident in her ability and buoyed by her success, but now she wasn't quite so sure that she could make it in the cutthroat entertainment industry.

'You would say that, Megan,' Ruby says, linking arms as the two of them head down a short flight of stairs towards the dressing rooms beneath the stage. There are only a couple of girls still to perform before they all need to take their place back on stage to receive the adjudicator's placings. 'But, as my best friend, you might be a little biased.'

'You know that's not true,' Megan protests, opening the door to the communal dressing room and standing aside to let Ruby enter first. 'I can only imagine what it must feel like to be you. You're so talented and clever and pretty. The world is your oyster,' she says, dramatically flinging her arms wide to demonstrate the expanse of possibilities open to her friend. 'Whatever you choose to do with your life, you'll absolutely smash it,' she adds, heading towards her metallic make-up box on the table in front of the mirror and rooting around in it for a moment before extracting a lipstick in an animal print casing.

Ruby's smile wavers, despite the compliment. She knows Megan is referring to the choice she'll soon have to make between studying at university or taking her chances with the thousands of other hopefuls in the entertainment industry. But it's not that straightforward anymore.

'Megan,' she says tentatively. 'Can you keep a secret?'

'I'm a bit hurt that you need to ask,' Megan replies, momentarily pausing the lipstick application she'd started and eyeing her friend through the lightbulb-framed mirror. She was the second to perform in the song and dance section and it was a class of twenty-seven, so her shocking pink lipstick has long since been licked off.

Ruby waits until Megan has completed her Cupid's bow and pressed her lips together to make sure the coverage is even before continuing.

'It's a biggie,' she says.

Megan turns to face her friend, her expression showing her concern. 'What is it, Ruby? You're not sick, are you?'

Ruby shakes her head. In the background, she can hear applause. There is only one more contestant to dance and Ruby is wishing she'd chosen the moment to tell her friend the secret she's been hiding since New Year's Eve a little more carefully.

'I think they're almost ready for us,' Ruby says, tilting her head in the direction of the stage. 'I'll have to tell you later.'

'That's not fair, Ruby. You've got me worried now. What's wrong?' Megan asks, taking hold of Ruby's forearm and looking directly into her violet-blue eyes.

Ruby returns the gaze, wondering what will happen to the mix of concern and adulation in her friend's eyes when she reveals her secret.

I don't have to tell her, Ruby thinks. *It may lead to nothing, and I will have risked ending a twelve-year friendship.*

A strident voice delivering a slightly out-of-tune version of 'As Long as He Needs Me' from *Oliver!* breaks into the silence.

'Please,' Megan says, applying a little more pressure to Ruby's arm.

'I-I've been seeing Kyle,' Ruby confesses.

Megan's chocolate-brown eyes blink rapidly. 'K-Kyle, as in Sasha's brother? As in Kyle who you know I've had a crush on forever?' Megan says in a faltering voice.

Ruby drops her gaze so she doesn't have to witness the bottom falling out of Megan's world. 'I'm sorry...' she starts to say.

'Why? Why Kyle?' Megan asks, the colour rising in her

cheeks. 'You could have anyone you want, but you've chosen him. Why, Ruby?' she demands, the volume of her voice rising. 'You're supposed to be my friend. How could you do this?'

Ruby's heart is pounding in her chest. She's known for a while that this moment was coming. She hated deceiving her best friend but hadn't wanted to hurt her in case the whole thing with Kyle was just a passing attraction for him and he moved his attentions elsewhere.

'It wasn't intentional,' she eventually says, acutely aware that 'As Long as He Needs Me' is rushing inexorably to its conclusion, at which point the two of them will be called back to the stage with their fellow contestants. 'We got talking at the New Year's Eve party and I guess I'd had a bit too much to drink because I let him put his number in my phone. Honestly, I had no intention of messaging him because I knew that you liked him,' she rushes on. 'But I couldn't stop thinking about him, so we arranged to meet at Daisy's for a coffee. He was even nicer second time around, so different from the boys at school with their immature comments.'

A smattering of applause signals the end of the performance and a crackling voice from a battered old speaker mounted high on the dressing room wall requests all competitors to gather in the wings.

'Can we talk about this later?' Ruby says, grateful for the intervention. She'd expected Megan to be upset but was shocked by the level of anger and accusations fired at her. She hadn't set out to hurt Megan but once she'd fallen for Kyle it was almost inevitable. 'W-we need to get back to the stage.'

Ruby heads towards the dressing room door, but Megan is rooted to the spot.

'Have you and he... you know?' Megan asks.

The two girls have previously indulged in many conversations about boys, kissing and sex and both agreed that they were not in a desperate rush to experiment, but Ruby has moved the goalposts and she's done it without telling her best friend.

'Not now, Megan. Miss Grace will be furious if we miss the adjudication. We could even get disqualified.'

'Like that matters to me,' Megan says, sounding utterly broken. 'You'll win, Ruby, just like you always win at everything.'

'Final call for the eighteens and under song and dance competitors to come to the side of the stage,' a voice crackles from the speaker.

'Come on,' Ruby pleads. 'We can sort this out later.'

Megan shakes her head. 'I can't. Tell them I'm sick or something.'

Ruby hesitates for a moment before taking the steps up to the wings two at a time and slipping into her number twenty-five position just as competitor number one leads the line out onto the stage.

As expected by everyone who witnessed the performance, Ruby is given first place. Once the adjudicator finished awarding places and commendations, one of which was for Megan's rendition of 'The Winner Takes It All' from *Mamma Mia*, Ruby rushes from the stage, ignoring all the praise she normally accepts so graciously.

She hurries back down the stairs to the dressing room and flings open the door. And gasps in horror.

There is no sign of Megan, but scrawled across the mirror in bright pink lipstick is the word BITCH.

FIVE

MELISSA

24 June 2023 – the day after the party

Mum leaves just before midday, refusing the lift I offer her, just as I knew she would. For once, I'm quite relieved because it gives me the opportunity to have a quick look around in Ruby's room before she gets back from her walk with Baxter. I have no idea what I'm looking for and I hate the idea of going behind my daughter's back, but the note and Mum's comments this morning have convinced me that my daughter has a secret.

As soon as Mum is out of the house, I rush upstairs and retrieve the crumpled note from my evening bag. Just as I remembered, the note is written in block capitals, giving no clue as to who may have written it. I stare at it for several moments, wondering how those few words can possibly have struck such fear into my heart. Am I genuinely concerned for Ruby's well-being, or do I merely hate the idea that she has things going on in her life that she no longer wants to tell me about now that she's older?

Part of me wants to leave things alone and give Ruby space to tell me her secret in her own time, if in fact she has one, but the caring mum in me thinks it's too risky. If something is happening in Ruby's life, something she's too afraid or embarrassed to tell me about, I simply must know.

I strip the sheets off Mum's bed and leave them in the doorway of the spare bedroom so that I'll have an excuse for being upstairs if Ruby returns while I'm having a bit of a snoop.

I take a breath before pushing the door open. I've always trusted my daughter implicitly. What I'm about to do feels wrong on so many levels, but I've convinced myself that I'm doing it with Ruby's best interest at heart. My mind is already reeling with awful possibilities. She might have got in with a bad crowd at school who are encouraging her to do drugs, or she might have been talking to someone online who is pretending to be someone they're not. There are so many tragic stories that I have come across in my work as a radio presenter where teenagers have been duped into taking revealing selfies which they later regret, by which time it is too late. Ruby is pretty savvy, but no one is immune to all the dangers of living in the goldfish-bowl world of social media.

Ruby's room is immaculate, just as it always has been since she was very young. I've never had to moan to her about clothes or toys being strewn around the floor. Everything has a place and that's where it lives. As soon as she could write, Ruby made labels from Post-it notes with some very inventive spelling and stuck them onto her drawers so that when her clean washing was put away, she would know precisely where to find it. The chair in the corner of her room only ever housed cuddly toys, never dirty clothes, which always went straight into the white wicker laundry basket next to the door of her small en suite shower room. That chair is now free of toys, most of which went to the Royal Alexandra Children's Hospital in nearby Brighton to be replaced with cushions, but Teddy still has a place on Ruby's bed and in her heart. He's perched on top of Ruby's pillow and it's almost as though he is watching me disapprovingly as I pad quietly across the cream-coloured carpet in his direction.

I pull open the drawer of the bedside table. I'm guessing that if Ruby keeps a diary, as I used to at her age, she probably writes it at night-time and slips it into her drawer before she goes to sleep. Facing up at me is the glossy printed prospectus for Laine Theatre Arts. Ruby passed her audition with flying colours, as we all expected she would, and has had to accept the offered place as the college is so oversubscribed, even though she hasn't made her mind up yet.

I'm just lifting the brochure to look underneath it when I hear Ruby call out, 'Mum, where are you? Don't tell me you're still in bed!'

I hastily close the drawer and hotfoot it out of Ruby's room. I grab the pile of dirty laundry and make my way to the top of the stairs just as Ruby appears at the bottom of them.

'Up here, darling,' I say, half-hiding my guilty face with Mum's bed linen.

'Wow, you don't waste any time, do you,' she says, eyeing up the sheets.

'I might as well get them in the washing machine and out on the line to dry while the sun is still hot,' I reply, making my way down the stairs and following Ruby into the kitchen.

She reaches a glass down from the cupboard, fills it with water from the dispenser in the fridge door and takes a long drink.

'I was ready for that,' she says, smacking her lips together. 'I take it Nana has gone?'

'Yes, you've missed her by half an hour or so,' I reply, bundling the washing into the machine, followed by a wash tablet, and turning the dial to quick wash. I keep my back to Ruby for a few more moments while I try to steady my heart-beat. If she hadn't called out, I would have been caught red-handed going through her bedside drawer. It doesn't bear thinking about. 'She was hoping you'd be back in time for her to say goodbye, but you were out for ages. Poor old Baxter looks shattered,' I add, looking over to where our Cavapoo is noisily slurping water from his stainless-steel bowl. He's a bit of a messy drinker and there is almost as much water on the floor as he will have consumed. As though he knows I'm talking about him, he wags his tail but doesn't lift his head from drinking.

'Sorry, I didn't realise I was being timed,' Ruby says, immediately jumping on the defensive.

There have been a few occasions in the past couple of months when Ruby has overreacted to innocent comments, which, since discovering the note, all add weight to the fact that she might be hiding something from us.

'Don't be silly, darling,' I say, trying to defuse the situation. 'Of course you're not. It would have just been nice if you'd been back before Nana left.'

She gives a slight shrug.

'I take it Dad got up for golf this morning,' she says. She knows he did as he wasn't in bed with me when she stuck her head around our bedroom door earlier, and his plate and mug were left on the draining board, along with hers, for the dishwasher fairy to load into the machine.

It feels like an attempt to be less snippy with me, so I respond with, 'Yes, much to my surprise.'

'Seven thirty was a bit of an ambitious tee-off time after getting in so late, particularly at his age.'

'Oi, less of your cheek,' I say, continuing the banter. 'Your dad and I are the same age, as you full well know.'

'Ah yes, but you look so much younger.'

'Now you've got me wondering what you're after,' I say, bending down to stroke Baxter, who has come over to me for a fuss, leaving a watery trail in his wake.

'I was just wondering what's on the menu for lunch,' she twinkles. 'I'm starving after all that walking.'

'Well, I'm doing a salad for your dad and me, but he won't be back for another hour or so. I can do cheese on toast for you if you like.'

'Thanks, Mum, you're an angel,' she says. 'I'll have time for a quick shower first, won't I?'

'Go on,' I say. 'You've got about ten minutes,' I add, calling after her as Ruby bounds up the stairs. 'You know, Baxter, I can't help thinking that my mum might have a point when she goes on about me pandering to my family's needs.'

He lifts his whiskered chin, still dripping with water, and cocks his head to one side as though he's waiting for me to continue my conversation with him. I'm amazed at how fond of Baxter I've become, having never had a dog in my life before.

We eventually gave in to Ruby's pleas for a puppy during lockdown. It was difficult for all school-age children to be couped up in their homes twenty-four seven with all their lessons online. Ruby didn't particularly struggle with that as she just got her head down and completed her work as she would have done had she been in the classroom. No, for her the main issue was the isolation of not being in physical contact with anyone apart from me and Steve. And the problem was amplified because there were two sets of people that she was being denied access to: her school pals and her friends from dancing. She and Megan stayed in contact, talking every day on FaceTime, but it wasn't the same as being in her physical presence.

Steve and I felt it too because Megan spent a lot of her free time at our house. She often stayed over at weekends because the girls had dance class or competitions and she occasionally holidayed with us too when her parents allowed her to. Megan was like the sister Ruby never had, so her absence from our lives was especially noticeable. She hasn't been around so much lately, but that's probably because of her Saturday job.

So, the main reason we caved in about getting a puppy was because Ruby was lonely. We didn't take the decision lightly, going through the pros and cons of the different types of dogs and also taking into consideration our lifestyle when everything returned to normal. After a lot of research and a fair amount of asking around, we settled on a Cavapoo and it has turned out to be the perfect choice, I think, giving Baxter's ears another fondle before washing my hands to make a start on Ruby's lunch.

I suppose I always knew that the bulk of looking after Baxter would fall on my shoulders once the lockdown was lifted and Ruby was back at school and dancing, but I don't mind. I don't see much of Steve during the week, so it's nice to be welcomed home from my shift at the radio station with a few happy barks and a very waggy tail.

He's whining softly now because he's heard me opening the packet of cheese and probably thinks it's something for him.

'You can't have any of this, boy, it will upset your tummy and we all know who'll end up clearing up after you,' I say good-naturedly.

To be fair, walks are pretty evenly split between us depending on who's around, and we all have an ample supply of poo bags in every coat pocket along with the dispenser attached to his lead. Considering it's the first time any of us has had a family pet, we're not doing too bad a job, I think as Baxter settles on his bed at the side of the back door, having given up on an unexpected treat. It will be a terrible wrench for Ruby when she has to leave him to go to university or Laine Arts, but it might go some way to filling the massive hole her leaving home will leave in our lives. Although Steve and I are both still working, our nest will feel very empty when Ruby has flown from it, something I try not to dwell on too much.

SIX

RUBY

January – five months before the party

It was tricky explaining to her mum why Megan had left the dancing competition early the previous day, given she was supposed to be in Melissa's care.

Her mum had wanted to call in at Megan's house on the way home to make sure she got back safely, but Ruby had managed to dissuade her, saying that maybe Megan needed a bit of space for herself.

'Have you two had an argument?' Melissa had persisted.

'Not exactly, Mum, just a bit of a disagreement, and Megan might have felt a bit awkward in the car with you. I'll message her in a bit.'

Ruby had been economical with the truth when Melissa had asked her about it later in the evening. She'd messaged Megan as she'd said she would but hadn't received a reply. That was the part she didn't tell her mum and it played on her mind, especially as she'd had no reply from two further WhatsApp messages. The only thing stopping her from going round to her friend's house to make sure she was okay were the two blue ticks by each of her messages signifying that they had been read.

The pale green gate squeaks as Ruby pushes it open and walks down the path to her nana's front door. It opens before she even has the chance to knock on it. Ruby has suggested on numerous occasions that a drop of oil would stop the squeaking, but her nana says she likes it making a noise because it alerts her to visitors, welcome and otherwise. She has a point as Linda's maisonette isn't in the best of areas.

'Come in, come in,' her nana says, ushering Ruby into the small hallway and closing the door behind her. 'Let's get you warm. It's freezing out there.'

'Don't fuss, Nana. I've just been sat in Mum's car with the heat turned up, and it's not as though you kept me waiting on the doorstep,' she says, giving her nana a hug. A wave of heat from the gas fire which must be turned up to maximum hits her as she pushes open the lounge door. 'I'll need to strip off in a minute. It's boiling in here and really stuffy. Don't you ever open the windows?' Ruby adds, unzipping her quilted coat and draping it over the back of one of the four dining chairs huddled around the small square wooden table.

'No point having the heating on if it's all floating out of the window,' her nana says. 'And besides, I might forget I've opened it, pop out to the shop and come back to an empty house.'

It wouldn't be the first time her nana's home had been burgled. There was precious little of any value to take, and the thieves were never caught, but that isn't really the point. Someone had been in her property, touching her things and tipping out the contents of drawers. It had left Linda feeling violated, but she still refused Melissa's offer of financial help to move her into a flat closer to the rest of her family and in a nicer area.

From the small kitchen area at the far end of the open-plan living space, she asks, 'Do you want coffee or tea, darling?'

'I'll have a coffee please, Nana. I didn't sleep very well last night, so I'm struggling to stay awake, and I've got more revision to do when I get home for my last mock exam tomorrow.'

Ruby chooses not to elaborate on her reason for not sleeping well. Not only was she feeling pretty upset about the whole situation with Megan, but she was also terrified that her friend might not keep the secret she had shared. Her relationship with Kyle is still in the very early stages. She isn't intending to permanently keep it from her parents, but neither is she ready to tell them about it. Being an only child has several positives: not having hand-me-downs, not having to share with siblings and having your parents all to yourself, to name a few. But the downside is that they can be overly protective, particularly in respect of boyfriends. Although Ruby had occasionally fancied one of the older boys at school when she was in the lower school, they'd been unaware of her existence. When she became a senior herself, she deemed her contemporaries too immature to bother with. But Kyle showing an interest in her is different; more grown-up. Her fear is that her parents will think he is too old for her and simply not good enough for their precious daughter. Until it's clearer where their relationship is heading, she can't see the point in having a confrontation with them.

'There you go, love,' her nana says, handing Ruby a mug of coffee.

'That was quick, Nana.'

'I flicked the switch on the kettle the moment I heard the garden gate,' she replies with a wink. 'Now, tell me all about yesterday. How did you get on?'

'Good,' Ruby answers, having a sip of her drink. It's just the perfect temperature. Unlike her mum, who pours boiling water onto coffee granules because she usually drinks pod coffee so is unaware of the difference it makes to the taste, her nana is an expert in instant coffee and always lets the water cool slightly after boiling. 'I got first in all my solos, and we won both group dances that I was in too. I guess you could call it a clean sweep,' she adds, trying not to sound smug. 'Miss Grace said the adjudicator really liked me. She apparently asked her if I'm planning on making it my career.'

'And are you?' Her nana settles into the armchair on the opposite side of the gas fire.

'I don't know, Nana,' Ruby sighs. 'It's one thing being the star pupil in your dancing school, but something else entirely competing for jobs with people who've been at full-time stage school since they were eleven.'

'But you're not just the star of your dancing school, Ruby. Doing so well in all the competitions you enter, including the Nationals and the Worlds, surely must give you confidence that you have a special talent.'

'I suppose,' Ruby says. 'But what if I don't make it and I haven't got a degree as a back-up? Where would that leave me in terms of a career?'

'Thankfully, I don't think so much importance is placed on degrees anymore. When I was young, only the elite students went to university to study academic degrees,' her nana says, a wistful expression momentarily clouding her face. 'But then things changed. Everyone wanted to go to university, and they developed degree courses in all sorts of subjects. It was a money-spinning exercise, if you ask me, and has left the students in debt up to their eyeballs. The trouble was, most employers wouldn't even look at your CV if you didn't have a degree, but I think things have come full circle, although a lot depends on the career choice. Any thoughts on what you'd like to do if the uncertainty of show business isn't for you?'

'Something to do with languages maybe?' Ruby shrugs. Her natural ability to learn languages helped her select French and Spanish alongside English to study at A level, but she has no idea what kind of job that might eventually lead to.

'You can't go wrong with languages. The world quite literally would be your oyster.'

Her nana's use of the same phrase Megan used the previous day before their argument has Ruby reaching into her pocket for her phone to check if she's had a message from her friend. She hasn't and her nana must have noticed the disappointed look on her face.

'Is everything okay, Ruby? You've seemed a bit off since you got here.'

'Sorry, Nana,' she replies, slipping the phone back in her pocket. 'It's just, I had a bit of a disagreement with Megan yesterday and now she's not talking to me.'

'I thought something wasn't quite right. Was it because you were doing so well in the competition? Try to put yourself in her place for a minute. It must be difficult always playing second fiddle.' At Ruby's puzzled expression, Linda tries to explain. 'You know, like in an orchestra?'

'Oh right,' Ruby says. She's not sure what a fiddle is and what it has to do with an orchestra but it's not a conversation she wants to have. 'It wasn't about the competition,' she begins tentatively, unsure whether she should confide in her nana or not. 'I... I told Megan a secret without thinking it through properly, and now she hates me,' Ruby concludes, a tremor in her voice.

'She doesn't hate you.' Her nana puts her mug down and moves across to sit next to her granddaughter on the sofa. 'Whatever the secret was, you two have been best friends for far too long to let it come between you. Do you want to tell me about it?' she adds, putting her arm around Ruby.

'I can't. You might tell Mum and Dad and then I'll really be in trouble.'

Her nana clears her throat.

'Erm... you're not pregnant, are you?'

'What? No, of course not. I haven't even got a boyfriend...'

Ruby stops. 'At least, not a boyfriend that I've got that kind of relationship with.'

Her nana appears to be weighing things up before she says, 'So, is this disagreement with Megan about a boy that you both like?'

Ruby nods.

'Okay. Let me guess. You knew she liked him, but he asked you out and you said yes. Am I close?'

'Spot on, Nana,' Ruby says, relieved that she won't have to find the words to explain the situation. 'Should I have said no when he asked because I knew how much Megan liked him?'

'That's a tricky one. I'm assuming you like him a lot too otherwise you wouldn't have said yes.' Ruby nods again. 'So, it's not as though you did it out of spite. You said yes because you like him and in my mind that makes it okay.'

'Really?' Ruby asks.

'Yes, really. It's not your fault that you both like the same boy. It would be different if Megan had been dating him and he dumped her for you, but that's not the situation. She'll come around eventually. She's hurting at the moment and that's understandable, but I'm sure the two of you will work it out.'

Ruby exhales heavily but doesn't speak.

'You know, it's not dissimilar to the way that me and your grandad got together. We were at school together too. My friend, Valerie, had a crush on him, and we ended up falling out over it.'

'Did the two of you make it up?' Ruby asks.

Linda pauses, realising she's backed herself into a corner that she can only get out of by telling the truth. 'No actually. She went around telling everyone that I'd stolen her boyfriend, even though they'd never gone out together, and everyone believed her. I was sent to Coventry by my whole year group,' she adds, shrugging her shoulders dismissively.

'Coventry? Why would you go there?'

Her nana smiles. 'It was a saying we used to use when people refused to speak to you because you'd done something wrong – not that we had, of course. The funny thing is, it made us stronger as a couple. We ran away to Gretna Green to get married as soon as we were old enough. I often wonder if we would have done that if our friends hadn't shunned us.'

'But you stayed married until Grandad's accident, so it was the right thing,' Ruby says.

For a moment, her nana looks as though she's going to respond to Ruby's comment before thinking better of it.

'That's history,' she says instead. 'I was just pointing out that you're not the first two friends to fancy the same boy, and if you handle it right, Megan will be more understanding than Valerie was.'

'My situation is a bit different though, Nana. He's not a boy from my class at school. He's the brother of one of my dancing school friends and he's a bit...' She pauses. 'Older than me.'

'How much is "a bit"?' her nana probes.

Ruby hesitates. 'Three years,' she admits, her cheeks flushing slightly.

As though the penny has suddenly dropped, her nana says, 'So that's why you don't want your parents to know? You're afraid that they'll think he's not a suitable first boyfriend?'

'Something like that,' Ruby says vaguely. 'You won't tell them, will you?'

'It's not up to me to tell them, darling. I hope you will when you're ready because it's never a good idea to keep secrets from your parents, but they won't hear anything about it from me,' she replies, holding her index finger to her lips.

'Thanks, Nana.' Ruby puts her mug down on the stone hearth to free up both arms to fling them around her grandmother. 'You're the best!' She pulls away. 'But what should I do about Megan?'

'When are you next at dancing?'

'Tuesday evening.'

'Why don't you try messaging her to see if she'll meet you before class and you can explain your feelings to her,' she suggests.

'She's not replying to my messages,' Ruby says.

'Well, send another What's Up now that she's had time to calm down a bit.'

Ruby doesn't bother correcting her. She and her mum have tried previously, but it always seems to fall on deaf ears and, in this instance, Ruby thinks it's probably more accurate. She pulls her phone out of her pocket and types a quick message before hitting send and holding her crossed fingers up in the air.

SEVEN

MELISSA

24 June 2023 – the day after the party

'Your idea of a musicals theme went down really well,' I say, handing Ruby a plate with two slices of cheese on toast, with the cheese still bubbling. 'Be careful, it's hot.'

It smells appetising and has had my stomach rumbling while it's been under the grill. It's only a couple of hours since I finished my breakfast, but I've helped myself to a digestive biscuit from the tin to accompany my cup of tea to stave off the hunger pangs. I'm seriously reconsidering my plan for a salad lunch with Steve as I pull out a chair to sit down opposite Ruby at the kitchen table.

Ruby heeds my warning and takes a nibble from the edge of her cheese on toast, managing to incorporate a small amount of the dollop of tomato pickle I've spooned onto the centre of each of the four toast halves.

'Right?' she says after savouring the mouthful for a few seconds. 'I knew my friends from dance class would be on board with a themed party, but I have to admit some of my school-mates really surprised me, particularly the boys,' she continues before taking a slightly larger bite of her lunch, sinking her teeth into the melted cheddar atop the crunchy slice of granary toast.

'Was it Troy dressed up as Shrek?' I ask. 'I spent half the evening wondering if he'd given any thought as to how he was going to get the green make-up off.'

We both laugh.

'At least he'll be able to use the excuse of the make-up for the green tinge to his skin today after the skinful he had to drink. I'm not sure how some of the others will explain it to their parents, though.'

'There did seem to be a few tipsy people last night,' I acknowledge. 'Do you think they'd been drinking before they arrived? Because we were very firm with the bar staff that alcoholic drinks were limited to one per token and everyone was only given two tokens.'

Ruby rolls her eyes and shakes her head in disbelief. 'Mum, you really are quite naïve for your fifty-eight years. Of course they had been drinking before they arrived, and then they were scrounging alcohol tokens off my friends that don't drink. It was a good plan to try to keep a handle on people having too much, but in reality it was never going to work.'

'Well, at least no one was staggering around in an obviously drunken state,' I say.

'And no one vommed,' Ruby adds, popping the final bite of her first piece of toast into her mouth before greedily starting on the next, 'which is always a bonus. At Lily's party in April, someone threw up in the planters by their front door on their way out. Her mum and dad were furious.'

Although it had never been a consideration to have the party at our house because of the number of guests, I think we made the right decision in hiring the golf club despite the expense.

While I'm imagining the nightmare of cleaning up after vomiting teenagers, Ruby says, 'Maybe Dad should have had a couple more drinks so that he would have been able to give the speech. I'm assuming he bottled it?'

Ruby's tone is playful but I suspect it might be hiding her disappointment that her dad hadn't delivered the speech despite promising to.

'Well, that's a little bit harsh, but yes, the nerves were obviously getting to him. Even the night before when Auntie Sadie was here for dinner, he wasn't his usual relaxed self,' I say.

'Yeah, I noticed that. It was almost as though they'd had an argument.'

'I can't imagine what about,' I remark. 'Unless he'd already voiced his concerns to her about getting up to do the speech. She was quite adamant he should deliver it,' I add, thinking back to the look she gave me across the top table as the two of us got to our feet simultaneously.

The image of the note flashes into my mind. Sadie had been surprised when I'd stood up to deliver the speech that she thought Steve was giving. And she'd been slightly critical of my delivery. With the benefit of hindsight, it's almost as though she was trying to find out if I'd seen the note. There's no question that Sadie and Ruby are close. What if Ruby told her a secret that Sadie feels uncomfortable knowing?

I didn't mention the note last night because we didn't have the chance for a quiet chat, but I'll have plenty of time over dinner tonight.

'So, when did you know that the speech was going to be down to you?' Ruby asks.

'About five minutes before your dad was due to take to the stage.' She raises her eyebrows and gives a slight shake of the head. 'Were you terribly disappointed that it was me rather than him?'

'More disappointed for him really. You've always done stuff like that, so I was surprised when he agreed to do it, rather than letting you take control like you normally do. Although I thought you seemed a little less fluent than usual. It must have been the short notice,' she says.

Ruby makes no attempt to hide either the accusation of me taking control or the criticism of my delivery, but rather than defending myself, I seize the opportunity to mention the note concealed within the pages.

'Actually, Ruby, there was a reason for that.' *Apart from the short notice I was given*, I add in my head. 'Did you notice me bending down to pick something up just before I started speaking?'

'Vaguely,' Ruby replies, wiping her mouth with a piece of flowery kitchen towel. She screws it up and drops it on the plate. 'What was it?'

I take a breath. I'd intended to ask Steve's opinion before mentioning it to Ruby, but I haven't had the chance and now an opportunity has presented itself to slip it into the conversation without making too much of a big deal about it.

'It was a piece of paper with the words "she's not who you think she is" written on it.'

I'm watching my daughter carefully for her reaction. She shrugs her shoulders. 'What does it mean? Who's not who you think she is?'

'I don't know, sweetheart, but I was rather hoping you might have an explanation.'

There's a brief pause while she examines my face with her piercing blue eyes.

'Oh, right, so you think the note is referring to me?' she bristles. 'Are you accusing me of something, Mum? 'Cos that's what it feels like.'

'No. No, of course not. It's just that if there's some kind of issue, you know you can talk to me about it. I'm always here for you,' I say, reaching my hand across the table towards hers.

She snatches her hand away from mine as though my touch has scalded her. 'Really? Is that what you think, Mum? You're never around for me to talk to. If you're not working, you're at the gym or volunteering for one of your charities. Charity is supposed to begin at home, but I certainly haven't seen much evidence of it.'

I can feel my cheeks heating up as if to remind me of all the work I've been doing recently with a menopause charity. Is it a fair criticism? Have I neglected my daughter when she needs me to confide in?

'I'm sorry if it feels that way to you, Ruby, but I think you're being a little unfair. I'm always driving you to dance practice and giving up my weekends to take you and Megan to dance competitions.'

Ruby claps her hands together repeatedly in a mock round of applause. 'Is that enough of a thank you, Mum?' she asks, her voice dripping with sarcasm. 'Or maybe you'd prefer one of my dance trophies because you think you're some kind of super parent for spending a few hours with your daughter at the weekend. You've gone on often enough about how much you longed for a baby and were finally blessed when you became pregnant with me. I wouldn't have thought actually looking after your yearned-for child would have been such a burden,' she says, pushing her chair back from the table, the legs scraping against the tiled floor, and getting to her feet so that she's looking down on me.

I have no idea how this has escalated so quickly, unless Ruby is using her anger to distract me from asking anything further about the note. Maybe she's got something to hide after all and this is her way of throwing me off the scent. There's no doubt that her words are cruel and uncalled for, but will anything be gained by having an argument with her?

I push down my own anger that is starting to bubble. 'Come on, Ruby. Let's not fall out over a stupid note on a scrap of paper that was intended for your dad's eyes, not mine. It probably doesn't even mean you.'

'But you automatically assumed it did, Mum, and that's what really hurts,' Ruby says, heading towards the kitchen door, wrenching it open and slamming it so hard behind her that my cup rattles on its saucer.

I hear her thundering up the stairs and then banging around in her room for a few minutes before stomping back down the stairs and throwing something onto the hall floor.

She flings the door open. 'Have you been snooping around in my room?' she demands, her eyes blazing.

I can feel the heat as my cheeks colour up, but before I can speak, she continues, 'Don't bother trying to deny it. Teddy has fallen off my bed. What were you looking for, Mum? Evidence to confirm your suspicions? Well?' she asks defiantly, her small frame filling the doorway, her hands on her hips. 'Did you find anything?'

My resolve from a few moments earlier not to rise to her provocation deserts me. 'How dare you speak to me like that? This is my house and I'll go wherever the hell I like in it. I don't hear you complaining when I've been in your room to clean or change the sheets on your bed.'

'But that's different. We both know what you were doing in my room today. I'm not ten years old anymore. I don't have to tell you every tiny aspect of my life,' Ruby says, the volume of her voice increasing with every word she utters. 'I'm an adult now. You don't control me, is that clear?'

I shake my head in despair. It's pointless denying why I was in her room when she knows exactly the reason I was there. Lying to her now will only make matters worse. My eyes rest on her striped canvas overnight bag leaning drunkenly against the radiator in which she usually takes her dancing shoes and make-up to competitions.

Obviously noticing, Ruby says, 'I'm going to stay at Nana's.'

'Can't we talk about this, Ruby?'

'There's nothing to talk about.'

'Okay,' I say, trying to remain calm. 'Well, can I at least give you a lift?'

'Don't bother,' she says over her shoulder as she grabs her keys off the rack in the hall and opens the front door. 'I wouldn't want to take up any more of your precious time. I'll get the bus.'

And then she's gone, leaving silence and emptiness in her wake.

I'm not sure how long I sit at the kitchen table, my hands in my lap, staring into space and wondering how I could have handled the situation so badly. Maybe it's only a few minutes, but the next thing I'm aware of is Baxter whining softly and looking up at me with his big brown eyes. I reach to stroke his head, but he intercepts my movement and starts licking my hand with his lolling pink tongue.

'Where did I go wrong, Baxter?' I say, sliding off my chair to sit on the floor next to him, my arms around his neck, my face buried in his soft fur.

He wriggles free and rolls onto his back for me to tickle his tummy. If only humans were as uncomplicated and loved as unconditionally as dogs.

'I wish I'd never persuaded her to have a birthday party,' I sob.

As far back as her seventeenth birthday, Ruby was adamant that she didn't want or need a big flashy party to celebrate her eighteenth. In fact, ever since the subject was first mentioned, she said she didn't want a party at all. She'd provided us with endless excuses and reasons why it wasn't a good idea, but none of them rang true. In my heart, I suspected that she was still afraid of a repetition of her disastrous sixth birthday party, even all these years later.

The memory of my daughter sitting at the head of a long trestle table wearing her pretty pink party dress, her blonde hair freshly washed and curling over her shoulders, has haunted me for years.

Ruby was a very popular child and had a constant stream of different friends over for play dates, so deciding who to invite to her birthday party and who to leave out was making her anxious. In the end, we rented the local village hall so that she could invite the whole class and nobody would feel excluded.

On the day, though, the table which should have been set for thirty was eventually reduced to just seven, including me and Steve.

My phone had rung on and off during the evening before Ruby's party, with apologetic mums saying that their child wouldn't be able to come because they'd been struck down with a sickness bug. By the following morning, it was clear that the numbers attending would be dramatically reduced and I'd warned Ruby over breakfast that a lot of her classmates wouldn't be able to come because they weren't feeling well.

Even I wasn't prepared for the number of no-shows, as not everyone had had the courtesy to ring and cancel. Watching the excitement drain from Ruby's face as the clock ticked past 2 p.m. and only two of her Year 1 classmates had arrived to help her celebrate, neither of whom had ever been to our house for play dates, had been heartbreaking.

In the end, Megan, Ruby's new friend from the dancing class that she'd recently started attending, and our babysitter's daughter, Jade, along with Caleb and Flo from school, were the only other children present.

Even my mum had refused to change her plans when I'd rung to explain the impending disaster. She'd booked tickets to go to a theatre matinee in preference to attending the party with 'a crowd of shrieking children', as she'd described it. Despite my pleas and telling her how upset Ruby was, she'd simply said she would see her granddaughter on the Sunday as originally organised. The offer to pay for her unused ticket and buy her a new one fell on deaf ears.

'Disappointment is something we all need to learn to deal with in life, as I know only too well,' she'd said, unable to keep bitterness from her voice. 'The sooner Ruby realises that she can't have everything she wants, the better, in my opinion. It will manage her expectations.'

It wasn't the first time that a disparaging remark about the way Steve and I were parenting Ruby had been expressed by my mum. I'd wanted to say, 'She's six years old, Mum. There's plenty of time to learn life's lessons.' But rather than getting into an argument about it, I'd forced a smile into my voice and said we'd see her the following day.

So, Steve and I sat down with the children to bulk out the numbers, forcing ourselves to eat sandwiches and crisps washed down with lemonade drunk from paper cups emblazoned with the words 'Happy Birthday Ruby' which I'd had specially made for the occasion. Even Mr Sausage, the children's entertainer we'd booked, couldn't raise a smile on Ruby's tear-streaked face with his balloon animals and dubious magic tricks.

Had I known that so few of Ruby's class would be well enough to attend, it would probably have been better to cancel or try to rearrange the party for a different day, but hindsight is a wonderful thing. At the time, it had been difficult to predict what would have caused the least amount of upset.

When I collected Ruby from school on the Monday after her party, she burst into floods of tears. Apparently, Flo had told her classmates that it was the worst party she'd ever been to and some of them had then told Ruby that they weren't actually sick, they just hadn't wanted to go. Children can be so cruel, and the fact that Ruby has refused to have a birthday party every year since shows the lasting impact the whole incident had on her.

It was no surprise that Ruby was adamant that she didn't

want an eighteenth birthday celebration, but Steve and I had hoped for a softening in her attitude as we got closer to the big day.

We broached the subject again over Christmas lunch when we were all feeling full of festive cheer, not to mention a little tipsy. Ruby had already attended several of her friends' celebrations and really enjoyed them, so we were hopeful that her resistance to having her own party would begin to wane.

At the Christmas lunch table, she hadn't outright refused to have a party, which Steve and I took as an encouraging sign. All we wanted was to celebrate Ruby, give her a night to remember, something wonderful and magical that would live in her memory forever.

Looking back, if we hadn't started making tentative plans and secretly enlisted Megan and a couple of Ruby's friends from school to help make it possible, I wouldn't be in possession of a note suggesting that my daughter has been lying to me. If we'd accepted Ruby's wishes, none of this would have happened and I wouldn't be distraught on my kitchen floor crying into my dog's fur.

EIGHT

MELISSA

February – four months before the party

'Did Ruby say why she didn't need picking up from dancing tonight?' Steve asks, reaching his arms around my waist and kissing the back of my neck.

If I wasn't busy whisking the skimmed milk into the flour and butter mixture so that my white sauce won't be lumpy, I'd turn to give him a proper kiss. Some couples cease to be outwardly affectionate the longer they are in a relationship, but Steve and I still have our moments. He buys me flowers every week and we curl up watching television together on the sofa on the evenings Ruby is staying over at her nana's.

'She said she and Megan were going for a coffee after class, and that they'd get the bus back to save me a second journey. I think me mentioning that I would have time to make lasagne might have coloured her decision,' I say.

'Oh, is Megan better now then? Poor kid sounded terrible during our call last week when I was trying to get an idea of how many of the dance class would want to come to Ruby's party. If we manage to convince her to have one,' Steve adds.

'She hasn't been at dancing since the competition. Maybe she wasn't feeling well then and that's the reason she went home early. Ruby said it was a nasty chest infection and she couldn't shift it,' I say, turning the gas ring off before adding the grated cheese to my perfectly smooth sauce. It was a trick I'd learnt from a celebrity chef who'd guested on my radio show a few years previously and I've used it ever since because it gives a cheesier flavour.

'I hope you don't get it, Mel. It's not ideal when you talk for a living,' Steve says, getting the place mats out of the drawer and positioning them around the kitchen table.

'You're optimistic,' I remark, nodding in the direction of the table. 'I haven't finished the layering yet and then it's half an hour in the oven.'

'I'm a boy scout at heart,' he replies. 'Nothing wrong with being prepared. And anyway, I need to get changed out of my work clothes before sitting down to eat.'

I'm just sprinkling the parmesan on the top of the lasagne before putting it in the oven, and Steve, now wearing his grey tracksuit bottoms and a polo shirt, is pouring us both a glass of red wine, when I hear Ruby's key in the lock. I slide the dish into the oven just as our daughter forcefully slams the front door, and the house shakes in response. We exchange a quizzical look as Ruby appears in the kitchen doorway, a thunderous expression on her face.

'How dare you interfere in my life and try to force me to have a party that I don't bloody want!' Ruby shrieks.

'Whoa there, Ruby. Calm down,' Steve says. 'Let's talk about it like adults, shall we?'

'You had no right to speak to my friends behind my back,' she continues with no decrease in volume.

It's clear that someone has spilled the beans about our tentative early planning for Ruby's eighteenth birthday bash and more than likely that someone is Megan. I'm disappointed that she has broken our trust in her and now our daughter is livid.

'What part of "I DON'T WANT A PARTY" did you two not get?' Ruby demands.

She clearly has no intention of calming down and a quick glance in Steve's direction tells me he is now almost as wound up as she is.

There have been very few arguments between the three of us over the years, but after a moment of shocked silence, Steve replies at a similar volume to Ruby. 'We'll speak to whoever the hell we like!'

I now feel like a spectator as the two of them lock eyes, glinting dark with anger. I'm pretty sure Ruby wasn't expecting that reaction from her normally placid dad, and to be honest neither was I.

'We're your parents,' he continues equally forcefully. 'While you live under our roof, you'll show us a bit of respect, young lady.'

'Respect is not a given, it's earned,' she flings back. 'How can I respect people who clearly have such little regard for my feelings?'

I've been holding back tears as I witness the spectacle of the two people I love most in the world hurling abuse at each other, but now they pour freely down my cheeks.

'Stop it!' I scream, stunning them both into momentary silence.

Steve starts towards me, but I hold my hands up, the palms facing outwards as though to push him away if he tries to come any closer.

'Let's just forget it. If Ruby doesn't want a party to celebrate her eighteenth birthday, that's up to her.'

He examines my face intently, searching for my true feelings. It seems like an age but is probably only a fraction of a second before he turns away from me to face our daughter. 'No, I'm not having that,' he says, his voice more controlled but his anger still evident. 'It might be your birthday, Ruby, but it's also the day your mother gave you life. You have no idea what she went through before she finally became pregnant with you; the years of negative pregnancy tests, hormone injections, miscarriages, until, when she had long since given up hope of having the one thing she craved more than anything in the world, she finally conceived you; our little miracle.'

My chest tightens at the words 'our little miracle'. Ruby is not the only one who has no idea of the lengths I went to in my efforts to become pregnant. My breath is coming in shallow gasps, and although I've never previously experienced a panic attack, I fear I'm about to have one.

Ruby's cheeks start to colour, but my normally mild-mannered husband hasn't finished.

'She endured thirty-six hours of torturous labour,' he continues, emotion now fuelling his anger, 'before conceding that she would need to have an emergency caesarean section because your life was in danger.'

Ruby is gripping the edge of the table, and her eyes are filling with tears. I want Steve to stop, but he clearly isn't done yet.

'She literally bears the scars of giving birth to you and you want to deny her the chance to celebrate your coming of age because of something that happened twelve years ago and was totally beyond our control?' The volume of his voice is increasing with every word. 'I thought we'd raised a nicer human being than that. You're pathetic! No, I take that back,' he rages. 'You're selfish and cruel.'

Steve has gone too far, but before I can voice my opinion he slams out of the room, leaving silence in his wake, only broken by Ruby's sobs. It takes all my self-control to resist the urge to rush over to comfort my daughter. The blood is pulsing through my veins. I can barely breathe, waiting for her next move. I've no idea if she's crying tears of self-pity, remorse or if she's angry with me because her father has firmly taken my side over hers. What she does next could colour our relationship forever.

'I'm so sorry, Mum,' she finally manages to mumble, lifting her eyes to look into mine. 'I've never thought of my birthday as your celebration too. Dad's right, I'm selfish and thoughtless. Each year that I haven't wanted a party to celebrate my birthday has made the idea of having one the following year even more unthinkable. But I realise now that my refusal to have birthday parties all these years has denied you both so much happiness. Can you forgive me?'

Unable to hold back any longer, I'm by her side in moments, scooping her into my arms. We cling onto one another, neither of us speaking. My initial feeling is one of relief that Steve's honesty hasn't driven a wedge between me and my beautiful girl, but it's quickly replaced by the unconditional love I've felt for my child since she let out her first cry to announce her arrival to the world.

Eventually, she eases herself away from my embrace.

'There's twelve years' worth of catching up to do, Mum,' Ruby says, her voice calmer but still shaky. 'It'll take a bit of planning, but we're going to throw the best eighteenth birthday party ever.'

'Oh Ruby, I'm so happy to hear that,' I say. And I am. Turning eighteen will be a hugely significant moment for her.

Clearly warming to the idea, she says, 'Do you think we can have a musicals theme?'

'I don't see why not,' I reply.

'Maybe we could ask Auntie Sadie to help.'

'Great idea. What time is it in New York?' I say, glancing at the kitchen clock. 'We could call her now if you like,' I add, anxious to set the wheels in motion before my daughter can have second thoughts.

'There's something I need to do first,' Ruby says, her eyes moving towards the kitchen door through which Steve had stormed minutes earlier.

I nod.

'Go and make your peace with your dad and then we'll eat. We can call Auntie Sadie later. Thinking about it, she'll probably still be working.'

NINE

SADIE

February – four months before the party

Sadie cups her oversized wine glass in her hand and gazes out at the myriad of lights reflecting on the dark expanse of water below her floor-to-ceiling windows before flopping down onto the chaise longue. It's only a little after 4 p.m., but at this time of year, it's already starting to get dark, which is the criteria for Sadie allowing herself her first drink of the day.

From her vantage point on the twentieth floor of her apartment block, she has a perfect view of the East River. It was what had encouraged her to sign the lease on the apartment when she'd first viewed it the year after her interior design business had really taken off. It was a view that could never be interrupted as her building was right on the waterfront. It's heartbreaking to think that she might soon have to leave this place she has grown to love.

It wasn't a particularly luxurious apartment and not decorated to her taste at all when she first moved in, but the landlord had been very receptive to the idea of her remodelling and redecorating at her own expense as he would be the one to ultimately benefit.

At the time, Sadie had thought her landlord would have a very long wait before he would make a profit, thanks to the money she had invested in his property and her home. She had every intention of renewing annually, as was written into her contract. That was when she could afford to pay the extortionate rent on a river-view apartment, but it's no longer her situation.

Since the meeting with her last client, Tonya Hammer, four weeks previously, Sadie's work has completely dried up. She contacted the clients she'd met at the Hammers' Christmas party as she'd felt compelled to. She kept the emails simple, saying that due to unforeseen circumstances she would no longer be able to undertake their projects and would be returning any advance payments she'd received.

Sadie doesn't know for sure whether Tonya had told people the real reason for the unexplained cancelling of their projects, but rumours quickly circulated that Sadie was unreliable and in financial difficulty. She was a pariah. From a diary filled with appointments that were scratched out with red ink to page after page of virtual white-out. The only entry in her diary now is Ruby's eighteenth birthday in June.

The idea had been to surprise her goddaughter by turning up at the house unannounced. Sadie was prepared to put aside her reluctance to return to the UK to try to make the occasion memorable, but now the visit is in serious doubt because of the cost of the flights and hotel.

Sadie had vowed never to return when she'd left England nineteen years ago. There was too much pain associated with her last few months in her home country. A clean break was needed from her past and she'd stuck to the promise she'd made to herself, even making an excuse not to return for Ruby's christening despite accepting the role of godmother. But turning eighteen is a huge moment in anyone's life and it's time to put Ruby before her own feelings.

Sipping the Malbec that she's been cradling in her hand, Sadie appreciates the warm feeling in her chest. She's grateful that her bar area was well-stocked when disaster struck as she's relied fairly heavily on alcohol to get her through the past few weeks, and good wine is a luxury she can no longer afford.

If I do manage to rustle up the cash for my UK trip, she ponders, *will it just be a flying visit or will I be forced to return to England on a permanent basis?*

She sighs heavily. One thing is certain: she can't stay in New York.

Of course, New York isn't the only American city, but building a reputation in any industry takes time and Sadie doesn't know whether she has the energy to start over in America.

Maybe I should return home, she thinks, taking another sip. *I could probably get a set-design job if I start throwing out a few feelers among my old contacts. I need to earn some decent money before I retire.*

She allows herself a wry smile.

Until that fateful afternoon in January when her world had come crashing about her ears, she'd felt a million miles away from retirement. She's always been young at heart and, thanks to a few subtle cosmetic interventions, looks fifteen to twenty years younger than she is. But she must face up to the facts. She's not that far away from pensionable age. *Nine years, give or take,* she thinks, *that's more or less all the time I have to reinvent my life.*

Lost in her thoughts, the shrill ringtone of her mobile phone startles her. It barely rings at all these days. It's unsurprising how quickly acquaintances that had been keen to form friendships during her success have faded into the background and no longer return voicemail messages.

Glancing at her screen, she can see it's Melissa calling. It's tempting to let it go to voicemail as she's not sure she's up to putting on an act for her best friend. One wrong word and Mel would suspect something's up and start asking questions. That's the problem with close friends, Sadie thinks. No matter how infrequently you see them or talk to them, they seem to have a sixth sense.

Maybe that's why she's calling. Perhaps she's got a feeling that something's not right with me.

After the eighth ring, the call will go to voicemail. Sadie knows she is only putting off the inevitable if she doesn't answer now, as Mel always rings again.

She hits the green button.

'Hi, Mel. How are you?' she asks in an artificially bright tone of voice.

'It's not Mum, it's me, Auntie Sadie,' Ruby says excitably.

'Ruby! My favourite person in the world,' Sadie replies, her voice now genuinely bright. 'Does your mum know you've got her phone?'

'Yes, of course. And I probably should have told you you're on speakerphone,' she adds, giggling. 'Mum's not looking too pleased that she's been bumped into second place on your list of favourite people in the world.'

'Oops. Sorry, Mel,' Sadie says.

'Apology accepted,' Melissa replies.

'So, girls, what's happening?'

'Well, you know it's my eighteenth birthday in June,' Ruby says.

'Is it?' Sadie says in a teasing tone. 'What date? I'd better make a note in my diary.'

'Very funny. Anyway, guess what? We've decided to have a party,' Ruby says.

Sadie almost drops her phone in surprise. Not only is Ruby going to have a party, but she sounds genuinely pleased about it.

Although there was nothing she could have done to change what happened at Ruby's sixth birthday party even if she'd accepted Melissa's invitation to attend, Sadie has always felt guilty for not being there to support her best friend and her goddaughter when they needed her.

'Amazing,' Sadie says. 'Am I invited?'

'Is that even a real question?' Melissa chips in. 'Although I did warn Ruby that you've refused all my previous attempts to get you home for a visit so not to get her hopes up.'

'You will come, won't you?' Ruby pleads. 'It's going to be the best party ever with your help.'

'My help?' Sadie says, immediately panicking about what that might entail. By June she will more than likely be homeless as well as broke and won't be in a position to help anyone. 'What did you have in mind?'

'I'm coming to that,' Ruby says. 'You know I love musicals and theatre? Well, I wondered if we could maybe have a themed party, and who better than you to design the room?'

'I know you're always super busy, Sadie,' Melissa adds, 'but if you could maybe jot a few ideas down for us to work from, that would be great.'

'I'm never too busy for you guys,' Sadie says, remembering the time she'd almost lost a potential new client when the two of them were over on one of their visits. Ruby had asked if they could go to a matinee performance of *Waitress* on Broadway and Sadie, not wanting to disappoint her, had left the potential client a voicemail to reschedule her 4 p.m. meeting that day so that they could all go. Unfortunately, the client hadn't picked the message up and had waited for Sadie for over an hour. It had all been smoothed over eventually, but Sadie had so many clients at the time that if she had lost one new one, it wouldn't have mattered. That contract had ended up earning her a hundred thousand dollars, but she would still have traded it to spend time with Ruby and Mel if it hadn't worked out. Those were the days when she could afford to pick and choose. 'Send me an email with some of your favourite shows, Ruby, and I'll make a start,' Sadie adds, thankful that her days will be filled with something other than regrets and worrying about how to pay the bills.

'Will do,' Ruby says.

'And you'll have to start thinking about who you want to come as too,' she adds before ending the call.

Sadie stares down at her phone for a moment, watching until the screen fades to black. She's shocked that Ruby is having a party and is clearly so excited by the prospect of it.

If Ruby can overcome her fears and move on with the rest of her life, maybe it's time for me to do the same, Sadie thinks, getting up off the chaise longue, walking over to the kitchen island and tipping the remainder of her wine down the sink. *Everything happens for a reason. Maybe the time is right for me to go home.*

TEN

RUBY

February – four months before the party

The days after she told Megan about Kyle were some of the most difficult in Ruby's life. Even though she was an only child, she'd never felt so completely alone before, because from the age of five, she always had her best friend. So, when Megan refused to respond to Ruby's calls and WhatsApp messages, it was like her friend had died. It was Ruby's first experience of grief, and not one she was keen to repeat. She was used to waking up in the morning and having a chat with Megan while she was getting ready for school. And then again at night-time, the two of them would chat long after they should both have been asleep.

It was bad enough not speaking to her friend for the first couple of days, but Ruby had managed to appear outwardly calmer than she was feeling because she was expecting to see Megan at dancing class on Tuesday evening. Ruby had sat quietly in the passenger seat of her mum's car on the journey from Brockledean to Brighton. She was anxious to see her best friend to try to rebuild bridges but was nervous about how her attempts to patch this up might be received.

But Megan wasn't at dance class, nor did she attend on the Thursday or Friday, which was when Miss Grace informed the class that Megan's mum had rung to say that she had a bad chest infection. 'Apparently, it's not Covid, but it might be a good idea for us all to do a test to be on the safe side,' Miss Grace had said.

One week stretched to two weeks and then three, during which time Ruby kept checking Megan's social media accounts to see if she was online. She'd posted nothing since the morning of the dance competition, when the two of them had taken a laughing selfie in the dressing-room mirror before it was defaced with pink lipstick. Time and again, Ruby questioned whether she could have broken the news to Megan differently, or if in fact she should have told her at all so early in the relationship.

It had made things a bit uncomfortable between her and Kyle for a while too because he couldn't understand what the issue was. He knew who Megan was because, like Ruby, she was in the same dance class as his sister, but that's where his knowledge of her ended.

Just as Ruby was starting to really worry about her friend, Megan messaged her out of the blue saying she would be back at dancing the following Tuesday. Could they grab a coffee after class and try to smooth things over?

It was a bit awkward in class, but neither of them drew attention to it, concentrating on the correct positioning for their bodies in the barre work and then focusing on learning the intricate steps in the enchainment. Ruby and Megan weren't particularly keen on ballet, but both understood its importance as a basis from which to learn other forms of dance.

They leave dancing class together, but the walk to the coffee shop is in virtual silence. Ruby's stomach is in knots. She's wondering if the two of them will ever truly be able to reconcile.

The lack of conversation continues as they wait by the counter to place their orders before making their way to a table towards the back of the café. No sooner are they seated than the words of apology spill from Megan's lips.

'I'm so sorry, Ruby,' she says. 'I completely overreacted.'

'I'm sorry too,' Ruby replies, the pent-up emotion of the preceding three weeks releasing like steam from the valve on a pressure cooker.

'It... it was just a bit of a shock,' Megan continues. 'You've never shown any real interest in boys and suddenly you're dating someone I've been crazy about since I was fourteen. You know that I fell for him after the first time he picked Sasha up after dancing, because I told you as much.'

Ruby did remember, and Megan was right about her never showing any interest in boys, but she might have been surprised by the reason. Her hormones were equally as rampant as all the other girls of her age. Of course, Ruby had crushes on people, but she kept them to herself because she couldn't bear the thought of possible rejection once they'd got to know her better. She had the appearance of being supremely confident in everything she did, but that was her outer shell, which she'd developed over a number of years to protect herself from ever feeling as crushed as she had after her disastrous sixth birthday party. Underneath it, though, she had the same self-doubts as most of her contemporaries and the idea of everyone knowing she had been dumped was something that terrified Ruby. It was easier to not lay herself open to the possibility in the first place, until Kyle had come into her life.

'The thing is,' Ruby says, 'I did notice Kyle, but there didn't seem much point in mentioning it because I never imagined in my wildest dreams that he would be interested in me. And I've liked other boys from a distance too if I'm honest, but despite what everyone thinks, I'm not as confident as you, particularly around the opposite sex. You've always been comfortable having a bit of banter with them while I get all tongue-tied. It's the one part of my life where I feel less in control.'

'I wish you'd told me all this before,' Megan says, an element of reproach in her voice.

'About my feelings towards boys generally, or Kyle specifically?' Ruby asks.

'Both, I guess. It's history now though, I hope?' Megan asks, tentatively reaching her hand across the table separating the two of them. 'I had a horrible attack of jealousy and you didn't deserve the mean things I said.'

'Or what you wrote on the mirror for that matter,' Ruby replies, laughing. 'That was a bit tricky to explain when the others followed me into the dressing room, I can tell you.'

'Oh God, I'd forgotten about that,' Megan says, the colour rising up her cheeks in her embarrassment. 'What did you say?'

'You'll like this,' Ruby replies conspiratorially. 'Talk about quick thinking. I said we'd been talking about Baxter maybe fathering a litter of puppies before his operation and couldn't remember what a female dog was called.'

'You're joking? Don't tell me they fell for it?' Megan laughs.

'If they didn't, nobody said anything,' Ruby replies, just as Megan's phone, which is lying on the table between them, pings to alert her to a WhatsApp message.

Ruby's eyes automatically drop to the illuminated screen and she registers the words 'Ruby's dad' before Megan can snatch the phone up.

There's a 'deer in the headlights' moment for both girls before Ruby demands, 'Why is my dad messaging you?' When Megan doesn't immediately reply, she continues in a panicky voice, 'Have you told him about me and Kyle? How could you? You promised to keep it a secret.'

'If he knows, I didn't tell him,' Megan replies.

'Then why is he messaging you?' Ruby insists, a threatening tone to her voice.

'I'm not supposed to say anything,' Megan pleads.

'I'll count to three and then we're done. One... two...'

'Okay, okay,' Megan says, raising her hands in submission, her face deathly pale. 'It's supposed to be a secret, but I don't want to risk losing you again.' She takes a deep breath and continues. 'Your parents have contacted a few of us from dancing class and school. I think they want to organise an eighteenth birthday party for you.'

Ruby is momentarily stunned into silence, before grabbing her dancing bag and rushing out of the coffee shop, Megan's calls for her to wait falling on deaf ears.

ELEVEN

LINDA

24 June 2023 – the day after the party

'Well, this is a nice surprise,' Linda starts to say as she opens her front door before her granddaughter has even raised her hand to knock on it. One look at Ruby's red-rimmed eyes and she knows something is wrong. Then she notices the striped canvas bag slung over her granddaughter's shoulder. 'Take your bag up to your room if you're stopping and I'll make us a cuppa.'

Five minutes later, the two of them are sat either side of the fireplace, each with a mug of tea in hand.

'So, what's all this about then?' Linda asks. 'I'm assuming you haven't popped in because you missed seeing me this morning.'

'I needed to get away from Mum,' Ruby says, sighing deeply.

'Why? What's happened? Did she find out about you and Kyle?'

True to her word, Linda hadn't mentioned the blossoming relationship between her granddaughter and her boyfriend to Melissa and Steve. The longer it went on though, with the youngsters becoming closer and closer, Linda tried to encourage Ruby to tell them herself.

'No. But there was an anonymous note left between the pages of Dad's – or should I say Mum's – speech last night and now she suspects that there is something going on.'

'What did the note say?' Linda asks.

'"She's not who you think she is",' Ruby replies.

'So, it didn't mention you by name?'

'No. But Mum just assumed it meant me. That's what really upset me, Nana. She jumped straight to the conclusion that the note was about me,' Ruby says, her voice wobbling.

'Well, I suppose that is a fair assumption,' Linda says, trying to be the voice of reason. Ruby opens her mouth to speak but Linda stops her. 'Let me finish. The whole evening was dedicated to you, so why would anyone choose to reveal a secret about someone else at your party?'

Ruby appears to consider what Linda has said.

'I suppose so,' she agrees grudgingly.

'I know you and Kyle are very careful, but is it possible that someone apart from Megan has found out about your relationship and has decided not to be such a good friend to you and reveal your secret?'

'Maybe,' Ruby says distractedly, focusing more on Linda's comment about Megan being a good friend. Since February, the two have been back to being virtually inseparable.

'Well, perhaps have a little think about who might have seen you and Kyle together,' Linda suggests. 'Jealousy is a terrible thing and teenage girls can do very hurtful things without considering the consequences.'

Ruby shakes her head. 'Honestly, Nana, I have no idea who would leave a note like that at my party. Everyone was really looking forward to it. Why would anyone want to risk spoiling the whole evening? And, to be honest, if it had been Dad giving the speech as planned and he'd found the note, I'm pretty sure he'd have gone ballistic right then and there.'

'So, who else could it have been if none of your friends had any reason to spoil your evening?' Linda watches as the colour seems to drain from her granddaughter's face. 'What is it, Ruby? Have you thought of someone?'

'Kyle,' Ruby says in a voice barely above a whisper. It's a statement, not a question. 'Kyle had reason to spoil my evening.'

'Why on earth would you say that?' Linda asks.

'He was annoyed that he couldn't sit at our family table because our relationship is secret. He was stuck on a table at the back of the room, "babysitting" his sister, as he described it. He doesn't understand why I haven't told people about us when we've been going out for five months.'

From Kyle's perspective, Linda could appreciate that there might be some justification in him trying to force Ruby's hand, but there was also the risk that it could force them apart. Would he really be prepared to take the chance?

'You know my view on that, Ruby,' Linda says. 'It will be far worse if your parents find out from someone else that you've been dating behind their backs. Is it just because he's older than you that you're reluctant to tell them?'

Ruby shakes her head. 'No. This sounds awful, Nana, but I'm afraid they won't think he's good enough for me because he didn't go to university and get a degree. They might try to stop me from seeing him.'

'They wouldn't do that if you explain how much you like him. Your happiness is the most important thing to them,' Linda says.

'Are you sure about that?' Ruby asks. 'They've got me on some sort of pedestal. They love the fact that I'm good at school and good at dancing. They see me as their perfect daughter; but nobody's perfect, Nana.'

Linda suppresses a smile. She had used those exact words

earlier when she was talking about Ruby to Melissa. It's not only a problem with Melissa and Steve, it's parents of only children generally. They lavish a lot of time and love on their sole focus of attention, which can result in the child excelling but can also lead to the child feeling pressurised and afraid to fail.

'I know, love, and it must be hard for you trying to live up to their expectations,' Linda says.

Ruby nods. 'Don't get me wrong, Nana, I like working hard at school and I love my dancing, but I want to have a life as well. I don't think Mum and Dad realise the pressure I feel to please them. I don't know what they would do if I decided to run off with Kyle and get married like you and Grandad did, but it's my life and I should be able to live as I want to.'

'You're not planning anything like that are you, Ruby?' Linda says, a knot of anxiety forming in her gut. Her already fractured relationship with Melissa would fall apart completely if the youngsters eloped and she subsequently discovered that Linda had known they'd been seeing each other.

'No. But it worked out all right for you and Grandad. You were happy together and you've already said that's all Mum and Dad care about.'

Linda wishes she could backtrack on her earlier words. Of course Melissa and Steve want their daughter to be happy, but they also want the best for her. While Kyle seems nice enough from what Ruby has told her about him, he doesn't appear to have a lot going for him in terms of career prospects. He works in a local gym teaching classes and has a few personal training clients, but there's only really room for one Joe Wicks per generation. Linda suspects that might be as much the reason that Ruby has kept quiet about him as anything else.

'I'm not sure that being kept a secret is enough of a reason for Kyle to spoil your evening?'

Ruby sighs. 'We had a big argument a couple of weeks ago,'

she says. 'We normally get on so well that it caught me by surprise.'

'What did you argue about?' Linda asks.

'Me potentially going away to university,' Ruby responds.

'Well, that's a bit selfish of him,' Linda remarks.

'That's what I said. I told him we could still be boyfriend and girlfriend. Lots of people have long-distance relationships that work out, but he wasn't sure. So, I suggested that he could maybe move as well, as there are gyms in every town, and he flipped! He thought I was saying that his job is less important than my education, but I wasn't, Nana.'

'I know, love, but it's difficult if one person in a couple feels inferior to the other. Did it get resolved?' Linda asks. 'You two seemed fine at the party last night.'

'We were, but now I'm wondering if he left that note to get back at me.'

'Well, there's only one way to find out,' Linda says, taking Ruby's mug from her hand.

'You mean just ask him outright?' Ruby says, looking worried. 'Won't that just make things worse if he had nothing to do with it?'

'You could tell him that your mum found a note and how upset it made you that she assumed it was about you. Then ask who would do something like that? He might not admit it even if it was him, but you've known him long enough to gauge his reaction, I would have thought?'

Ruby swings her legs down from where she has tucked them under her on the sofa and gets to her feet. 'You're right, Nana. Now that I've got a doubt in my mind, I'd rather find out the answer sooner rather than later.'

'What are you waiting for then?' Linda asks.

TWELVE

MELISSA

24 June 2023 – the day after the party

'Hi, honey, I'm home!' Steve calls out in an American accent while dropping his golf bag on the hall floor with a clatter. He and I stumbled across the sitcom by the same name on an obscure TV channel during lockdown and, since then, Steve has found it hilarious to announce his return home from golf in that fashion.

Normally, I would fire back an equally comedic response, but right now I can't get the words out.

'Don't tell me you're still hungover...' Steve starts to say before stopping dead in his tracks. 'What are you doing down there? Is something wrong with Baxter?' He drops to his haunches with an anxious expression, which I see the moment I lift my tear-stained face away from Baxter's furry neck.

Baxter seizes the opportunity to wriggle free from my grasp and slinks over to Steve, whining softly. It's almost as though he's trying to tell Steve how upset I am.

'What the hell's going on, Mel?' Steve says, reaching for my hands and pulling me gently to a standing position and into an embrace.

'It's Ruby,' I say. I feel his body tense up immediately. 'She's okay,' I say to allay his fears, 'it's just we had a big falling-out.'

The tension relaxes slightly. Ruby and I don't often argue, but neither is it the first time.

'About what?' he asks, taking my face gently in his hands and searching my eyes for answers. 'She was in such a good mood after her party. What happened?'

'There's something I should have told you last night,' I say, 'but it was so late by the time we got home, and I knew you had to be up early. I wasn't going to mention it to Ruby before speaking to you,' I rush on, 'but the opportunity presented itself and I thought it was better to ask the question right away.'

'Mel, you're not making any sense. I have no idea what you're going on about. Sit down and let me get you a cup of tea,' he says, obviously noticing the barely touched one from earlier.

It's the second teabag I've wasted today, is all I can think as he flicks the switch on the kettle and ushers me into a seat.

'Is Ruby in her room? Do you want me to fetch her down so that we can hash this out together?' he asks, heading towards the doorway.

'She's not here. She stormed out after our argument.'

Worry flicks across my husband's face. While he's always tried to take my side in anything to do with disciplining Ruby because he believes a united front is the best way to parent a child, things are a little different now that our daughter is of an age where 'storming out of the house' is an option.

'It's okay,' I add. 'She's gone to my mum's.'

'Well, it's not okay because she's clearly upset you, but at least she's safe. What's this about, Mel?' he asks, reaching a fresh cup down from the cupboard and proceeding to make me a tea. 'What should you have told me last night?'

'It was when I got up to deliver the speech you were supposed to give. There was a note slipped between the pages.'

'A note? What did it say?' he asks, his back to me as he replaces the milk in the fridge.

I get a sinking feeling. I wish I'd either told Steve about the note last night or not mentioned it to Ruby, but it's too late for both of those options now.

I take a deep breath.

'It said, "She's not who you think she is",' I reply.

'And you assumed the note was about Ruby?' He stirs my cup of tea before slowly and deliberately placing the teaspoon on the draining board. It's like watching him in slow motion. It's almost as though he doesn't want to turn and face me.

'Well, who else could it mean?' I ask with a hint of irritation in my voice. 'It was slipped between the pages of a speech about our daughter. It must be referring to her, surely?'

Steve turns to face me and offers me my tea while massaging his forehead with his free hand. 'I agree, that seems most likely, but you don't know for sure. Please tell me you didn't actually accuse Ruby.'

I'm trying desperately to remember how the conversation went. It escalated into confrontation so quickly, I genuinely don't know if I out-and-out accused her.

'I don't think so,' I say. 'I think I just asked her if she had any idea what the note might mean.'

'So, as good as then. Honestly, Mel, you should have waited for me to get back and we could have handled this together.'

I don't understand why Steve is attacking me like this. If he'd found the note, which is what should have happened if he'd given the speech as planned, I'm pretty sure the accusations would have been flying last night when we got home, if not at the party itself. At least I've had the good sense not to ruin her actual birthday, which she properly enjoyed for the first time in thirteen years.

If Steve is waiting for a response, he can wait a bit longer. If I speak now, I can't be held responsible for what I might say and that will only make matters worse.

He gives a deep sigh. 'Look, surely you can appreciate that if Ruby is hiding something and you've called her out on it, she's not likely to tell us what it is now.' When he receives no response from me, he continues. 'And if this isn't about her, you've made her feel like we don't trust her at a time when she's about to go out into the world on her own and needs our unconditional support more than ever. Either way, and I'm sorry to say this, Mel, but you've made a bit of a mess of the situation.'

I'm furious that Steve is speaking to me like this, but I know giving in to that anger isn't going to calm the situation.

'I know,' I say, biting down on my lip so hard that the metallic taste of blood enters my mouth. 'You're right. I shouldn't have mentioned anything to Ruby until we'd had the chance to discuss it. But, in fairness, I wasn't the one who was supposed to find it. It should have been you.' A thought suddenly occurs to me. What if Steve deliberately asked me to make the speech knowing that I would find the note because he put it there? 'Why did you change your mind about giving the speech?' I ask.

'You know why. I've never been comfortable in the limelight. That's your forte. I thought I could do it and then realised I couldn't. It's as simple as that,' he says, spreading his hands as though laying his explanation out on a plate.

'But how can I be sure of that? For all I know, you put the note there for me to find,' I persist.

He's looking at me with what can only be described as an incredulous expression on his face. 'You can't be serious,' he says. 'Why would I do that?'

'I don't know,' I say. 'Maybe you discovered something about Ruby and didn't know how to tell me.'

'Trust me, if I found something out about her, you'd be the

first person I'd talk to about it and I would expect you to do the same.'

I drop my gaze. 'Of course,' I say, but I can't look my husband in the eye.

'We've never had any secrets where Ruby's concerned,' he says.

By adding the words 'where Ruby's concerned', I immediately wonder if there are other secrets he's keeping from me, but I'm hardly well-placed to be judgemental, so I don't pursue it.

'You know, she said some pretty unkind things to me,' I say, moving the conversation away from talk of secrets.

Steve raises his eyebrows in question. 'Like what?'

'She said I'm never here for her. That's so damned unfair. I've always put her first from the day she was born.'

'I'd say it was long before that,' he mutters.

'What's that supposed to mean?' I demand.

'Nothing. Just forget it,' he says, starting towards the door, then turning back to face me. 'Look, all I'm saying is, what makes you so certain that the note was about Ruby?' He's looking straight into my eyes and for a millisecond I wonder if he knows.

A sudden chill runs through me, turning the blood in my veins to ice, despite the heat of the June day. I assumed that the 'she' mentioned in the note was Ruby, but what if the words weren't about our daughter? What if they were about me?

The only person who knows anything about my terrible secret is Sadie, and even she doesn't know the whole story. Is it possible that someone else has found out? Because I'm pretty sure she wouldn't betray my trust.

'How well do you really know Sadie?' Steve asks. 'Maybe you should have thought about that before jumping to conclusions about Ruby.' He turns away from me again and goes out into the hallway. 'I'm going for a shower now and then I'll probably have a nap. I'm knackered.'

I have no idea what his comment means, but he's clearly not intending to discuss it with me.

'What about lunch?' I demand, struggling to keep my tone civil.

He's already halfway up the stairs but turns back to say, 'I don't know about you, but I've lost my appetite.'

There's a saying that Steve and I have always tried to stick to in our marriage: never go to bed on an argument. It feels as though that is what he is doing now, although it was less an argument, more a disagreement, and he's only going for a nap. Even so, not only is he judging my parenting ability in a tricky situation, which, to be honest, I doubt he could have handled better, but he's also left me wondering whether my best friend has betrayed me.

A part of me wants to storm up the stairs after him and demand to know what he means, while the rest of me wants to slam dramatically out of the house as Ruby did earlier. The trouble is, where would I go? Unlike my daughter, I don't have the best relationship with my mum, and since Ruby is with her, it wouldn't be an option anyway. I'm glad Mum was able to quit drinking after I told her that Ruby wouldn't be allowed sleepovers at her house unless she did, but it makes me sad that she couldn't have done it for me when I was young.

I'm due to meet up with Sadie in a few hours for dinner at her hotel, which I'd been looking forward to, but now Steve has cast a shadow over that too. I can't bear to be in the house knowing we're barely on speaking terms. My eyes rest on Baxter, who is lying on his bed with his chin on his paws giving me the side-eye.

'Sorry, Bax. You're my only option,' I say, reaching his lead down from the peg and attaching it to his collar.

He barely has the energy to wag his tail, but he trots into step at my side as we head down the back garden path and through the gate at the bottom leading onto the open fields behind our house just as it starts to spit with rain.

THIRTEEN

SADIE

May – six weeks before the party

Tapping her foot on the marble floor tiles in the entrance hall of her apartment building, Sadie is waiting impatiently for the lift as it continues its slow descent from the twenty-fifth floor. She'd known the timing of the video call with Mel and Ruby would be tight, but she hadn't wanted to change it and 3.30 p.m. was the only time her bank manager could squeeze her in for a face-to-face appointment. She knew seeing him in person would be essential if she was going to have any chance of extending her overdraft facility.

She'd set everything up ready for the FaceTime call from the UK before leaving earlier that afternoon. Her laptop had been positioned on a small table in front of the chaise longue, with the screen angled down slightly so that the view of the New York skyline would be visible over her shoulder. Keeping up the appearance of normality was important; Mel was like a sniffer dog. If she got the slightest whiff of something being wrong, she would pursue it relentlessly and that was the last thing Sadie needed. She was going to tell Mel everything eventually, but now was not the right time, with Ruby's party arrangements in full flow.

The meeting at the bank hadn't gone as well as she'd hoped. In fact, it hadn't gone well at all. Sadie had taken as much care over her personal appearance as she had for the set-up in her apartment. She'd spent time blow-drying and styling her hair, applied subtle eye make-up but with a strong red lipstick and had worn a blouse that showed a suggestion of cleavage without being too obvious. A tight-fitting pencil skirt with a high enough split to show off her shapely legs had completed the look. She knew she'd achieved the desired effect when the concierge who had been largely ignoring her over the past few months when she'd slunk in and out of the building in a tracksuit and trainers with a baseball cap obscuring her hair and most of her face offered to hail her a cab and then held the door open for her. It was an expense she could ill afford, but neither did she want to arrive at her appointment a hot dishevelled mess. It was her final opportunity to try to secure a further overdraft facility, having been declined in her online application.

She wasn't asking for a huge amount of money, just enough to make the rent on her apartment until the end of her year-long contract so that she wouldn't lose a large percentage of the hefty deposit she paid up front each year, which was the landlord's guarantee of a year's worth of income. If she defaulted on her monthly rental payment, she would lose most of the deposit but would still be evicted within thirty days. None of it seemed fair. Apparently, it had always been in the small print of the contract but had gone unnoticed by Sadie previously because money had never been an issue before.

She'd been kept waiting for over half an hour at the bank and when she was eventually shown into the bank manager's opulent corner office on the forty-fifth floor, it was not Dan Lazenby behind the oversized desk as Sadie had expected. The woman, who'd introduced herself as Liz Durrant, had apologised both for keeping her waiting and also for the fact that Dan had been called away unexpectedly, but said she was happy to help if she could. Sadie had the distinct impression that she'd been set up.

She'd had a brief fling with Dan in the early days of her interior design business when she was redesigning his family's beach house in Cape Cod. It was part of an already established pattern that satisfied Sadie's physical needs without any emotional attachment and had been useful leverage when she'd needed a bridging loan during the pandemic. Apart from that, she hadn't been in touch with Dan for years. One look at her account and he would have known what today's meeting was likely to be about. He'd clearly decided to delegate the meeting to a colleague.

Liz Durrant was an altogether different kettle of fish. It was still fairly unusual for women to break through the glass ceiling and climb to the top in the older established companies. There was no way Liz was going to put her career on the line for someone who had no clear way of illustrating how she would be able to pay back any money loaned to her.

Sadie was in the impressive office with its floor-to-ceiling windows and view over the financial district for a total of twelve minutes. She had left feeling humiliated and even more desperate than when she'd arrived. At least it had removed all possibility of her being able to stay in her New York apartment until the end of the year. In a way, that certainty removed some of the stress from the situation. Her time in New York was nearly done and there was nothing more she could do to delay her departure.

The lift finally trundles its way down to the lobby and then climbs back up again to the twentieth floor, stopping several times en route to let people off. Sadie can feel her anxiety levels rising along with the ascent. By the time she slots her key in the locked apartment door, her phone is showing 17.23.

With only seven minutes to spare until the scheduled call, she moves quickly across to the set-up in front of the windows to wake her computer from sleep mode and lay her phone next to it on the table, checking that she's flicked it from silent.

On the way to the bathroom for a quick wee, she stops off in the kitchen to pour herself a large glass of red wine, leaving it on the countertop to grab on her return.

She's just drying her hands when her phone starts ringing. They're early, she thinks, hurrying across the room to answer the call, picking up the wine glass on her way.

'Hi, you two!' she says, her voice artificially bright. 'I thought we were doing a video call,' she adds before taking a large swig of wine.

There is silence from the other end of the line.

Glancing down at her phone screen, Sadie can now see that it's not Mel's number. Her hand starts to shake, causing the wine in her glass to slosh around dangerously close to the rim. She quickly puts it down next to her computer. The last thing she needs is a red wine stain on the off-white carpet that she would have to pay to have cleaned. Despite having the carpets fitted at her own expense, like every other improvement she has made to the apartment, it's now regarded as fixtures and fittings, which she is responsible for keeping in good condition if she wants any of her deposit back.

'Who is this?' she hisses into the phone.

More silence. It is the third time this week that her phone has been contacted by the same number which she doesn't recognise, but the anonymous calls have been happening on and off since the middle of March. Normally, the caller hangs up after a few seconds, but today is different. Sadie can hear breathing.

'Is that you, Tonya?' Sadie demands. 'If it is, what more do you want from me? You've destroyed my business and I'm being forced out of my home because no one in this town will lend me any money to pay my rent,' she continues more forcefully.

Still nothing.

'Look, I totally get why you might think it's nothing more than I deserve because I brought all this on myself, but haven't you exacted enough revenge now? I have nothing – as in, absolutely nothing – left,' Sadie says, her anger giving way to emotion at the desperate situation she finds herself in.

'We need to talk,' says a quiet female voice from the other end of the line.

Sadie is taken aback. The voice doesn't belong to Tonya. Unless she's very much mistaken, the woman sounds young and has a British accent.

'Who is this?' she says, repeating her earlier question.

'I'll call again,' the woman replies, and then the line goes dead.

Sadie sinks onto the chaise longue, staring at the phone in her hand. Her heart is pumping hard, but before her mind has time to properly process the call, her computer screen lights up and her phone starts to ring.

For a moment, Sadie contemplates not answering the call, but she can't bear the thought of disappointing Ruby.

'Get a grip,' she mutters to herself. 'It wasn't her. It can't be.'

Taking a deep breath and a large swig of wine, she presses the accept button. Her computer screen is immediately filled with Ruby's and Mel's happy smiling faces.

'Hi, you two!' she says, repeating her earlier greeting, her face emulating their expressions. 'Welcome to a sweltering-hot New York city. Apologies for any visible damp patches. I just got in and I can't tell you what a relief air conditioning is. I don't know how you manage without it over there.'

'You've obviously forgotten what English summers are like because you've been away for so long,' Melissa says in reply. 'I almost put the heating on this morning.'

'She's joking, Auntie Sadie, but it has been raining and miserable today. I hope it will be brighter by my birthday,' Ruby says.

'I'll order it especially,' Sadie says. 'Speaking of which, did the fabric to cover the boring wooden panels arrive okay? You really couldn't have chosen a less inspiring function room for Ruby's big do, Mel.'

'It turns out that the twenty-third of June is a very popular date for birthday celebrations, so it kind of chose us,' Melissa says, glancing at her daughter with such love in her eyes that Sadie feels like an intruder.

'True,' she manages to reply. 'But we're going to make this June twenty-third celebration the best one ever.'

They stay on the call for ten minutes or so before Sadie makes the excuse that she has a call waiting. She doesn't, but there is only so much happy smiley enthusiastic Sadie she can muster given the disappointment of her meeting at the bank and the shock of her earlier phone call.

She carries her glass of wine over to the windows and stands gazing down on the East River, watching the boats receding into the distance until they are tiny pinpricks on the horizon, before they disappear completely.

Just like my life in New York, Sadie thinks, turning her back on the view that she has come to love but can hardly bear to look at.

Sitting down on the chaise longue, she opens her email and searches for her landlord's address. With a heavy heart, she starts to write the letter giving a month's notice on her home.

FOURTEEN

RUBY

March – three months before the party

Ruby waits until her parents are ten minutes into watching their new favourite thriller series before excusing herself, saying she is too tired to concentrate on the intricate twists and turns of the plot. Melissa immediately offers to turn it off and record the rest of the episode so that they can all watch it together, but that is precisely what Ruby doesn't want. She wants them to be so totally engrossed in the drama that she can make the phone call from her room without fear of being overheard. After explaining that she will catch up in the free period she has at school the following day, she gets herself a glass of water and heads upstairs to her room.

She has timed this perfectly to account for the time difference in New York. Any earlier and Auntie Sadie might not answer her phone as she would probably still be working, but she likes to finish for the day at 5 p.m. in order to have her evenings free.

Ruby is quite enamoured with Sadie's way of life, maybe because it's so different from what is perceived to be 'normal'.

She has no husband and children to consider which gives her free rein to do exactly as she pleases. Ruby has loved the idea of all that freedom and devoting herself to her career, but since Kyle has entered the frame, she's no longer sure if she's cut out for a similar lifestyle.

He is part of the reason for the call. Ruby had confided in her nana when she told her that she was dating Kyle without her parents' knowledge, but that was as far as it went. She didn't feel comfortable talking to her about the intimacies of their relationship and also felt it would be an unfair burden for Linda to keep it a secret. Ruby has come close to telling her mum about Kyle on a couple of occasions but stopped herself, remembering that her mum shares everything with her dad. There's no way he's ready to accept yet that she's no longer solely his little girl. The air has been cleared with Megan, but Ruby is acutely aware how insensitive it would be to have the conversation she wants to have with her too. Which only leaves Sadie, who has been her confidante on a previous occasion and who Ruby feels she can trust.

A couple of months after the incident where a dance competition adjudicator had body-shamed her, she and her mum had gone on a visit to New York. Maybe it was because Sadie didn't see Ruby on a daily basis as her parents did, but she immediately noticed Ruby's dramatic weight loss and wasn't afraid to question her about it. Melissa had readily accepted Ruby's explanation of how she had dropped a few pounds through sensible eating and additional exercise, but Sadie was harder to fool. It was true that Ruby had been eating better, cutting out calorific snacks and milky coffees, but she'd also started forcing herself to be sick after eating family meals.

Fortunately, Sadie had been able to empathise as she'd gone through a similar phase herself in her teenage years. She'd been able to nip in the bud something that could have developed into a much more serious problem with devastating consequences.

Sadie had agreed to keep her secret so long as Ruby kept her end of the bargain and stopped sticking her fingers down her throat as a method of controlling her intake of calories. It had strengthened an already close bond between the two of them.

Even so, it has taken Ruby several weeks to pluck up the courage for the call she is about to make.

The phone only rings out twice before it is answered.

'Hi Ruby, how are you doing?' Sadie's voice sounds bright and cheerful, as it always does. 'How are the party ideas coming along?'

'Oh yes, good,' Ruby replies. 'We should be able to send you a more or less complete list of people by the end of the month. Everyone I've told about fancy dress with a musicals theme seems really on board with the idea.'

There is a short pause, each waiting for the other to speak before they both speak at the same time.

'You go,' Ruby says.

'After you,' Sadie replies. 'You rang me so I'm guessing you have something on your mind?'

'Well, yes actually. But this is just between us, right?'

'It's always just between us, Ruby, if you want it to be,' Sadie replies. 'I'm pleased that you feel you can talk to me about awkward stuff. It's probably way easier for me to be objective than it is for your mum and dad, even though I'd say they are pretty liberal thinking.'

'Maybe with some things, but when it comes to me, they still see me as a ten-year-old. I think the thought that I'll soon have a life away from them and everything that entails absolutely terrifies them.'

'So, is this the debate between university and stage school? Whichever you choose, you'll be living away from home, and they'll just have to come to terms with it. Are you any closer to making your mind up?' Sadie asks.

A vision of the girls in the pop group Bucks Fizz ripping off their colourful skirts midway through a rendition of their Eurovision song flashes into Ruby's head. She hadn't been around in 1981 when the UK's entry had clinched the top spot in Dublin, but she has seen the clip many times as it's often shown in the lead up to the song contest having only been achieved on one more occasion in the following forty years.

Although it isn't the actual reason for her call, Ruby decides to play along so that she can ease her way into the trickier conversation later on.

'Not really. I had to accept the place offered at Laine Theatre Arts because there were so many people auditioning and so few places, but it doesn't mean I'll be going there. I just don't know if I'm pushy enough to make it in that field,' Ruby says.

She's had the conversation with both her mum and nana. It's not merely about talent. Ruby knows that there are plenty of people who went to stage schools with high hopes for a glittering career who are waiting tables and making cold calls from a call centre, their lives on hold until their big break comes along. But it doesn't come along for everyone and that's the bit that scares Ruby. She's so used to being rewarded for the hard work she puts in, and the thought that it might not be that way in the real world is paralysing.

'Of course I want it,' Ruby continues. 'But I'm not sure I'd do absolutely anything to get it like some people would, and I don't know how much of a fighter I am. My parents, particularly Mum, have never let me fight any of my own battles.'

'Then maybe that should be what pushes you to try for it,' Sadie says, her tone considered rather than persuasive. 'They won't always be there to fight your corner. You don't want to live the rest of your life wondering if you could have been in that top few per cent.'

'True, but I also hate the idea of wasting my brain for a slim chance of making it in the entertainment industry, especially as

Dad's not so keen on me taking that risk. I've never felt the pressure of being an only child more than I do right now,' Ruby sighs.

'Have you tried to have a conversation about your future with them both at the same time?' Sadie asks.

'It doesn't work. They both voice their opinions, but nothing gets resolved. I seem to be the only thing they ever argue about. Maybe it will be better for them when I'm not living at home anymore. Oh, I just don't know. Everything is so much more complicated than it used to be,' Ruby says, rubbing her forehead with the palm of her free hand as though trying to clear her thoughts.

The call to her godmother was supposed to be for non-specific relationship advice that she hadn't felt able to talk to her mum about without having to answer a ton of questions. While she wasn't exactly lying to her mum, nor was she telling her the truth about having a boyfriend. Ruby had thought it would be easy to steer the conversation with Sadie, but it hasn't gone the way that she'd hoped.

'I agree, it's a tricky decision, but don't go stressing over it too much,' Sadie says. 'It doesn't have to be for the rest of your life. Look at me. I was happily muddling along as a set designer in a London theatre when the chance came for me to come here and work in New York. Accepting that job changed the course of my life.' Sadie pauses. 'Did I make the right decision? I guess I'll never know, but once I'd made my choice, I committed wholeheartedly to that path, and it's been amazing.'

'*Been* amazing?' Ruby says. 'You make it sound as though you're ready for a new challenge.' When Sadie doesn't respond, Ruby adds, 'You're not, are you?'

'Even I get homesick from time to time,' Sadie says vaguely. 'Then I gaze out of my window at the view over the East River and remember what I looked out onto from my pokey flat in West Kensington. There really is no comparison.'

'I love your apartment. Wouldn't it just be the best thing if I got into a show on Broadway? I could come and stay with you, and Mum and Dad wouldn't need to worry,' Ruby says, momentarily allowing her imagination to run riot as she pictures the two of them walking arm in arm down Fifth Avenue laden with designer shopping bags.

'Be careful what you wish for, Ruby. New York in small doses is very different from living here all the time. I love the hustle and bustle and the constant noise, but it's not for everyone. It takes a long time to get used to, especially if, like you, home is more rural. And then there's the people you are forced to leave behind,' Sadie says. 'Would that be a problem for you?'

With that one sentence, Ruby realises that she hasn't been quite as clever as she thought in going along with talking about her career. Sadie has been playing her at her own game, guiding the conversation to eventually ask if Ruby has a special someone that she would be sad to leave back in England. It's a question that Sadie has asked a few times previously and one to which Ruby has always been able to truthfully answer no. But her situation is different now. It would be a little obvious if she were to ask the ambiguous questions she'd been intending with Sadie's boyfriend radar already on high alert.

'Not at all. New York is only an eight-hour flight away for anyone who really wants to stay in touch, like you do with Mum. I'm sure Megan would love to come out for a visit given half a chance,' Ruby says, hoping that she's done enough to throw Sadie off the boyfriend scent. 'Actually, I should probably get some sleep. It's ten thirty here and I've got school in the morning. Thanks for the career advice. Speak again soon,' she adds, tapping the screen on her phone before Sadie can reply and letting it fall onto her bedcovers.

Although Ruby feels a bit annoyed and disappointed in herself that she wasn't brave enough to come straight out with her questions about sex and when it's the right time, it had become too risky by the end of the call.

If she'd asked the generic questions about the point where a relationship should turn from casual dates to something more intimate, Sadie would probably have caught on and asked the direct question, 'Are you seeing someone?' If Ruby told the truth, she would be going behind her parents' backs again, and once was bad enough. Besides, she'd more or less reached her own conclusion by the end of their conversation: if she needs to ask for someone else's opinion, then she isn't yet ready for the next step. Kyle wants her to be sure before they take things further, and by needing to ask, it's clear that she hasn't reached that point yet. After all, she would know when she's ready, wouldn't she? Perhaps feeling uncertain is just a part of growing up, but Ruby doesn't like it at all.

FIFTEEN

MELISSA

24 June 2023 - the day after the party

Pushing the glass door to the hotel bar open with one hand, I wave to Sadie, who is perched on a stool at the bar, with the other. It's weird how some people can look so elegant balancing on a small, padded leather circle with no back support and others look like a sack of potatoes. While Sadie is definitely in the former category, I would be the latter, which is why I'm going to suggest going straight to our table.

She asked me to book Highbourne House for her trip to the UK as it has a good restaurant and is closest to our home, although why she refused the offer to stay with us, I'll never know. Even with Mum unexpectedly agreeing to spend last night at ours, there are two more spare bedrooms, one of which has an en suite bathroom, and Ruby and I always stay at her apartment when we visit New York. She mentioned not wanting to get under our feet while we were so busy organising the party, but something about her excuse didn't quite ring true. At least she's allowing me to pick up the tab for this whole visit, which seems only right after all the work she put in to making

Ruby's party a success. And it was a success, even if it doesn't quite feel like it now that the note has cast a shadow over everything.

While I was out walking Baxter, I more or less convinced myself that someone had found out about the secret I've been harbouring for nearly nineteen years. Whoever it was had chosen Ruby's party to reveal the truth to Steve. What I can't figure out is, who? No one at the party, not even Sadie, knows all the facts about Steve's company's family barbecue in 2004 that changed my life.

I also haven't entirely ruled out Steve's suggestion that the note might be written about my best friend, although I find that less likely. The only people at Ruby's party who have any connection with Sadie are me, Steve, Ruby and Mum. I know I didn't write the note and I'm fairly sure that Steve didn't. That only leaves Ruby and my mum. It's true, Mum was never Sadie's biggest fan, but I can't imagine what she could possibly know about her that would prompt her to leave the note; and anyway, she would have been more direct. As for Ruby, she adores her Auntie Sadie to the point where I've sometimes felt a little jealous of their closeness. I suppose it's possible that the two of them have argued about something, but not very likely. In the taxi on the way over to meeting Sadie, I decided that I need to pay close attention to her reaction when I mention the note.

'Sorry I'm late,' I say, air-kissing either side of Sadie's face, 'I got caught in the rain so had to do something with my hair.'

I hadn't banked on the light drizzle as I set out on my walk with Baxter turning into a heavy downpour just as we were at our furthest point from home. We both got drenched, meaning a bath for him and an unscheduled hair wash and blow dry for me. It was annoying as I loved the way my hairdresser had styled it for Ruby's party, and I was hoping that would do me for a few days.

'No worries,' Sadie says, raising her almost empty glass. 'You know I'm quite happy drinking at the bar on my own. Let's face it, I've had plenty of practice. Shall I get you a drink and me a refill or do you want to go straight through to the restaurant?'

'We should probably go through,' I reply. 'This place gets packed on a Saturday night, so I doubt they will hold our table for more than fifteen minutes.'

'True,' she says, draining the remaining liquid from her glass and sliding off the bar stool as elegantly as she'd been perched on it. 'Anyway, I'm starving,' she adds, linking her arm through mine. 'And we've got a lot of catching up to do.'

It could be my imagination, but she made it sound as though there's something she wants to tell me.

Our dinner is every bit as delicious as the five-star reviews on Tripadvisor suggested it would be. We chose different starters so that we could each sample the other. I went for baked provolone cheese on a tomato and garlic sauce base with two pieces of flat bread to ensure that none of the sauce was left in the piping-hot glazed terracotta dish in which it was served, while Sadie opted for truffle and parmesan arancini balls. They were crispy on the outside and succulently moist inside, very different from the pre-made ones I buy from the supermarket.

We've chosen a Pinot Grigio to accompany our food and I was quite surprised by the speed at which we got through the first bottle. Sadie ordered another before we'd been served with our main course, so I was glad I'd opted to get a taxi each way rather than drive. Normally, Steve would have offered to drop me off and pick me up, but following our earlier disagreement, I didn't want to ask him. There was also a part of me that wanted him to be at home in case Ruby changed her mind about staying at her nana's.

Maybe it's because we were surrounded by Ruby's friends from school and dancing last night, but we've spent most of the evening so far reminiscing about our own school days.

'It's funny isn't it,' Sadie says, sticking her fork into the ribbed tube of pasta coated in a tomato and chilli sauce and popping it into her mouth. 'Who'd have thought we'd have stayed friends all these years after such a rocky start.'

She's right. The two of us did not have the most promising of beginnings and neither of us can remember why. What we both have crystal-clear recollection of is the fight we had during a lunchtime netball practice, although again neither of us can recall what caused it. Sadie had launched herself at me and slapped my face, her nails catching my skin in the process and drawing blood from my cheek. I'd responded by grabbing her hair and jolting her head backwards, more to keep her at arm's length and prevent further attack than anything. That was not the way Miss Peake, our PE teacher, saw it. We were both sent to the headmaster's office to await the arrival of our parents, or, in my case, my mum, and that was when I'd started to cry. Sadie didn't know anything about my dad's accident and subsequent death. I can still visualise the look of horror on her face as it all spilled out of me. Before we were even called into the office to be reprimanded and handed our punishment, which was two weeks' worth of after-school detentions, she'd thrown her arms around me and our friendship was born.

We all say things as teenagers that prove impossible to maintain as we get older and life gets in the way, but our friendship has endured the best of times and the hardest of times too. It may have helped that when we left school, Sadie and I went to the same university, although it still wasn't a given. In a fresh environment with an abundance of new and interesting people, some childhood friends drift apart. That was not true for me and Sadie. If anything, it seemed to cement together any minor cracks.

'Do you remember us standing on the corner of Melton Road, talking about what we wanted to be when we grew up and how many children we were going to have?' I say, skewering a prawn soaked in bubbling garlic butter. I blow on it lightly before putting it in my mouth. The flavour explodes on my tongue. It is nothing short of divine, I think, making a mental note that Steve and I should book this place for our anniversary dinner in August.

'Yep,' Sadie replies. 'Four each, wasn't it? Two boys and two girls. If I try hard enough, I can probably remember the names I was going to call them.'

There is an undeniable sadness in her voice. We rarely talk about the affair she had with a married man that was the catalyst for her move to New York, but I'll never forget her devastation the night after he told her it was over. She'd called me in floods of tears and begged me to go over to her flat. The image of her sat on the floor in her tiny lounge, rocking back and forth as she sobbed uncontrollably, the whole story pouring out of her now that the flood gates were open, will live with me forever.

The saddest thing for me was that I had never known Sadie to be so completely and utterly happy in a relationship. I honestly believed, as did she, that he was the love of her life, the man she was going to spend the rest of her life with. Maybe the two of them were destined to be together, but he wasn't brave enough to leave the family he already had. Or perhaps he'd lied to her, having never truly loved her at all and it had been just a fling for him. Either way, the affair has shaped Sadie's life and from the snippets she shares of her life in the Big Apple, a husband and children have never featured in her plans since she broke up with him.

'Neither of us had the easy ride we innocently expected regarding children, did we?' I say, helping myself to another garlic prawn and surreptitiously mopping the dribble of butter from the corner of my mouth with the linen napkin.

'No, but at least you got your beautiful girl in the end,' Sadie says.

I keep my head down and concentrate on the fat juicy pink prawns. I was relieved that they'd arrived without their heads. I love the taste, but there is something so accusatory in their black unseeing eyes. They might not be looking at me, but I'm pretty sure Sadie is, and I hope she hasn't noticed the redness creeping up my neck.

She's right, I did get my beautiful girl in the end, but at such a huge cost.

Whether she notices me colouring up or not, she chooses to ignore it. Perhaps she thinks it's a menopausal hot flash. 'Did you see the way all the boys were looking at Ruby at the party last night?' Sadie continues. 'She looked stunning. No, I take that back, she *is* stunning. Dressed up as Elsa or fresh-faced from a dog walk, that girl is special. Are you sure she isn't dating yet? Honestly, I find that so hard to believe.'

Is this what Sadie has been leading up to? Does she know something I don't about Ruby? Maybe it was her who left the note last night to prepare me for what she is about to divulge. Then I remember that she knew it was supposed to be Steve giving the speech. There's no way she would have wanted him to find a message like that about his daughter at the party. His reaction might have cast a shadow over the event that Sadie had planned so meticulously but, more importantly, could have ruined Ruby's birthday, which Sadie wouldn't have been prepared to risk. I'm pretty sure the note wasn't left by her, but this is my opportunity to test the waters.

'Actually,' I say, laying my fork across my now empty dish and mopping my mouth with my napkin for a final time, 'something happened last night that I wanted to run past you.'

She seems to stop mid chew, raising her eyebrows questioningly. 'What?' she manages through her mouthful of food.

I reach down to my handbag under the table and retrieve

the crumpled piece of paper. 'Someone slipped this between the pages of the speech,' I say, handing it over.

Sadie's eyes scan the words, connect with mine briefly and then drop back to the note. She turns the paper over in her hand to look at the reverse side of it, almost as though she's expecting a signature or some other clue as to who might have written it.

'You think this is about Ruby?' she asks.

'Well, it was Ruby's party. I can't imagine who else it would be referring to, can you?'

A half moment of concern flashes into Sadie's eyes. Could Steve be right? Is Sadie hiding something?

'Has Ruby seen this?' Sadie asks, regaining her composure.

'No,' I sigh.

'But...' she presses.

My friend knows me so well. She can tell that 'no' isn't the end of the story.

'I did mention it to her and asked if she knew what it meant. I know, I know,' I say, responding to Sadie's disbelieving expression. 'We had a massive row over it earlier and she stormed off to her nana's.'

'So, you haven't had a chance to talk to Ruby since accusing her of something she may or may not be guilty of?' Sadie asks.

I shake my head.

'Well, I know you're the experienced parent here, but if it was me, I think I'd try to speak to her before it drives a wedge between you that you might not recover from.'

'I tried to call earlier while I was out walking Baxter, but her phone is going straight to voicemail,' I say. She's got me worried now. The last thing in the world that I want for Ruby and me is to have the fractured relationship I have with my mum. 'Should I go round to my mum's, do you think?'

Sadie appears to consider the suggestion for a moment before saying, 'She's probably feeling pretty pissed off with you right now and needs some space. Going round there might exacerbate the situation.'

'I can't just do nothing.'

'Look, why don't you ring your mum's phone instead? At least that way you'll have reached out an olive branch, even if Ruby won't speak to you.' She must be able to see from my expression that I'm undecided because she adds, 'And it will set your mind at rest that she's safely where she said she was going.'

To be honest, it hadn't crossed my mind that Ruby would be anywhere other than where she said she would be. I wonder where that implicit trust was when I decided to go through her private things earlier. Maybe I am beginning to have doubts about her?

Now that Sadie has mentioned it, I'm desperate to check with my mum that she's there. My mind runs wild with a sudden onset of worries. Such terrible things can happen to young girls when they are out on their own. I can't bear the thought of Ruby becoming a crime statistic.

'Good idea,' I say, starting to reach into my bag for my phone.

'I think that's probably a call best made from the privacy of my room,' Sadie says, gesturing to the waitress for her to bring the bill with the globally recognised air signature.

SIXTEEN

RUBY

April – two months until the party

'Does it ever get boring?' Megan asks, biting into her hummus and falafel wrap and wiping the bit of filling that escaped from the corner of her mouth with her finger, then licking it.

'Enjoying that, are we?' Ruby says. 'Anyone would think you haven't eaten for a week, and I know that's not true because I watched you tuck away that bacon roll for breakfast.'

'I just love my food,' Megan says, taking another bite. 'Anyway, stop changing the subject.'

'I'm not sure what the subject is,' Ruby replies, carefully peeling the skin away from the sides of her banana and taking a bite of the creamy white inside. Ruby is very particular about the ripeness of her bananas. If they are underripe and have even a hint of green to the skin, she won't eat them at all. Similarly, if they have more than a couple of brown spots, she fears the inside will be too soft, almost floury in texture, and they will most likely end up in the food waste bin unless intercepted by her mum. It is amazing how adept Melissa has become at gauging them when she is out doing the supermarket shop, but also how good she is at making banana bread if they've gone just over.

'The subject is winning,' Megan says, screwing the wrapper from her lunch into a ball and aiming it at the bin in the corner of the dressing room. It catches the rim and bounces off it and onto the floor. 'For me, part of the adrenaline rush that fuels my performance is wondering if I might get a place or a special mention from the adjudicator. It must be hard for you to always deliver your best performance if you kind of already know that you're going to win.'

Ruby shrugs. 'I don't think I compete to win,' she says.

'Oh right,' Megan says, struggling to keep the sarcasm from her voice.

'No, really,' Ruby responds. 'It's lovely to win, of course it is, but I genuinely love the freedom I feel when I'm on stage performing. It's like all my worries just disappear when I hear the first note of the music. I've always felt that way about dancing, even before I started winning.'

'That's one of the things I've always liked about you,' Megan says.

'My love of dancing? You love it too, don't you?' Ruby asks. 'You must do, otherwise why would you give up so much of your free time to do it?'

'No, I mean yes, of course I love my dancing, but it's your honesty I've always liked,' Megan says. 'It's why I was so upset back in January when you told me that you'd been seeing Kyle. No' – she intervenes when Ruby tries to speak – 'let me finish. We've always told each other everything and then suddenly you kept a massive secret from me. Not only that, but I was also worried that the more you saw of Kyle, the less time you would have for me. I was being selfish on all sorts of levels,' she admits.

'But you needn't have worried about us seeing less of each other,' Ruby says, expertly aiming her banana skin at the bin, where it drops neatly inside. 'Bullseye!' she shouts.

'OMG, Ruby. Even chucking your rubbish in the bin you're better at than me,' Megan says, rolling her eyes.

Ruby gets to her feet, bends at the waist to give a small bow as though accepting her friend's praise, then crosses the space to pick up the wrapper that had fallen short of its mark.

'And now you're tidying up after me,' Megan says.

'We do things for each other, Megan. That's what friends do. It's why I felt so terrible not telling you about me and Kyle,' Ruby says, undoing the hook and eye fasteners down the back of a pale green ballet tutu before lifting it off the rail where it had been hanging next to five other similar garments all in different pastel shades. She gives it a little shake to froth up the layers of net before stepping into the leg openings. 'I know I've said it before, but I hope you know how genuinely sorry I am that I wasn't honest about it from the beginning. No more secrets, okay?' she adds, facing the mirror, in which she is making eye contact with her friend. Her hands press into the satin fabric at her waist, and she raises her eyebrows at Megan in expectation.

The two of them have been involved in dancing competitions for enough years for Megan to know that her help is required to do up the row of hooks and eyes that will give the perfect figure-hugging fit, but she doesn't move. Her eyes are fixed on Ruby's in the mirror.

'What is it?' Ruby asks.

'The thing is...' Megan starts to say and then falters. She tries again. 'The thing is, I've been keeping something from you too. I was going to tell you that night in the coffee shop when I'd come back to dancing after being off sick, but you stormed off before I had the chance.'

'That was two months ago,' Ruby says. 'We've seen each other loads of times since then.'

'I know,' Megan replies, 'but this is something I've known about for a while and not told you. While I was off sick, I realised how unfair I'd been in criticising you for not being honest with me for a couple of weeks when I'd been keeping a secret since I was twelve years old. I'd properly psyched myself up to tell you and then the moment was gone.'

'Okay,' Ruby says, trying to keep her voice calm. 'Do you want to tell me now?'

Megan nods. She gets up off the plastic chair and walks over to where Ruby is still standing in front of the mirror holding the fabric of the bodice of her tutu into her waist. She pulls the two sides of the satin fabric together until they meet and starts securing them in place with the fasteners, slowly moving up the centre of Ruby's back, giving it her full attention. The fit of a tutu is always quite snug, requiring the dancer to breathe in while being fastened into it, but Ruby is holding her breath for quite a different reason. She has no idea what Megan is about to divulge, but judging by the way her friend is building up to the revelation, it must be serious.

After Megan has fastened the top hook, she refocuses her gaze on Ruby in the mirror and takes a deep breath.

'I'm adopted,' she says in a voice completely devoid of emotion.

There is an often used expression about someone's jaw hitting the floor when they've had a big surprise. While the floor is still some distance from Ruby's chin, her mouth has fallen open in shock.

'What the actual...?' Ruby says, spinning around to face her friend. 'Are you winding me up?'

'Does it look like I'm winding you up?' Megan replies.

Ruby examines her friend's face. Even covered in the heavy stage make-up the girls must wear, she can see that Megan is pale and her eyes are sad.

'No. It looks like you are deadly serious,' Ruby replies, reaching out to touch her friend's arm. 'Are you sure you're okay talking about it here? We can go somewhere afterwards if you'd rather.'

'There's not a lot to talk about really.' Megan shrugs. 'I had no idea I was adopted until I overheard my mother during one of my parents' many heated arguments.'

'What did she say?' Ruby asks, still trying to process what Megan has just told her.

'I can tell you to the precise word. Try as I might to block it from my mind, I'll never forget what she said. "Adopting her was supposed to bring us closer together, but it's done the exact opposite. If we're being honest, that was the next biggest mistake of our lives, after making our wedding vows",' Megan says as though she's reciting part of a script from a play.

Ruby gasps. 'That is a dreadful thing to say. How could she be so cruel?'

'In fairness, she didn't know I was listening. The words weren't meant to hurt me, they were directed at Paul.'

'Do they know that you know?' Ruby asks.

'They do now,' Megan says. 'I didn't let on straight away, but it was around that time that I began calling them Paul and Anna, so they probably had their suspicions. Maybe that's why they started to take even less of an interest in me. They didn't have to pretend anymore that they loved me. I'm pretty sure we'll all go our separate ways once I leave home to go to uni.'

Ruby remembers quite clearly when Megan started calling her parents by their first names instead of Mum and Dad. She'd asked about it at the time and Megan had been dismissive, saying, 'Loads of kids do it now. You're so old-school, Ruby.' As a twelve-year-old, she'd totally bought the explanation and even explained it that way to her parents when they'd questioned it. Her dad had been very quick with his response. 'Don't you go getting any ideas like that, young lady.'

'Oh Megan, that's so awful,' Ruby says. 'I can't believe you've been dealing with this by yourself for all these years.

You're so brave. I'm sure I'd have had to have some kind of therapy. It's huge, Megan, really it is. It's incredible that you've turned out to be such an amazing human being and such a good friend too.' Unable to hold back, she encases Megan in her arms and hugs her tightly.

'Careful or you'll burst out of your tutu,' Megan eventually says as she releases herself from Ruby's grasp. 'It's old news for me now. I struggled a bit at first, but we all find our own ways of dealing with stuff and I've got mine. I'm glad I've told you though,' she adds, turning to the mirror to reapply the lipstick that had come off while she was devouring her lunch. 'A problem shared and all that.'

There was something in Megan's tone of voice that isn't sitting right with Ruby. She sounded matter-of-fact, as though she was completely in control of her feelings, but Ruby has known her friend for a long time and is worried that Megan is hiding her true emotions.

'I'm just thinking about the timing of you finding out about being adopted,' Ruby says. 'Was that around the same time as you developed a crush on Kyle? Do you think you were searching for someone a bit older to love you because you no longer believed that your parents did?' she adds, reaching for her satin pointe shoes and unravelling the ribbons before slipping her feet into them.

Megan is holding her lemon-coloured ballet dress, about to put it on, but stops to fix Ruby with a stare. 'And that is precisely why I never told you or anybody else that I'm adopted,' Megan replies, clearly irritated. 'Everyone seems to think they're a therapist these days, searching for reasons behind certain types of behaviour.'

Ruby can feel herself colouring up so keeps her head down, concentrating on tying the ribbons of her left pointe shoe while Megan steps into her tutu. Outside of the foot, ribbon under, inside of the foot, ribbon over, then taking both ends round to the back, returning them to the front and securing with a small knot on the inside of the ankle before tucking the ends in neatly.

When Ruby doesn't comment, Megan continues.

'So, no, Ruby, that's not why I fell for Kyle. It was another couple of years before I first laid eyes on him when he picked Sasha up from dancing class shortly after passing his driving test. I saw him and fancied him. It's as simple as that. And, unfortunately for me, he didn't feel the same way. While I was worshipping him from afar, he probably didn't even know I existed. And after the initial shock and disappointment, I'm now okay with that too.'

Megan is back to sounding calm and measured. Her words were obviously meant to reassure Ruby that she's no longer jealous of her friend's budding relationship with Kyle, but they haven't rung true. Ruby knows she should respond but doesn't know what to say.

Animated chatter in the corridor outside the dressing room signals the imminent arrival of the other girls whose ballet dresses are hanging up on the rail.

'Thanks, Megan, for being so understanding about Kyle and telling me about the other thing,' Ruby says in a hushed voice, carefully avoiding the use of the word adoption for fear of being overheard. As the door is pushed open, she adds at normal volume, 'I'll do you up when I've finished my other shoe.'

SEVENTEEN

MELISSA

24 June 2023 – the day after the party

No wonder Sadie has chosen to stay here. I'm following her into room 7 on the first floor of Highbourne House. It's been sympathetically converted from a family home into a boutique hotel in a building project that started around five years ago but was then interrupted by the pandemic. Every time I drove past after the building work had stopped, I was sad to see the glorious Georgian windows that would usually let in so much light boarded up with metal grilles to prevent break-ins and squatters. Although the refurbishment was completed late last year, in time for company Christmas parties and family Christmas lunch bookings, this is the first time I've been inside since the reopening. It won't be the last.

'Wow,' I say, taking in the ornate fireplace and window seat, both of which have been restored to their former glory, 'I'll bet you wish you'd had a hand in this refurb, don't you?'

'They clearly didn't need me,' Sadie replies. 'They've done an excellent job on modernising, keeping original features where they could and maintaining the style with things that had to be replaced. Do you want a glass of Dutch courage?' she asks, opening the door of a mini fridge which is cleverly disguised behind a wooden front designed to look like a chest of drawers. 'Or would you prefer a hot drink?'

'Coffee would be lovely, thanks,' I reply. 'Two bottles of wine between the two of us on top of drinking last night is probably enough for me. I don't want to wake up with another thumping headache like I did this morning,' I add.

'I'd forgotten what a lightweight you are when it comes to drinking,' Sadie remarks, carrying the kettle through to the en suite bathroom to fill it with water.

'And I'd forgotten how you can pack it away with seemingly no ill effects afterwards,' I counter.

'You used to match me drink for drink back in the day,' she says, coming back into the room and repositioning the cordless kettle on its base before flicking the switch.

'That was pre-Ruby,' I say. 'I didn't touch a drop from the moment I suspected I might be pregnant until I stopped breastfeeding completely at nine months. It obviously affected my tolerance to alcohol because, as you so astutely point out, I'm done after three or four drinks.'

'Speaking of Ruby,' Sadie says, glancing at her watch, 'do you want to give your mum a ring now before it gets too late?'

I suppress a laugh. 'Mum might be a pensioner but, trust me, she isn't one to go to bed at nine o'clock with a cup of Horlicks!'

'Horlicks! That's a word I haven't heard in a while. Do they still make it? And what about Ovaltine? I'm pretty sure that was my mum's favourite bedtime drink.'

My mum's bedtime tipple was brandy for a long time after my dad died, although I didn't know that at first. Mum was difficult to wake up in the mornings and I remember being terrified that she too had died on the days she was particularly unresponsive. I only started to realise that she was drinking heavily when she became careless with the bottles, leaving them on the kitchen table at night for me to deal with in the morning before I could sit down for my bowl of cereal. I wasn't prepared for Ruby to go through the same experience, which is why I'd issued Mum with an ultimatum. If she wanted her granddaughter to spend time with her alone, she had to promise she would always be sober in her presence. I didn't force Mum into total sobriety, that was her decision, and credit where it's due, she's stuck to it. Sadie knows my mum had a drinking problem, but she doesn't know the full extent of it. Now it's no longer an issue, she doesn't need to know. We share most things, but not quite all.

'I have no idea about either. You're right though,' I say, taking my mobile phone out of its dedicated pocket in my handbag. 'I'll make the call now to set my mind at rest that Ruby is safe.'

'Hold on a minute. You don't want Ruby thinking you're checking up on her. If your mum sees your number, she's bound to give the game away that it's you calling. Use mine,' she offers, unlocking her phone with her pin and handing it to me. 'Tell her straightaway not to let on that it's you and frame your questions carefully as though you are some kind of cold caller from her internet provider or something,' Sadie says as I key in Mum's number.

It all seems a bit cloak-and-dagger, but necessary to make sure Ruby is okay.

Mum answers on the fourth ring. 'Hello?' she says warily.

I'm pleased she is on her guard answering a call from a number that she doesn't recognise. There are so many scams around, particularly directed at older people. Although she's pretty savvy, I've drummed it into her never to give any bank details or pin codes to anyone without checking with me first.

'Mum, it's me, but please pretend it's not because I don't

want Ruby to know I'm checking up on her,' I say, rattling my sentence out like machine-gun fire.

There's a small pause.

'Yes, this is Linda White. Who's calling?'

Good, she is playing along.

'Thanks,' I reply, keeping the volume of my voice low so as not to be overheard. 'Did Ruby come over to yours this afternoon?'

'Yes, that's right,' Mum answers in the telephone voice she uses when she's talking to a random cold caller.

I give a thumbs up to Sadie before continuing.

'Was she very upset?'

'I wouldn't say that,' my mum says in the same neutral tone.

Much as I don't want my daughter to be upset, I'm quite surprised at that response.

'Did she tell you we had a row?' I persist.

'It was mentioned, yes,' Mum says.

'How is she now?'

'Fine,' is the clipped response. Mum is doing a good job of keeping this phone conversation anonymous.

'Do you think she'll talk to me?' I ask.

'Maybe another time,' she says in quite a dismissive tone, as though she's preparing to hang up. She's probably worried that Ruby may start to suspect something is not quite right if we stay on for much longer.

'Thanks for looking after her for me, Mum,' I say, but she has already ended the call.

'Happy now?' Sadie says, handing me my coffee.

'Happy is probably an overstatement,' I reply, taking the mug and walking over to sit down in one of the two velvet upholstered chairs either side of a round table to one side of the window. I was pacing up and down while I was on the phone to Mum, but I feel more relaxed now knowing that Ruby is safe.

'How beautiful are these curtains, by the way?' I say, indicating the floral silk fabric framing the square-paned windows.

'God, it's nice to hear them called curtains,' Sadie says. 'It's a much nicer word than "drapes",' she adds, wrinkling her nose.

'I don't know if I agree with you there. Drape is more descriptive of the falling fabric.'

'It depends on the fabric,' she counters. 'I guess it just gets a bit wearing hearing the American version of the English language constantly,' she adds.

'Don't tell me your love affair with New York is finally over?' I say, blowing gently on my coffee.

I can feel excitement bubbling when she doesn't speak. Could it be possible? Is my best friend really considering coming back to live in the UK?

'I'll never fall out of love with New York,' she says, her voice tinged with sadness. 'I love the energy and vibrancy and optimism. And I adore my beautiful apartment.' She pauses.

Unless I'm very much mistaken and I don't know my friend as well as I think I do, there's a 'but' coming just as there had been in our conversation about Ruby and the note earlier. I give her the space to formulate her next sentence.

'But... New York has fallen out of love with me,' she eventually says.

EIGHTEEN

SADIE

January – five months before the party

Sadie drops her chin further into her cashmere scarf and thrusts her hands deeper into the pockets of her goose-down padded jacket, but nothing can insulate her from the icy chill permeating her bones.

Since moving to New York in 2004, Sadie is all too familiar with the weather extremes the city's residents endure. There is the intense oppressive heat of the summer months when the New Yorkers who can afford to abandon their high-rise apartments for the relative cool of their houses on the coast. And then there are the freezing temperatures of January and February, when the wind blowing in off the East River cuts through outer layers of clothing like a hot knife through butter. But it isn't the swirling snow and the sub-zero temperatures that are chilling Sadie to her core, it's fear.

Standing in the street looking up at the impressive brownstone house in Greenwich Village, Sadie acknowledges that she has been summoned rather than invited to today's meeting by her most recent client, Tonya Hammer.

Sadie had been introduced to Tonya and her husband, Alec, at a party following the refurbishment of a thirty-second-floor apartment overlooking Central Park. It was the latest of several apartments that Sadie had remodelled in the same block, so it had been an easy job as she already knew all the potential problems. The line in the contracts that she insisted all her clients sign about hosting and inviting her to post-refurbishment parties had initially raised a few eyebrows, but it turned out to be an ingenious way of growing her interior design business. Personal recommendation in any walk of life is almost always preferable to finding someone online, but being able to show clients the quality of work you produce is even better. As compliments abounded, Sadie would be introduced as the designer and project co-ordinator. She never left any of the parties without a handful of business cards or mobile numbers from people wanting their home to be upgraded to a similar standard.

Tonya and Alec Hammer were effusive in their praise of what she had achieved in their friend's apartment and when they mentioned that they had bought a brownstone in Greenwich Village that needed completely gutting, Sadie had jumped at the opportunity to get creative. Within a week, she'd been invited to the house for a recce and had produced her initial design thoughts and costing. It was ludicrously expensive, but Sadie always went in high with the initial estimate in expectation that she would be asked to cut costs to the actual amount she wanted to spend. But that wasn't the case for the Hammers. Budget was not a problem. She was given virtual carte blanche to spend on the best of everything. The only minor issue was the deadline. She knew it would be tight to get the entire project completed in eleven months but was confident it was doable with the list of reliable contractors that she'd built up.

The restoration of the house was exquisite and had been finished two weeks ahead of the deadline, giving plenty of time to organise the lavish Christmas party that Tonya and her husband threw every year on the second Saturday in December. As per the contract, Sadie had attended and been introduced to a host of potential new clients, some of whom she was already in preliminary discussions with.

So why am I here? Sadie thinks, climbing the steps leading up to the front door, as though trying to lift her feet from quicksand. There is a heavy feeling in the pit of her stomach as each step brings her closer to finding out if her worst fears are about to be confirmed.

At the top of the steps, she pulls on the wrought-iron handle and can hear the clanging sound of the doorbell echo from deep within the house. *For whom the bell tolls* springs unbid into Sadie's head as she waits for the door to be opened by the Hammers' Filipino maid, Remedios. The sense of foreboding is almost overwhelming, as is the urge to make a run for it while she still has the chance. But where would she run to? New York is a mighty metropolis, but there would be nowhere to hide if Tonya decided to start throwing mud in her direction. And, as everyone knows, mud sticks.

After a few moments, the door swings open to reveal the double-height hallway and the magnificent marble staircase leading to the first-floor drawing room where the initial design meetings between Sadie and Tonya had taken place. Alec had not been that involved, at least not with the renovation work.

She follows Remedios up the stairs, allowing herself a virtual pat on the back for her choice of paint colour, a rich petrol blue on the walls married with champagne gold wallpaper panels. It works perfectly as a backdrop to exhibit the Hammers' priceless art collection.

The door to the Art Nouveau-inspired drawing room is open and Sadie can see Tonya outlined against the window. It is the perfect vantage point to watch Sadie ascend the front steps.

'Take a seat, Sadie,' Tonya says without turning to face her. 'Remedios will bring us some tea.'

Sadie unzips her coat and unwinds the scarf from around her neck before perching on the edge of the gold-coloured couch. Even knowing as she does that the American idea of tea is very different from that of her own Yorkshire roots, she's anticipating its arrival. Her anxiety is making her mouth as dry as the Sahara Desert.

The silence in the room is almost as heavy as the terracotta-coloured fringed velvet curtains – or drapes, as Tonya and all her other clients insist on calling them.

After a few moments where all Sadie can hear is the rhythmic ticking of the grandfather clock on the landing, she attempts to engage Tonya in conversation.

'Erm, is everything working well with the design?' she asks. When Tonya doesn't respond, she tries again. 'It's not a problem if there are some changes you want to discuss.'

Tonya turns to face Sadie for the first time, the expression on her face blank and unreadable. 'Everything about the refurbishment is completely fine,' she says. 'In fact, fine doesn't do it justice. It's little short of a masterpiece. It's a pity really; you are very good at what you do.'

Sadie's heart starts to thump a little louder in her chest. *What's a pity?* she wonders. There had been a firm emphasis on the word 'refurbishment'. If everything is fine in that respect, something else prompted the meeting this afternoon. A meeting Sadie sensed she would be unwise to turn down.

Before she can comment, Remedios enters the room carrying a tray on which there are two porcelain mugs each housing a teabag, an insulated jug of hot water more commonly associated with corporate meetings, a jug of milk and a sugar bowl.

'It's all right, thank you, Remedios, I'll pour,' Tonya says dismissing her maid who bows her head slightly before leaving the room.

Tonya appears to be taking her time as she pours the hot water from the flask before adding a splash of milk and a teaspoon of sugar without the need to ask how Sadie takes her tea. She's served her on many previous occasions throughout the renovation when they sat down together to discuss tiles and worktops and flooring, amongst other things. The unusual slowness of her actions feels deliberate, as though she wants to give Sadie a few moments to consider her words from a few moments earlier.

Eventually, she hands the mug to Sadie, picks up her own and settles herself into the multicoloured velvet armchair that looks nothing like it did in the flea market where Sadie had found it. The full reupholstery job has given it a new lease of life. In any other circumstances, Sadie would be basking in the warm glow of pride from a job well done but instead, all she feels is the chill of anxiety despite wrapping both hands around her mug of insipid-looking tea.

'So,' Tonya says, raising the delicate porcelain mug to her lips and taking a sip of her drink, her eyes firmly fixed on Sadie's, 'shall we dance around the issue with you denying having an affair with my husband? Or shall we just cut to the chase, and I'll tell you what I know?'

Sadie takes a gulp of her own tea, thankful that it wasn't as hot as it might have been if brewed correctly. She isn't normally one to regret indiscretions with clients. It suits her needs. She doesn't want the whole husband and children package, just some extravagant dinners out and some fun in the sack. Although morally wrong, Sadie always settled things in her own mind by believing she is doing the wives a favour. Couples get bored after years of marriage, which can ultimately lead to one or the other having affairs with people who they then decide to start over with. Sadie didn't want that. She always made it clear from the outset that it was a no-strings attached arrangement and that she had no intention of any kind of long-term relationship. The moment the refurbishment was over, and calls could no longer be explained by anything to do with the project, she ended things.

Her liaison with Alec had started off in a similar way to her other affairs, with clandestine meetings in areas of the city that neither of them would normally frequent. But in the autumn, he suddenly started taking her to some of his favourite haunts nearer his home. It was almost as though he wanted to get caught cheating on his wife and by the sound of things his wish has been granted.

'Well?' Tonya prompts, tapping the side of her mug impatiently with talon-like fingernails painted an imposing shade of red. 'Which is it to be?'

It had been clear to Sadie from the moment they'd met that Tonya was used to getting her own way. Her family, the Durlingtons, was part of the New York elite, the closest thing to royalty on this side of the pond. Her husband, on the other hand, had a middle-class upbringing but had excelled at law school. He'd risen rapidly through the ranks at Durlington and Travers, meeting Tonya at one of her father's social gatherings. Despite her mother's reservations, the pair started dating and Frank Durlington saw it as a smart business move for the future of his company when his daughter had declared her intention to marry Alec.

Not normally one to be intimidated, Sadie is almost squirming under Tonya's steely scrutiny.

'I... I don't really know what to say, Tonya. I guess I got caught up in the heat of the moment and things just happened,' Sadie mumbles, wishing the ground would open and swallow her up.

'Right. So, according to my private detective,' she says, reaching for some papers from the Queen Anne table at the side of her chair and scanning them before locking her eyes on Sadie's, 'you got caught up in the heat of the moment seventeen times over the course of the nine weeks I had him watching you.'

Sadie has no answer. She and Alec have clearly been caught red-handed. After his initial caution, Alec became almost reckless in his choice of meeting places, taking her to restaurants and hotels where the waiters and concierges greeted him by name and deliberately avoided eye contact with her. The two of them hadn't been in touch at all since the Christmas party a month ago, so why had Tonya waited until now to confront her?

Having no way of knowing how Tonya is planning to punish her for sleeping with her husband, Sadie takes the stance that the best form of defence is attack. There is no way she's prepared to accept all the blame.

'Clearly it would be pointless to deny that Alec and I were seeing each other,' Sadie says, indicating the papers in Tonya's hand, 'but it's only fair that you should know that I didn't start it.'

Tonya raises her eyebrows expectantly but says nothing.

'Alec invited me to lunch with the two of you to discuss the project and when I arrived, and you weren't there, he made an excuse that you had another appointment that you'd forgotten about but had to attend. We had lunch, talked about the house and I left thinking nothing of it. It was only when he contacted me a few days later saying that he had tickets to the theatre but you were unable to go that I began to suspect he might have an ulterior motive.'

'So you suspected an ulterior motive, but you accepted the invitation anyway,' Tonya says, her gaze cold and unsympathetic.

'He put me in a difficult position.' Sadie tries to maintain her composure. 'Your renovation was the biggest and most elaborate project I've ever undertaken. It had the potential to bring me in a lot of new clients, which I really needed as I was only just breaking even again after not being able to do anything during the pandemic. I didn't want to jeopardise anything by refusing to go,' she finishes somewhat lamely.

Like a lot of businesses, Sadie had almost gone bankrupt during the lockdown that had prevented her from doing her job. The good reputation she had speedily built up in the years since she'd had a change of career direction could just as quickly be forgotten.

It had all come about following a chance encounter in a coffee shop opposite the theatre where she was working at the time. It had been busy, and Sadie was occupying a table for two on her own, so when a smartly dressed man had asked if she minded him taking the other seat, she had shrugged and carried on sketching on her computer. It hadn't taken long before the man introduced himself as Cameron Todd and asked what she was drawing. The play she had been working on the set design for was set in a luxury penthouse apartment and when she swiped through her sketches on the computer, he'd asked her if she'd ever considered designing homes for real. Cameron had explained he was a realtor specialising in homes for the mega rich. By the time the two of them had finished a second flat white, Sadie had been persuaded to give high-end interior design a go. He'd emailed her first potential client there and then, sending over the set designs she'd been working on as examples of her work, and Sadie was hired on the spot for her first interior design project.

It had been tough at first, making contacts in the construction industry and with tradespeople, not to mention getting to grips with planning restrictions and building regulations, but Cameron helped where he could. She knew he was married, but it hadn't stopped her from having a fling with him, as had been her modus operandi since arriving in New York. Having short affairs with married men and not allowing any emotional attachment meant she would never again experience the heartbreak of being rejected by someone she had fallen in love with totally and utterly.

Tonya places her mug down on the table and leans towards Sadie, holding her with an intense stare. 'You know, I'd like to believe you, really I would. I liked you and I loved your energy, enthusiasm and creativity when you were working on my house.'

The use of the past tense is unnerving for Sadie.

'You're probably wondering why I've waited until now to confront you with this when you've long since stopped seeing my husband.' She raises her eyebrows in a question, the intensity of her stare not wavering for a moment.

Sadie nods in response.

'Because I was prepared to give you the benefit of the doubt. You must know that you're not Alec's first affair and, goodness knows, he can be very charming and persuasive. Your problem is that I had my private detective do a bit more digging and it seems that you too make a habit of this sort of thing.'

Sadie can feel the heat rising in her cheeks. If any of her previous clients have suspected anything, it has never previously been raised.

Tonya continues. 'My problem is that I don't want you doing this to any of the friends who I introduced to you at my party and who, unlike me, actually still like their husbands.'

'It won't happen again,' Sadie says, gripping her delicate mug so tightly that she is afraid it might break. 'You don't have to worry about them, I promise.'

'You're right,' Tonya replies. 'It won't happen again because you won't have the opportunity. I'm giving you a choice, Sadie. Either you contact all the people whose numbers you took at my Christmas party and make an excuse as to why you won't be able to work on their refurbishment projects, or I'll contact them and tell them the truth – that you're a great designer but you can't be trusted around their husbands.'

The heat from moments earlier disappears from Sadie's cheeks to be replaced with an icy chill. It isn't that easy. Tonya comes from money. She has no concept of what it's like to be broke, particularly in New York where everything costs a fortune. Some of the deposit money Sadie has already been paid by her next client has been allocated to pay the rent on her apartment over the coming months, the annual contract on which had renewed on the first of January. She will have to return the deposit and that will make things very tight until she gets her next commission.

'Okay...' Sadie starts to say but is stopped in her tracks by Tonya.

'And don't even think of trying to work in this town again. I haven't told my father because I'm too embarrassed that Alec would choose a fifty-eight-year-old woman with loose morals over me, but it's an option if you want to try to fight me on this. No one – as in absolutely no one – gets one over on the Durlingtons. Have I made myself clear?'

Sadie, unable to see the point in prolonging the agony, gets to her feet.

'Crystal clear,' she says, tilting her chin upwards in a small gesture of defiance. 'I'll contact everyone I'm currently in discussions with and tell them I'll no longer be able to fulfil their briefs.'

Despite the gravity of the situation, Sadie allows herself an internal smile at her unfortunate choice of words. Removing briefs has been more her thing, she thinks, shrugging into her coat and twisting the expensive cashmere scarf which had been her final gift from Alec around her neck.

'I'm sorry for you that it had to end like this, Sadie, but hopefully this experience has taught you something,' Tonya says, picking up a small handbell to ring for Remedios, who appears a little too quickly in the doorway. 'Miss Appleton is ready to leave now, please show her out.'

Sadie follows Remedios back onto the landing and down the sweeping staircase, an image of Scarlett O'Hara in *Gone with the Wind* flooding her mind.

As the solid front door closes behind her, Sadie glances up at the drawing-room window, from where she knows Tonya Durlington will be watching, having exacted her revenge on 'the other woman'. Although Sadie can't imagine what her next steps in life will be, she raises a hand defiantly before thrusting them both deep into her pockets and descending the steps.

Scarlett O'Hara's famous line had been, 'Tomorrow is another day.' At that precise moment, Sadie can't visualise what tomorrow looks like in her life, the life she has painstakingly built up over the past nineteen years. It's tempting to head for the nearest bar and get blindingly drunk, but, realising the futility of it, she heads instead for the nearest subway station. She has no idea how much longer she will be calling her apartment home, but for now it's her sanctuary and the only home she has.

NINETEEN

MELISSA

24 June 2023 – the day after the party

Sadie has always been the more practical, less emotional of the two of us. When we were younger, I was the one who would throw myself dramatically onto the bed sobbing into my pillow when things didn't go my way, whereas Sadie would search for possible solutions. So, to hear the defeat in her voice when she said that New York has fallen out of love with her takes me by surprise.

'What do you mean?' I ask.

She's staring intently into her wine glass, almost as though she expects to find the answer to my question in there. When she does raise her eyes to connect with mine, I recognise the look in them.

It's one I haven't seen since she first went to America.

'I need to tell you something,' she says.

It had been nineteen years ago when Sadie had cooked her signature spaghetti Bolognese, in the small kitchenette of the flat she rented in West Kensington. It was one of her very small repertoire of dishes that was more than just palatable. We'd been chatting away throughout our dinner, but something hadn't seemed quite right. I put it down to a combination of her still getting over the end of her affair with the love of her life and the fact that unusually she hadn't joined me in a glass of Chianti to wash the pasta down.

We'd cleared away the pasta bowls, but instead of washing them, she left them to soak in the sink. 'I'll do those later,' she insisted, 'there's something I need to tell you.'

We sat in the two easy chairs with the table between us. Only, back then, it had been me with the glass of wine and her with a soft drink, the opposite of tonight. The pained expression in her eyes was the same though.

With the benefit of hindsight, I now understand why she kept bringing the topic of conversation around to me and Steve trying for a baby. At the time, I'd thought her persistence strange as she knew how sensitive I was about the subject because of all the failed IVF attempts. Eventually, I'd said that I didn't really want to talk about my inability to become pregnant and that's when she'd come straight out and asked if Steve and I had ever considered adoption. It was out of the blue and had caught me off guard, but I replied that we'd discussed it at length on numerous occasions, but Steve wasn't keen, and I was now too old to be considered. That's when she'd dropped her bombshell.

'You could adopt my baby,' she said.

I've relived that moment a thousand times since. The room had started to spin, and I'd battled with the urge to throw up. Steve and I had tried and tried to get pregnant over the course of our fourteen-year marriage, but it just hadn't happened for us. Now, if I was understanding things correctly, my best friend, who knew the anguish it had caused me over the years and wasn't in a steady relationship herself, was casually announcing that she was pregnant. I was stunned. I couldn't look at her. I know she continued to talk, but I didn't hear the words. It was all just a muffled blur.

After the initial shock, I felt anger. I was angry with my body for repeatedly failing me on the one thing I felt was missing from my otherwise perfect life. But, mostly, I was angry at Sadie for not taking precautions. A baby simply didn't fit into her lifestyle. Even at thirty-eight, she was a party-girl, not a homemaker. And then the penny had dropped. She clearly had no intention of keeping the baby herself. She was suggesting that Steve and I adopt her child as an alternative to something totally unthinkable to me. A tiny spark of hope reared its head that my husband might change his refusal to consider adoption if it was Sadie's baby. Then I remembered the last conversation we'd had about it.

'What's more important to you, Mel – a baby or us?' he'd asked, gently holding my face between his hands to maintain eye contact with me. 'Because you're going to have to choose. You can't have both, and as far as I'm concerned, this is the last conversation we ever have about it because it's destroying us.'

I knew Steve was right. My obsession was coming between us, but I didn't know if I could just accept his ultimatum. If we were to stay together, it would have to be on the understanding that I could never be a mother. I'd wrestled with my true feelings for days. I couldn't just give up on something I'd wanted for so long, but I knew I must because I loved my husband. Sadie was throwing me a lifeline, but it had come too late. He'd been clear that I had to make a choice and I'd chosen him.

I finally found my voice to reply to Sadie. 'No, we couldn't adopt your baby or anyone else's. Steve made his feelings quite clear to me and I don't want to do anything to jeopardise my relationship with him. He's my "one", Sadie. I love him more than life itself,' I said. 'He must come before everything else. You do understand, don't you?'

She'd seemed about to say something. Maybe she was considering questioning why Steve's feelings on the matter were more important than mine. There was a momentary pause before she simply nodded.

'H-how far along are you?' I managed to ask.

'Just a few weeks,' she replied. 'Under normal circumstances, I wouldn't have told you because anything could happen between now and the baby being viable, particularly at my age. I couldn't wait though. I needed to know as early as possible whether you and Steve would consider adoption.'

'What will you do now?' I had a feeling I knew, but I needed to hear her say it, even though I dreaded her response.

She gave a little shrug. 'Obviously, I can't keep it. I thought it might have been the answer to yours and Steve's prayers...'

'How can you be so cold and calculated?' I interrupted. 'It's a person we're talking about here, Sadie. You can't deny it the right to live.'

'I don't have a choice, Mel.'

'But what about the father? Doesn't he have any say in this?'

'You seem to forget he was a married man,' she replied. 'So, no. He doesn't have a say, because he doesn't know and I'm not going to tell him. Nobody knows apart from you, and it must stay that way. Promise me you won't say anything to anyone.'

I got up from the chair, knocking my glass of wine over in the process, but I didn't care. I had to get out of Sadie's flat. I needed to get away from the person who had been my best friend and confidante since we were eleven years old. The whole situation was overwhelmingly sad and unfair.

At that moment, rushing down the communal stairs from her third-floor flat and bursting onto the street below, gasping for air, I honestly believed I would never be able to speak to Sadie again. It was as though the bottom had fallen out of my world.

We didn't speak for several weeks. Despite her efforts, every time her number flashed up on my phone, I just hit the red button. I couldn't bear the thought of hearing her voice. And then I received a text message.

I couldn't do it, Mel. I didn't go ahead with the termination. But now I've had a miscarriage. The baby must have known that it wasn't wanted.

I stared at that message for a long time, tears streaming down my cheeks, not only for the loss of the unborn child but also for how close I had come to begging Steve to reconsider his stance on adoption. When I finally stopped grieving for Sadie's baby, my thoughts turned to my friend. I wanted to comfort her. Although she hadn't planned or even wanted the baby, she must still be suffering terribly. That was when an almost inconceivable thought entered my mind. What if she was lying? What if she was claiming that she'd had a miscarriage because she didn't want our friendship to be over? I had to know the truth, so I arranged to meet her in person.

I think I'd known the minute I walked into the café because she looked so dreadful.

We saw each other every day for the following two weeks and then she dropped a second bombshell. She needed a fresh start and had got herself a job working in a Broadway theatre in New York. She was saying goodbye.

A shiver runs through me as I look at her now, her eyes holding that same desperation as they had all those years ago.

Please, I'm thinking, *please don't tell me you've been lying to me all these years about terminating your baby.*

'I've fucked up big time, Mel,' she says, her voice barely above a whisper.

I can feel the thudding of my heart against my ribcage. If

she has been lying to me all along, why would she suddenly decide to tell me the truth? Nothing would be achieved and yet so much would be lost.

'What's happened?' I ask, inviting an answer that could end our forty-seven-year friendship. We've had our ups and downs over the years, it's only human, but if she outright lied to me about losing the baby naturally when in fact it had been induced, there is no future for our friendship.

'I had an affair,' she says.

TWENTY

LINDA

24 June 2023 – the day after the party

Linda hurriedly terminated the phone call with her daughter when she heard the squeak of the unoiled hinges of the front gate. It wouldn't do for Melissa to hear Ruby calling out to her nana if the front door wasn't opened immediately as was usual, after she'd conducted the telephone conversation as though her granddaughter was present.

Walking across the room, she pockets her phone and opens the door moments before Ruby knocks on it. Her granddaughter is on the front step but makes no attempt to enter the house, instead glancing over her shoulder at the young man standing on the other side of the gate. Even without the distinctive moustache, Linda recognises him as Freddie Mercury from the party the previous evening.

'Erm,' Ruby says, fidgeting with her fingers and looking uncharacteristically nervous, 'Kyle has walked me home and we wondered if you might like to meet him?'

'Well, that would be very nice,' Linda says. 'And not before time, if I'm honest.'

Ruby motions for Kyle to make his way down the path and reaches reassuringly for his left hand while he extends the other one to shake hands with Ruby's nana.

Linda can barely suppress a smile at the formality of the gesture but reciprocates by taking his hand in hers. It is clammy, which could be due to either the warmth of the June evening or his nervousness at finally being introduced to a member of Ruby's family.

'Nana, this is Kyle,' Ruby says, making the introductions. 'And, Kyle, this is my nana, Linda.'

'Pleased to meet you...' Kyle pauses, clearly unsure how to address Ruby's nana.

'You can call me Linda,' she says, recognising his dilemma. 'Come on in and let's get you a cold drink. You must be thirsty if you've walked from your flat in this heat.' She notices Kyle exchanging a questioning glance with Ruby. 'You're in Ellington Avenue, aren't you?' Linda continues. 'You don't really think I'd let my precious granddaughter go out without me knowing where she's going, do you? That wouldn't be very responsible of me, would it?' she adds, ushering them into her living room.

'No, I suppose not,' Kyle concedes, standing awkwardly next to the table.

'Sit yourself down on the sofa with Ruby,' Linda says. 'There's plenty of room for two and I'll get us some drinks. What would you like? I've got orange squash, lemonade or I can probably find a beer in the fridge, but no guarantees it isn't past its sell-by date as it might have been there for a while.'

'I'll just have water, thanks,' Kyle replies. 'I won't stop long as Ruby has to be up early for her dancing competition. Did you message your mum to make sure she's still okay to take you? If not, I can give you a lift.'

Linda smiles to herself as she reaches a couple of glasses down from the cupboard and starts to fill one of them with water from the tap. She likes the fact that Kyle appears to have a considerate nature.

'No, not yet,' Ruby says. 'I'll do it after you've gone. Thanks for reminding me.'

'I hope you're okay with tap water, Kyle? I don't hold with paying for something that should be free. And goodness knows what they might put in the bottled stuff to keep it from going off,' she says, placing the glass on the work top. 'Are you having a squash, Ruby?'

'Yes please, Nana,' Ruby says. She clears her throat and continues. 'I hope you don't mind Kyle coming around unannounced. It's just that we've had a long talk tonight about stuff, and we think it's time to stop being secretive about our relationship now that I'm officially classified as an adult.'

'I couldn't agree more,' Linda says, handing the cold drinks to the couple on the sofa and sitting down opposite them. 'I'm not going to lie; I haven't felt comfortable for a while knowing something that your parents don't.' Linda notices the look that her granddaughter gives her. 'But, no, I didn't write that note. You asked me to keep your secret, so I did, even though I had some reservations. I suppose I should feel honoured that you've chosen to introduce Kyle to me before your mum and dad,' she adds, a smile playing at the corners of her mouth.

'It was just easier,' Ruby says, taking a sip of her drink. 'You already knew about Kyle, so we were kind of hoping that you might be able to smooth the way a bit for us?'

'Ruby! That sounds really bad,' Kyle says. 'You make it sound as though we're using your nana.'

'It's fine, Kyle,' Linda responds. 'I don't have a problem with it at all. I think it's a sensible idea really. Melissa and Steve will probably be quite annoyed with me for not telling them I knew about all this months ago and that will hopefully take the heat off you two a bit.' Noticing Kyle's worried expression, Linda adds, 'This won't be about you as a person, Kyle. Dads never like the idea of their daughters starting to date, because they remember what they were like themselves when they were young, free and single. It's them being protective towards "their little girl",' she says, using her fingers as quotation marks, 'especially if, like Ruby, she's an only child.'

Linda allows her mind to wander back to the first time she had introduced Ruby's grandpa, Dave, to her family the day after her fourteenth birthday. It hadn't gone down too well and, ironically, given what she has just said to Kyle, it had been her mum, Shirley, who had been more disapproving of them starting a relationship at such a young age. Linda knew her mum had high hopes that her middle child, who was far and away the most academically gifted of her three children, would be the first family member to go to university.

Linda and Dave weren't actively prevented from seeing each other, but it was discouraged at every opportunity. Shirley and Tom suddenly started organising regular weekends away in their caravan in Hastings rather than only going there during the school holidays. On the weekends the family did stay home, the kids' help was required to give a fresh coat of paint to their bedrooms or tidying in the garden. Linda and Dave were virtually restricted to seeing each other in breaktime at school and walking home together. Although Shirley probably didn't realise, it was almost certainly what eventually prompted them to run away to Gretna Green to get married in the summer holiday after the two of them had sat their GCE O level examinations. They were very much in love, and they wanted to be together. Getting married had seemed like the only solution at the time.

That was part of the reason that Linda has been so concerned about keeping Ruby and Kyle's relationship from her daughter. She didn't want the responsibility of knowing about them and not telling Melissa about it, but she made a promise to her granddaughter, one that she wasn't going to break. It had put Linda in an impossible situation, worrying that Ruby and Kyle might make decisions that could affect their entire lives just as she and Dave had.

As the weeks had turned to months, it had crossed her mind to try to anonymously alert her daughter that Ruby was seeing someone, but she hated the idea of her granddaughter never being able to trust her again, so she'd kept quiet. Whoever had placed the note in Melissa's speech had inadvertently done Linda a massive favour and it was irrelevant whether or not it was about Ruby. Because Melissa had assumed it referred to her daughter, the need for Linda to reach a decision on betraying Ruby's trust was removed.

'Going back to the note for a minute,' Kyle says. 'Ruby told me about it. She even wondered if I might have written it, which she now realises is ridiculous.'

Ruby nods her head vigorously. 'Yes, thinking about it, Nana, although Kyle was against me going away to college or university because he didn't think a long-distance relationship would work for us, nothing would have been gained by telling my parents about us dating. It would probably have made them even more keen for me to go away and split us up before we got too deeply involved.'

'It's too late for that,' Kyle says, twisting Ruby's long blonde hair around his fingers and gazing at her with such an adoring look that Linda almost feels like an intruder in her own home. 'We've talked it through and whatever Ruby decides to study and wherever that is going to be, I'll be going with her. Getting a job in my line of work won't be difficult wherever we're living and at least it will give us the chance to get to know each other better, annoying habits and all,' he adds, dropping a kiss on the top of Ruby's head.

Before the couple can get into a discussion about annoying habits, Linda jumps in. 'So, how do you plan to go about telling your mum and dad, Ruby?'

'I'm at a dancing competition for most of tomorrow, but maybe I could suggest that you come round for dinner, Nana, and then you and Kyle could turn up together? They should be in quite a good mood if I've had a good day.'

'Won't they suspect something is up?' Linda asks. 'I've only been to your house a dozen or so times since you moved in and that would make it twice in a week, including an overnight stay. Mind you,' Linda adds, a smile spreading across her face and bringing a twinkle to her eyes, 'if I arrive with Kyle, they might think that I've got myself a toyboy.'

'Nana!' Ruby exclaims. 'You're old enough to be his grandma!'

The laughter that ensues is interrupted eventually by Kyle.

'Seriously though, Linda. Who do you think left the note for one of Ruby's parents to find? It wasn't me and it wasn't you. The list of suspects is getting shorter and the motive less obvious, if the words are about Ruby at all.'

'Have you confided in Sadie?' Linda asks, looking pensive. 'You two have always been close, but her friendship with your mum goes back nearly fifty years. If she felt it was something your mum should know but she didn't want to break a promise she'd made to you, there's a possibility she could have put her on the scent anonymously. It would mean she didn't have to choose between the two of you.'

'No, I haven't told her about Kyle. We've talked on the phone more generally about boyfriends,' Ruby says, a flush creeping up her neck, 'but that was more for some general advice.'

'I think she picked up on the chemistry between us at the party last night,' Kyle says.

'Yes,' Ruby agrees, leaning her head into Kyle's shoulder. 'But that was after Mum had found the note, so I don't think Auntie Sadie was responsible for it.'

'You know, I'm starting to have serious doubts whether the

note was about you, Ruby,' Linda says. 'But in a weird way it's worked out for the best because you two have decided to reveal your relationship regardless of the consequences, and in my opinion that is the right thing to do.'

'And at the right time,' Kyle adds, 'now that Ruby's exams are over.'

'Still, if the "she" in the note is not you,' Linda says, redirecting her gaze solely towards her granddaughter, 'then who does it mean?'

'You don't think it could be about Auntie Sadie rather than written by her, do you?' Ruby asks. 'There's been a weird kind of atmosphere between her and my dad. Do you think he might have discovered something and was trying to alert Mum to it without being the whistleblower?'

'It's possible, I suppose. Maybe that's why he asked your mum to do the speech at the last minute so she would find the note,' Linda says thoughtfully. 'That's the trouble with secrets. They have a habit of eventually coming to light and with them comes a whole heap of consequences.'

TWENTY-ONE

MELISSA

24 June 2023 – the day after the party

The relief that floods through me when Sadie announces she's had an affair is palpable. I'm assuming this is nothing new. Over the years, I've chosen not to delve too deeply into my friend's private life, but I do know she has a bit of an obsession for dating married men. Although it's not something I necessarily approve of, it's her life and she must have her reasons for choosing liaisons with no future prospects. She's never offered an explanation and I've never asked for one, but I suspect it might have something to do with trust issues after being dumped by the love of her life.

'Blimey, Sadie. Is that all?' I say. 'It's not exactly breaking news that you choose to sleep with married men. You had me really worried for a minute there.'

She shakes her head. 'This was different,' she says.

I'm about to ask her if she broke her own rules and allowed herself to get emotionally as well as physically entangled with someone else's husband when she continues.

'The affair was with the husband of a very well-connected

client, as in virtual New York royalty, if they have such a thing over there. Apparently, she began to suspect something was going on towards the end of the project on their house which, with the benefit of hindsight, is unsurprising as he'd started to get careless about where we met up. She had us followed by a private detective. About a month after the refurb was finished, she confronted me and told me that if I didn't sever contact with all the prospective clients she'd introduced me to, she would tell them about the affair with her husband and others previously. She said she'd make sure I'll never work in New York again,' she concludes, exhaling heavily.

I'm not sure what to say. It must be absolutely awful to have everything you've worked so hard to build start to crumble around you. Sadie has always prioritised her work, putting it before relationships and even friendships, as her going off to New York when I needed her bears testament to. Without it, what does she have left?

'Wow,' I say. 'That is a bit more serious than I was expecting. Do you think she would carry out that threat?'

No wonder Sadie is so worried. Her business has been built on personal recommendations. If they dry up, where would her work come from?

'She already has. My phone has stopped ringing. No one will touch me with a bargepole,' she confesses, her shoulders sagging and her chin dropping forward onto her chest.

'Bloody hell, Sadie. What an almighty mess,' I say, shaking my head.

'I know,' she replies. 'I haven't worked at all since January.'

'How on earth have you been managing?' I ask. New York is not the cheapest city in the world whichever part of it you're living in, but a front line, East River view apartment must be astronomically expensive.

'I was okay to start with because I had some savings. I guess I was hoping that everything might blow over eventually, but that was just me sticking my head in the sand. I got through my savings quicker than I thought I would, so I started selling off my furniture to pay the rent. The last time you called,' she says, raising her eyes to look into mine, 'I was sitting in an empty apartment aside from the chaise longue and the occasional table. Even they've gone now,' she admits, her lower lip trembling.

I can barely believe what I'm hearing. There's always been a small part of me that was envious of my friend and the life-style she was leading in New York, but she has managed to press the self-destruct button on it all.

'There must be hundreds of thousands of single men in a city the size of New York. Why on earth didn't you have a fling with one of them rather than risking everything you've worked so hard to build up?' I say, trying to keep the incredulity from my voice.

'I didn't want them,' Sadie replies miserably. 'I wanted Alec.'

'What was so special about him?' I ask, wondering how someone as worldly wise as Sadie could have been taken in by someone who was happy to cheat on his wife.

'None of us really knows what attracts us to one another, do we?' she says, giving a slight shrug of the shoulders.

She's right. I fancied Steve the moment I saw him but if asked, I wouldn't be able to explain why.

'I just loved being in his company,' she continues. 'He made me feel special, as though I was the only woman in the world, and I fell for it, even though I knew he was married to someone else. I think I was starting to fall in love with him,' she admits, blinking rapidly, presumably to keep tears from her eyes.

'Did you try to speak to him to hear his side of the story after your meeting with his wife?' I ask. 'If it was me, I would have demanded an explanation.'

'I thought about it,' Sadie says, nodding her head as though she agrees that an explanation was owed to her. 'After the devastating meeting with Tonya, I went home to my apartment and downed half a bottle of vodka. I almost called Alec then,' she says, a faraway expression on her face as though reliving the moment. 'My finger hovered over his name on my mobile phone, but I lost my nerve and threw the damn thing across the room instead. When I woke up the next morning, having eventually cried myself to sleep, I discovered that despite the protective film, my phone screen had shattered, just like my life really,' she says, her eyes connecting with mine as she sighs deeply.

She's not wrong. Not only is her business in tatters, but she's also had her heart broken again.

'By the time my replacement phone had arrived the following day,' she continues, 'I'd realised the futility of contacting Alec. Whatever his reason for behaving the way he did, our affair was over, and if he decided to tell Tonya that I'd been in touch, she might have carried out her threat to tell her father, not that it could make things any worse. The damage to my career was done, end of story,' she says, a sad finality to her voice.

'I'm so sorry it all ended that way, Sadie,' I say.

'Me too,' she says. 'You know, you asked me why I didn't date one of the thousands of single men in New York?'

I nod.

'It was a weird kind of self-preservation. My heart was in a million pieces when I arrived in New York. Fragment by tiny fragment, I was finally reconstructing it. Then I met Alec. What a fool he has made of me,' she says, still with no trace of anger in her voice.

'So, what are you going to do now?' I ask gently.

'Well, I'm not going back to New York. I've got nothing to go back for. When I ran out of things to sell, I had to come clean with my landlord and tell him that I couldn't afford the rent,' Sadie says sadly. 'I handed back the keys to my beautiful apartment before heading to the airport for my flight here. Everything I own in the world is in this room with me.' She indicates the four suitcases lined up against the wall like sentries.

I'd thought it was strange that Sadie had brought so much luggage for her four-day stay when Ruby and I had picked her up from the airport, but I could never have imagined the reason.

'So, I take it you won't be needing a lift to the airport tomorrow?' I say, stating the obvious. Selfishly, I'm pleased that Sadie is home for good, but I would never have wanted it to be in these circumstances.

She shakes her head again. 'That's why I wanted us to have dinner tonight so that I could explain why I'm not going back,' she says.

'Have you thought about what you're going to do?'

There is another deep sigh. 'I got in touch with a few people back here once it became clear that I wouldn't be able to stay in New York. There are a few irons in the fire, so hopefully I'll be able to pick up some freelance work in my old career.'

'And where will you live?' I ask. 'You know you can come and stay with us for as long as you need to.'

'Thank you, but I couldn't,' Sadie says.

'Why?' I persist. 'We've got plenty of room and you need a roof over your head.'

'The only thing I've got left is my pride,' she says, her eyes sparkling with the tears she seems determined not to cry. 'If I lose that, I really do have nothing.'

'You know,' I say, wondering if I'm doing the right thing in owning up to what I thought she had been about to confess, 'for one awful minute, I thought you were going to tell me that you'd lied about miscarrying your baby.'

Sadie's head snaps up from where it had been tucked against her chest. She looks alarmed. 'What do you mean?' she demands.

'I... I thought maybe you were going to tell me that you lied about not going ahead with the termination because you were so desperate for our friendship not to be over.'

I'm not sure what I see in Sadie's expression, but if pressed, I would say it's relief.

'It would have been, you know,' I continue. 'I couldn't have stayed friends with someone who had deliberately aborted their baby when there are so many people in this world who would do anything to become pregnant.'

Sadie's head drops forward again. She knows I'm including myself in that statement, because she knows just how far I was prepared to go. I watch her bring her hands up to her face, almost as though she is trying to hide from me.

A lead weight is forming in my chest where my heart normally beats.

'Sadie,' I say, urgency in my voice. 'Tell me that's not what happened.'

She shakes her head. 'It's worse,' she says, her voice barely audible.

To my mind, there isn't anything worse. I have no idea what she could possibly mean, unless she wasn't pregnant in the first place and had pretended to be. But that makes no sense. She's my best friend. Why would she play a cruel trick like that on me?

'I didn't lose the baby,' she says, finally lifting her face to mine. Her cheeks are wet from tears.

'I don't understand,' I say, struggling to recognise this version of Sadie as the strong confidant woman she has always been. 'Are you saying you were pregnant when you went to New York? Did you have the baby there?' I ask, the questions pouring out of me, such is my urgency for the answers.

She takes a moment to calm herself, wiping the moisture from her cheeks in an impatient gesture.

'I didn't go to America when I said I did. I moved out of my flat in West Kensington and into a women's refuge on the other side of Brighton until the baby was born,' she says.

My heart is thumping against my ribcage. My best friend has been keeping a huge secret from me for almost twenty years. I'm struggling to comprehend.

'Why a refuge?' I ask. 'Why would you do that? Why not be around people you knew who would have supported you and the baby?'

'By people, do you mean you and Steve?' she says with a hint of bitterness. 'Have you forgotten that I asked you if you and he would consider adopting my baby and you rejected the suggestion without even discussing it with him? I was desperate. I felt backed into a corner, knowing that I wouldn't be a good mother to my child. I booked an appointment and even turned up at the clinic at the appointed time, but I just couldn't go through with the termination. Your words kept running through my mind. I didn't want you to hate me, Mel.'

I can hear the raw agony in her voice all these years later and can only imagine how alone and afraid she must have felt. It's not something she would have felt able to go to her parents with, and her one true friend had stormed out of her home. I'm starting to feel guilty that I chose not to risk talking to Steve about adoption. But if we had adopted her child, there's every chance that my beautiful Ruby wouldn't exist because I'd have stopped trying to become pregnant.

'What happened to the baby?' I manage to ask, my voice shaking.

'She was taken from me after a few hours. It was the way things were done back then. I signed the papers, and she was given to the adoptive parents before I had a chance to change my mind, not that I would have done,' Sadie says, a flat finality to her comment.

'You had a daughter too,' I say. 'She and Ruby could have grown up like sisters if things had been different.'

'But things weren't different,' she replies, her voice devoid of emotion now that she's regained her composure. 'I couldn't wait to get away from England. I didn't want to accidentally see my baby with her new mummy out for a walk. I did what was right for both of us, but it didn't make the decision free from regret.'

I genuinely cannot imagine how Sadie could hand over the child she had just given birth to. I have never felt such pure love as the first time I held Ruby to my breast. All thoughts of the route I had taken to get me to the point of cradling my own baby in my arms were banished from my mind in that moment of agony and ecstasy and I know Steve felt the same way. We were both utterly besotted with Ruby from her first breath.

'But once you'd had your baby and had given her up for adoption, why did you go through with your move to America? You could have returned to London and made out that New York was a mistake,' I say, struggling to understand Sadie's motive. 'You must have felt so isolated and lonely out there.'

'Quite the opposite,' she replies. 'Being away from England was the best thing I could have done for my sanity. By distancing myself, it was as though it had never happened. I flew out to America the week after my baby's birth to start the job you thought I was already so busy doing that I never had time to call you. Remember all those letters you wrote and sent to the theatre?' she asks.

I nod in response.

'Well, they were redirected to the hostel by my colleague who got me the job in the first place. I'd told him my mother was terminally ill and had at best six months to live so I needed to stay close to her. That's why they held the job open for me even though they were short-staffed and all had to work overtime to cover for me. So, you see, my whole time in New York started with a massive lie. Maybe it was destined to come crashing about my ears as some weird retribution.'

I don't know what to say. I feel sad and shocked in equal measure and incredibly hurt that the truth is only coming out now.

'Why now?' I ask. 'Why are you telling me all this? Is it because the note is about you and not Ruby?' I say, my heart sinking that my immediate thought had been that it was about my daughter. What kind of mother does that make me?

'I was waiting for you to ask that,' she replies with a twisted smile on her lip. 'It could be, I suppose. Let's face it, just like the note said, I'm not who you thought I was.'

'Oh Sadie,' I say, going over to her and pulling her into a hug. 'I'm not going to lie. I wish you'd told me all this when it was actually happening, but it's all in the past and nothing will ever change the fact that you are my best friend in the entire world.'

She is clinging on to me as though she might never let go when the phone on her bedside table rings. She jumps almost out of her skin and makes no attempt to answer it, instead looking at the phone with what can best be described as a fearful expression.

'Blimey, is that the time?' I say after a quick glance at my watch. 'That'll be reception ringing to tell me my cab is here.'

'Do you have to go?' Sadie asks, releasing herself from our hug and going over to the bed to answer the phone. 'I could ask them to come back in an hour.'

'They'll be fully booked on a Saturday night. We can meet up tomorrow if you're free though,' I say in response to the disappointed look on her face.

'I can't do tomorrow,' she says. 'I'm meeting with an old colleague in London who might be able to pull a few strings to get me some theatre work. How about Monday morning if you're not working? There's more to the story, but it's not so urgent now that you know I won't be going back to New York,' she adds, picking up the telephone receiver. After a moment, she says, 'Thank you, she'll be right down.'

Obviously, I'm impatient to know the rest of the story, but it will have to wait.

'Monday works. I've taken the week off to recover from Ruby's party and catch my breath after all the planning. Let's meet here at eleven and then maybe grab a bite of lunch in the restaurant afterwards. My treat,' I say, picking up my bag and heading for the door. 'I hope tomorrow goes well.' I hold my hand up with my fingers crossed.

As the door closes behind me, I hear Sadie say, 'So do I.'

TWENTY-TWO

SADIE

22 June 2023 – the day before the party

Sadie can see a shadowy outline approaching through the frosted glass panels in the front door. She's arrived early for dinner at Steve and Melissa's house because she is hoping to catch Steve alone.

After pressing the doorbell, her mind transports her back to January when she stood waiting on a different doorstep. At least this time she knows why her stomach is in knots.

The door opens and Sadie is relieved to see it is Steve.

'Sadie! How lovely to see you,' he exclaims, the enthusiasm in his voice not quite matching the expression in his eyes.

It's the first time in almost twenty years that Sadie has set eyes on her best friend's husband, because he always made the excuse of being too busy at work to accompany Melissa and Ruby on their New York trips. She can't help acknowledging that time has been pretty kind to him. His hair is more grey than blond now, but he still has it in abundance and despite being slightly thicker set than he was in his late thirties, he doesn't have the middle-age paunch that so many other men approaching sixty have.

'Hello, Steve,' she says, taking a small step backwards as he seems to be contemplating whether or not to endorse his words of welcome with an affectionate hug.

'You've caught us out a bit, I'm afraid. Mel's not back from walking Baxter and Ruby's at dancing. But come on in,' he says, stepping to one side of the doorway to allow her to pass.

Sadie doesn't move.

'I wanted to get here a bit early, Steve, because we need to talk,' she says with a degree of urgency in her voice.

'Talk about what?' Steve asks, the warmth of his welcome replaced with anxiety. 'We haven't exactly kept in touch for the past twenty years; what would we have to talk about?'

'We both know the reason we didn't keep in touch,' Sadie replies, looking him directly in the eyes. 'And why you've avoided all the trips to New York. I'm just amazed that Mel was never curious as to why you didn't want to go.'

'It's called trust, Sadie. She believed that I had business meetings, which I did,' he adds, a cold edge creeping into his voice.

'Meetings you could have got out of if you'd wanted to,' Sadie persists.

'But I didn't want to,' Steve says. 'I never wanted to lay eyes on you again after what happened. You deciding to up sticks and go to America was a best case scenario as far as I was concerned.'

A few years ago, those words of rejection may have upset Sadie, but since the confrontation with Tonya Hammer in January, she's had more important things to worry about, not least of which was her reason for needing to speak to Steve in private.

'Well, that's as may be, but I'm back. Like I said, we need to talk and without danger of being interrupted or overheard. What I have to say can't be dealt with in five minutes.'

'Sadie, I genuinely have nothing to say about what happened between us twenty years ago. It's ancient history from a period in my life that I've since regretted with every fibre of my being.'

'Trust me, the feeling is mutual,' Sadie says.

'Look,' he says, glancing over his shoulder, his body language a clear indication of his anxiety. Although I've never been in their house before, I've seen lots of photographs and know that they take Baxter out for his walks through a gate at the bottom of their garden. He's clearly expecting Melissa will be back from walking their dog at any moment. 'I love my wife. I always have and I always will. There really is nothing more to say unless you're planning to destroy your best friend's marriage?'

Before Sadie can respond, Melissa's voice calls out, 'Steve, I'm back. Where are you?'

'Tomorrow morning at 10 at my hotel. You really should be there,' Sadie hisses, a hint of warning in her tone.

'It's Ruby's birthday for God's sake,' he hisses back. 'How am I supposed to explain disappearing for an hour?'

'I'm sure you'll find a way,' she says at the same low level, before cranking up the volume. 'Hi, Mel!' Her voice is loud and cheerful as Melissa's head peers around a doorway at the far end of the hall. 'I'm a bit early. I hope that's okay?'

Melissa lets out a squeal of delight and rushes towards Sadie, throwing her arms around her friend and squeezing her so tightly that eventually Sadie has to push her away.

'I can't believe you're really here,' Melissa says, still holding on to her friend's shoulders as though fearful that Sadie is a figment of her imagination and will disappear if she lets go of her. 'Why is she on the doorstep, Steve? Come in and let me show you around,' she continues, her voice filled with excitement, 'or did you want a drink first?'

She grabs Sadie by the hand and pulls her past Steve, who is standing like a statue, his back pressed against the front door.

'A water would be good,' Sadie replies as she follows her friend through the door from which she had emerged moments earlier. 'Wow! What a beautiful kitchen. It's so much bigger in real life. And the view out to the garden is lovely.'

'It's not the panoramic view over the East River that you have from your apartment,' Melissa says, reaching for a glass from the cupboard and filling it with chilled water from the dispenser in the fridge door. 'But we love it, don't we, Steve,' she adds, handing the drink to Sadie.

'It's home,' Steve says, briefly making eye contact with Sadie.

Sadie's stomach twists. He seems to be underlining what is at risk of being destroyed. *But I have no choice*, she thinks, draining her glass.

'Are you okay doing the tour with Sadie? I've got the barbecue to attend to,' Steve adds, letting himself out of the patio door and closing it quite firmly behind him.

Sadie notices the slightly puzzled expression on Melissa's face before her friend says in an almost conspiratorial tone, 'He takes his barbecue very seriously. Come on, let me show you around.'

TWENTY-THREE

MELISSA

22 June 2023 – the night before the party

Something seemed a bit off between my husband and my best friend tonight. I'm finishing loading the last few dishes into the dishwasher before heading up to bed after Sadie left fifteen minutes ago. We've agreed to meet at the golf club at midday tomorrow to start setting up the room for Ruby's party. As she was leaving, she gave me a massive hug but managed to air-kiss either side of Steve's face without physically coming into contact with any part of him. It seemed quite unnatural.

Immediately after she'd gone, Steve, who has had rather more to drink than he usually does, asked if I was okay to tidy the kitchen. Neither of us likes to get up to the detritus from the night before after hosting a dinner party and as he had done all the cooking, I was completely fine with it. Besides, it has given me a few minutes to myself to mull over the evening.

Earlier, I showed Sadie around our house, a tour which was accompanied by lots of oohs and aahs, and just as we were coming out of the master bedroom, Ruby arrived home from dance class and hurtled up the stairs, giving Sadie another full-on bear hug, not dissimilar to the one she'd received from me twenty minutes earlier. After a couple of minutes of excited chat, Steve called up the stairs that he was 'building the burgers' and we all made our way downstairs and out onto the decking that led off our kitchen.

While we were tucking into our food and wine, I didn't really notice that the atmosphere between Sadie and Steve was as chilled as the Chardonnay. There was a lot of chat about Ruby's party, but once our daughter had excused herself from the table, the conversation became a little stilted.

We'd always been extremely close friends, often going out to dinner in a foursome with Sadie's latest boyfriend. She had been a frequent visitor at our house for small dinner parties, although I don't remember us ever going for dinner at hers. Firstly, her flat was too small for a proper dining table so would have meant us eating off our laps, and secondly, and Sadie would admit this herself, she's not the world's best cook. Steve's reaction when I'd told him that Sadie was moving to New York was mixed. I hadn't mentioned anything to him about her pregnancy and subsequent miscarriage, so it was awkward trying to justify why she needed a new start on a different continent, particularly at a difficult time in our lives. Instead, I'd told him that she'd been offered a fabulous job working in a theatre on Broadway, which was the truth. He'd agreed that it was too good an opportunity to miss, although I do seem to remember him saying that he thought it was a bit selfish to be 'abandoning' me when she knew how much I needed her.

Although Ruby and I have been to visit Sadie in New York half a dozen or more times, Steve hasn't seen her since she moved. *Maybe he was just feeling awkward around her after all these years*, I think, pressing the start button on the dishwasher and giving a final wipe to the work surface before flicking off the light and heading upstairs to join my husband. Time changes people and we've lived very different lives, particularly since Steve and I became parents.

He has his back to me and is snoring gently when I go into our room, but by the time I've cleaned off my light make-up, had a wee and brushed my teeth and am flicking off the light in the en suite bathroom, he has rolled onto his back and appears to have his eyes open.

'Everything okay?' I ask as I slide between the cool cotton sheets. Even the lightweight summer duvet has been too warm for us this past couple of weeks. I say this past couple of weeks, but as anyone at a similar hormonal stage of their life as me knows, throwing the duvet off in the middle of the night because of personal tropical moments can strike at any time of the year.

'I was just thinking how unusual it is to still be so close to the people you were at school with,' Steve says. 'I have no contact with any of my old school friends and most of them still live in the area.'

His comment seems quite casual, but it's an odd thing to be lying in bed thinking about on the night before his daughter's eighteenth birthday.

'Well, it's person, singular, rather than people,' I say, turning on to my side to face my husband in the dark. 'I'm not close to anyone from school, or uni for that matter, apart from Sadie. I guess we just click.'

'But she's very different from you,' he persists.

'I suppose she is,' I reply, wondering what has brought about his sudden interest in why Sadie and I have stayed friends for so long. 'But they do say opposites attract,' I continue, laying my arm possessively across his chest. 'Look at us. I'm pretty sure not many people would have thought our relationship would have stood the test of time. And that includes me after that awful first date,' I add, digging him gently in the ribs.

I'd met Steve in the Easter holidays when I was home

before going back to university to sit my final exams. Sadie and I were at a party and Steve was with a bunch of his mates. They were knocking back the pints while we were on the cocktails. He later told me that one of his mates had egged him on to ask one of the 'posh birds' out. That had made me laugh as neither Sadie nor I could ever be described as posh, but it was obviously the impression given by the cocktails.

There almost wasn't a second date after an excruciatingly boring afternoon spent fishing at a local lake, which was little more than a giant pond in truth. We'd sat on camping chairs for hours barely talking because he didn't want to scare away the fish. He didn't catch anything, but I did – a streaming cold.

When he had the nerve to call for a second date, I initially turned him down until he admitted that 'the date' was part of a bet with his mates. If I agreed to a second date, which they were all certain I wouldn't, they would chip in and pay for us to have dinner in a fancy restaurant. I'd already made up my mind that our second date would be our last but thought the very least I deserved after the disastrous fishing date was a slap-up meal in a restaurant of my choice. He charmed me over chicken kiev and crème brûlée, and despite being very different in lots of ways, here we still are nearly forty years later.

I guess I'm expecting him to wander down memory lane with me and have a laugh about the fishing date. It's been a dinner party special whenever new people ask how Steve and I met, but tonight he's obviously not in the mood for reminiscing.

Now that my eyes have properly adjusted to the darkness, I can see his eyes are indeed open and he's staring up at the white expanse of our bedroom ceiling.

'Are you sure you're okay?' I venture, curling his sparse chest hairs in my fingers.

'Just nervous about tomorrow, I guess,' he replies.

'Don't worry about the speech,' I say reassuringly. 'You've been over it loads of times, and what does it matter if you make a couple of mistakes? The only people who will know about it are me and Ruby, and we're not going to judge you. She's just so pleased that you've agreed to stand up and deliver it even though it's outside of your comfort zone.'

'You're forgetting Sadie. She'll be aware of any mistakes too.'

'Well, yes,' I agree. 'But she's not going to judge you either.'

I don't quite catch what my husband mutters as he turns onto his side, facing away from me, but it sounded like 'I wouldn't be too sure about that.' I'm tempted to ask him to repeat himself, but he's clearly on edge about tomorrow, so I decide to leave it. I can't help wondering what has brought on the animosity directed towards Sadie that I'm sensing though. I kiss his shoulder before turning onto my other side, facing away from Steve.

Although I'm pleased that Ruby agreed to an eighteenth birthday party and I'm looking forward to celebrating with her tomorrow, I must confess I'll be glad when it's all over. If I'm being totally honest with myself, Steve is not the only one experiencing pre-party nerves, but mine are for different reasons. I can't stop my irrational fear that something will go terribly wrong in a repeat performance of her sixth birthday party.

I reach for the lavender pillow spray from my bedside table and apply a couple of spritzes to my silk pillowcase. It was a Christmas gift from Ruby which she claimed helps prevents wrinkles and makes your hair shiny. I'm not so sure about the wrinkles, but I've noticed a definite improvement in my hair.

With that thought in my mind and having taken a couple of deep lavender-infused breaths, I drop off to sleep.

TWENTY-FOUR

SADIE

21 June 2023 – two days before the party

Although grateful to Melissa and Ruby for picking her up from Heathrow airport, Sadie was relieved when they were happy to drop her at Highbourne House Hotel rather than coming in with her, after arranging to have dinner together the following evening at Mel and Steve's home. The flight from New York had been very full and she found it impossible to sleep. She was looking forward to soaking in a hot bath with a nap to follow, so was pleased when Melissa said that the hotel was allowing her an early check-in.

It had given Sadie a lovely wanted feeling to see Mel and Ruby's happy smiling faces waiting to greet her from behind the barrier after she'd cleared customs. They had no idea that she was here to stay. As far as either of them knew, she would be getting on a flight back to JFK on Sunday evening to resume her super busy life. They would find out soon enough that there was no return ticket, but it wasn't something Sadie wanted to share before Ruby's big day.

Ruby had squealed and rushed forward the moment she

had seen her Auntie Sadie emerge bleary-eyed from taking the overnight flight, which had been the cheapest ticket she could get. She'd flung her arms around Sadie like they were in the closing scenes of *Love Actually* – their must-watch Christmas movie. The excited chatter had continued non-stop for most of the hour and a half journey home, but even so, Sadie had been struggling to keep her eyes open.

Closing the door behind the porter who has shown her to her room, feeling slightly embarrassed that she hasn't had the foresight to get any English cash to give him as a tip, Sadie goes straight into the bathroom to start running her bath. She twists the dial to close the plug, but before she can turn on the taps, her mobile phone starts to ring.

She hurries back through into the bedroom and retrieves it from her handbag, wondering what tiny detail Mel or Ruby has forgotten to share with her that can't wait until dinner at theirs tomorrow evening.

'Hello,' she says, slightly breathless from rushing to answer before her voicemail kicked in.

'You're here then.'

It is the youthful English voice that Sadie last heard almost a month previously. She's been waiting for this moment, but now it has arrived, she's unsure what to say.

'Who is this?' Sadie asks, gripping the phone tightly, realisation dawning on her almost immediately that whoever it is must have watched her arrive at the hotel fifteen minutes earlier.

'Haven't you worked it out yet?'

Sadie is pretty sure she has worked it out, but it hasn't made it any easier to acknowledge the truth.

'Are you my... my daughter?' Sadie asks, struggling with the unfamiliar word.

'Very good. At least you remember that you have a daughter.' The sentence is dripping with sarcasm. 'Or should that be "had" a daughter, because that's all you did really. You gave birth to me, then got rid of me as quickly as you could.'

Sadie's heart is pounding. She's been waiting for a follow-up call, going over and over in her mind what she'll say to the young woman who shares her DNA, but no other aspect of her life. Nothing she has planned is forthcoming.

Eventually, she whispers, 'How did you find me?'

'It's all about you, isn't it? Not "how are you". But then I guess you've never cared about me, so why would you start now?'

I deserve that, Sadie thinks.

'But to answer your question, it was surprisingly easy,' the young woman says. 'I knew your name, because my mum let it slip in one of her endless screaming matches with my dad. Such a lovely family you chose to give me to.'

There is a heavy emphasis on the words 'lovely' and 'chose' which makes Sadie flinch. She was told about the couple who would be adopting her baby but she certainly had no choice in the matter once she'd made her decision not to keep her.

'Before signing the adoption papers, it seems my mother had been worried that you might change your mind and come looking for me, which we both know was never going to happen. Apparently, the agency that handled my adoption assured them it wouldn't be an issue because you were moving to New York, something else I overheard when voices were raised.'

Sadie can almost taste the bitterness in the woman's voice. She wants to tell her why she took the decision to give her baby daughter up for adoption. She senses that now is not the moment.

'How thoughtful of you to pass on that piece of information. It made it so much easier for me to find you when I started looking,' the woman continues. 'All I had to do was search the internet with your name, your nationality, and the year that you moved to New York, and hey presto, just like magic, there you were smiling out from the computer screen at me. You made it especially easy by being so high profile and successful. Such a shame that it's all come crashing down now,' the woman says, unable to hide the satisfaction in her voice.

Sadie is trying desperately to think how it would be possible for her daughter to have played any part in her fall from grace in New York. She's nervous to ask the next question but knows she must and that it must be phrased very carefully.

'How do you know about my business failing?' Sadie asks.

'You really should be more careful who you have an affair with. Is that why you ran away in the first place? Is my dad a high-profile married man that didn't want you once he discovered you were pregnant? Or maybe, like Tonya, his wife found out that her husband had been cheating on her?'

At the mention of Tonya's name, the blood in Sadie's veins turns to ice. How did her daughter know about Tonya? Had she somehow discovered the affair with Alec and tipped his wife off? What would be her motive? With her business in tatters in New York, she was having to return home to try to pick up the pieces of her life.

For a moment, Sadie allows herself to hope that her daughter might have engineered the whole thing because she wants her in England. Sadie is beginning to wonder if the two of them could try to build a relationship, but her hopes are dashed with the woman's next sentence.

'Don't get the crazy idea that I wanted you back in England so that we can play happy families and make up for lost time. I don't want you in my life,' the woman says spitefully, 'but I do want something from you.'

For the first time since the phone call began, Sadie can feel anger bubbling. She'd been faced with an impossible choice all those years ago and this young woman is clearly not in any mood to hear her side of the story, instead assuming that it had been an easy decision for Sadie to make.

'Well, if it's money, you're out of luck. You've shot yourself in the foot by destroying my business. I have nothing apart from the clothes I'm wearing and the contents of my suitcases.'

'If I'm supposed to feel sorry for you, I don't. They were your life choices, so you need to own the consequences. I wouldn't take your money anyway,' she adds.

'So, what do you want?' Sadie asks.

There is a very short pause before the woman answers.

'I want to know my father's name. I'm assuming you know who he is and that you weren't just sleeping around with anyone who would have you?' she says, clearly calculating every word to cause the maximum amount of pain.

'I resent that remark. I loved your father. He's the only man I've ever loved...' Sadie falters, the memories rushing back to her. 'But you're right in your assumption that he was already married to someone else.'

'Well, that makes it easier. Just give me his name and contact details and I'll disappear from your life again.'

'No,' Sadie says. She doesn't want her daughter to disappear from her life without her hearing her side of the story. She wants to lay eyes on the woman that she last saw as a tiny baby swaddled in a soft muslin blanket hours after she'd taken her first breath. There had been a moment as she held her newborn in her arms, gazing down at her smooth skin, upturned nose and inky blue eyes that were unable to focus on her, when Sadie almost changed her mind. Could she keep her? Could she make it work? The single tear that dropped off the end of her nose onto her baby's cheek as she was taken away was the final contact she thought she would ever have with her daughter. She isn't prepared to let this opportunity go.

'What do you mean, no?' the woman demands.

'I mean, I will give you the information you want about your father because I honestly think you have a right to know. But, in return, I want to meet up with you.'

There is another short pause from the other end of the phone call, suggesting to Sadie that her daughter had not been expecting a request to meet. She lets the silence hang.

'All right,' the woman says eventually. 'I'll meet you in Miss Daisy's, the café on the High Street, at 10 a.m. on Sunday morning.'

'How will I know it's you? I don't know what you look like,' Sadie says.

'Whose fault is that?' the woman retorts. 'But it doesn't matter. You seem to forget that I know exactly who you are. Don't be late, and make sure you have the information for me,' she adds before ending the call.

Sitting on the edge of the bed where she's been perched for the duration of the call, Sadie can barely believe what has just happened. The thought that the anonymous calls she started receiving in March could possibly be from the daughter she'd given up for adoption had begun to seem less and less likely the more time that elapsed without further contact. She'd started to believe instead that it was a sick joke. She had thought that perhaps one of the wronged wives who knew she was English had put on an accent, or that maybe it had been Tonya herself. Now she's had her original suspicion confirmed.

Sadie has sometimes allowed herself to imagine what it might be like if her daughter discovered she was adopted and chose to go in search of her birth mother, especially after some of the conversations she and Ruby had had recently. Every time she'd hung up the phone, she'd allowed herself to wonder who would be acting as a confidante to her eighteen-year-old daughter and giving her advice if it was needed. Eighteen is a difficult age in an unforgiving world, but it's also the age where adoptees can view their full birth certificate.

She never marked the day she gave birth or allowed herself to think about how it might be celebrated because she relinquished the right to have those thoughts when she handed over her child. She's thought more about her baby in the past few months than she has throughout the whole of her daughter's childhood. Being so closely involved with organising Ruby's party was undoubtedly a factor, as was having more time on her hands with the collapse of her business. But she suspects it's more than that. Becoming closer to Ruby brought with it the realisation of how much of herself she'd surrendered when she'd handed over her baby.

Apart from Mel, Sadie had no real friends. She never allowed herself to develop a close relationship with anyone, male or female, since moving to New York following the devastation of being dumped by the one person who she truly loved. No one, apart from Mel and Ruby, was permitted to stay over at her East River apartment. Even acquaintances who were occasionally invited round for drinks were never offered the spare room to crash in if they'd had a few too many. She'd specifically never permitted any of her married male friends access to her apartment.

It was a promise she'd made to herself after allowing the married man she had been sleeping with to come to her West Kensington flat for their assignations. Their child had been conceived in her bedroom, something neither of them had been aware of when he finished their affair, claiming that it had all been a terrible mistake. Once she knew about the pregnancy, Sadie had been unable to sleep in the bed where she'd foolishly dreamt that the married man might one day be hers. She was thankful for the temporary solution of the sofa bed in the lounge, but her home felt tarnished and no amount of scrubbing with bleach would ever make it feel clean again. Part of her reason for leaving the UK had been to get away from that flat and the unhappy memories it held. She'd needed a new beginning in a place where she knew no one, and no one knew her, and she was determined never to make the same mistake again. It hadn't crossed her mind that the New York apartment wouldn't be her forever home, and yet here she was again, forced to leave her home because she'd slept with the wrong man.

Her daughter explained in the phone conversation how she had been able to track Sadie down, but there are still many questions she hopes to get answers to at their meeting on Sunday. How could she have known that Sadie would return to England after the failure of her New York business? There is also a question mark over how her daughter knew her travel arrangements and which hotel she would be staying in. It's almost as though she was being fed information from Mel or Ruby, but, as neither of them is aware that she has a daughter, that can't be the case.

Tiredness from her lack of sleep on the flight is clouding Sadie's ability to think straight. Forgetting the bath she had been planning to take before the call, she slips her feet out of her shoes and climbs into bed fully clothed. Even with her mind in such turmoil, she's asleep within seconds.

TWENTY-FIVE

MELISSA

23 June 2023 – Ruby's birthday

I wake to a beautiful morning, exactly like the one on which Ruby made her entrance into the world and our lives changed irrevocably.

She was already six days late when I went into labour with her, but I knew she was all right because the hospital had me doing a kick chart for her for the previous three weeks. It was apparently something to do with her being quite a big baby for the size of me, which meant she would sometimes lie very still for long periods, probably because she simply didn't have much room to move. When she did move, though, she was a proper kicker, with odd shapes protruding at all sorts of angles beneath the taut skin of my belly. Even before she was born, Steve and I had joked that she would either be a footballer or a dancer. It seems our predictions about the latter have come true.

I really hadn't wanted to have the C section that we'd eventually had to resort to. I wanted to feel the exquisite agony of the final push, but that was denied me after the electrodes that the medical staff had attached to her head to monitor her progress indicated that she might be in distress. I'd waited so long to become a mother that I couldn't risk her life being snatched away from me in the final moments, so I reluctantly agreed to the caesarean section.

The screen across my rounded belly had gone up at around six o'clock in the morning, but Steve in his gown and his mask bravely stayed down at the business end of things. She was a bit bloody when she was first handed to me, my little miracle – although, to be fair, not as little as she might have been.

By nine o'clock, we were happily installed in our private room, me besotted with the beautiful baby who was already suckling at my breast, watched over by Steve, who had a look of pure wonder on his face.

There was no denying she was big, weighing in at over nine pounds, but there was no sign of distress and I have occasionally wondered if the C section was more for my benefit than hers. Maybe the midwife didn't think I would have enough energy left to push after thirty-six hours of labour, but I know I would have found it from somewhere.

The sky was still a perfect cloudless blue when I left hospital two days later. Steve was walking down the corridor ahead of me, swinging the baby carrier in what can only be described as a jaunty fashion. I didn't need to see his face to know that it was split with a grin from ear to ear.

Like most new parents, we suffered from sleep deprivation. If we got three consecutive hours sleep in the first six weeks, we thought we were winning. Although it was me doing the feeds, Steve would stay awake with me, offering to make me a cup of tea or fetch me a fresh glass of water. And he always did the middle-of-the-night nappy changes. Quite often it was accompanied by words such as 'gross' or 'disgusting', but I knew he wasn't complaining. Nothing could dull the brilliance of our beautiful little gem. She had arrived in the world healthy and strong, finally making us the family we had longed to be for so many years. And one of the pluses of having a bigger baby was that she could take on more of my milk at each feed than a smaller infant would. By three months, she was sleeping through the night, and we became the envy of all the other parents in our baby group.

Every twenty-third of June since that first one in 2005, I've sent up a prayer to heaven, even though I'm not particularly religious, in recognition of my incredible good fortune. This morning is no different. I have my eyes closed and am muttering my words of thanks when there is a sharp knock on our bedroom door before Ruby bursts in.

'It's official,' she says, unable to contain her excitement. 'I'm an adult.' With that, she launches herself onto our super king-size bed, bouncing up and down in a most unadultlike fashion. The image of Tigger from *Winnie the Pooh* is filling my mind.

'Please don't vote until you've read all the parties' manifestos,' Steve says, sleepily emerging from beneath the covers on his side of the bed. 'Happy birthday, sweetheart,' he adds, reaching his arms out to his daughter for a hug.

'Tell me you're not completely naked,' Ruby says, holding back from the invited embrace.

'Just the top half,' he confirms.

For the first time I can remember, Ruby is reluctant to give her dad a cuddle because of touching his bare skin, underlining the announcement she made moments ago about being an adult. I'm not sure of the specific significance at this point, but I'm certain it's merely the start of a new phase in all our lives. She is no longer our little girl and I'm suddenly overwhelmed by the thought. She has her whole life ahead of her and, increasingly as time passes, Steve and I will be less and less involved in it.

'What's for breakfast?' she asks, removing herself from her dad's embrace. 'I'm starving.'

'Anything you particularly fancy?' I ask as she leans into my outstretched arms. I must learn to cherish these special moments, which will undoubtedly become more infrequent.

'Smashed avocado and poached egg on toast,' she says decisively, smacking her lips together. 'That is a proper celebration breakfast.'

Ten minutes later, we're all in the kitchen, and Baxter seems to have got caught up in Ruby's mood. His tail is wagging wildly and he's barking excitedly, the latter of which is quite unusual for him, I think, as I watch him chase Ruby around the kitchen table. He's going to miss her almost as much as I will when she goes to university or dance college.

My throat closes and I turn away so that the tears currently poised and ready to roll down my cheeks will fall unnoticed by Ruby and Steve. *Focus on making today Ruby's best birthday ever*, I tell myself sternly. *There will be plenty of time to miss her when she's actually gone.*

'You do the dog's food, Steve, and I'll make a start on ours,' I say, reaching into the fridge for the avocados and eggs. 'Can you pour the orange juice, Ruby, and lay the table, please? I'm assuming food comes before presents?'

Keeping busy has always been my go-to when a situation threatens to engulf me.

Ruby loved the silver star necklace with her initial engraved on it that had been inside the first small gift box that Steve and I had directed her to open. In the second small box was a pair of ruby stud earrings, which she'd immediately put into her ears, making her dad squirm. Weirdly, people who don't have any piercings seem to think it hurts when putting in or taking out jewellery from the fully healed holes. Steve's worst nightmare are the thread-through earrings that I always take great delight in pulling through the piercing slowly, occasionally emitting pretend 'ouch' sounds when I know he's watching me.

Next, Ruby moved onto her present from my mum. It was a mobile phone cover with a beautiful marbled design in pink and red and the initial R in rose gold. After Baxter's gift to her – a bag of his favourite treats which she'd immediately opened and fed him several of even though he'd only just had his breakfast – there was only an envelope left on the table. Ruby's true reaction was difficult to gauge when she opened it to find a course of ten driving lessons, but she smiled and thanked us before excusing herself from the table to go and get showered.

Later, on her way out, Ruby almost knocked over the lady delivering a huge bouquet of flowers. They were from Sadie and the card read, 'Grown-ups get flowers on their birthday.'

I'm just arranging the flowers in the biggest vase I can find when Steve comes into the kitchen.

'I'm popping out for a bit,' he says.

'Oh?' I say, unable to keep the disappointment from my voice.

I'd been hoping that Steve and I might have time to celebrate our daughter's birthday by going back to bed. Ruby is spending the day at a spa with Megan. It's her gift to Ruby that she's thoughtfully organised for today to keep her away from the golf club while Sadie and I are getting it ready for the party tonight. We all agreed that we want her to walk into the room once it's been transformed rather than being part of the process.

'Yes,' Steve replies. 'I thought I'd go and look at a few possible cars for Ruby. The more practice she gets, the better. You're not that bothered about coming, are you?' he says, maybe noticing the look of disappointment on my face that I thought I was hiding. 'It's only a first look to see what's available at a decent price. Also, let's face it, I'm not likely to see much of you today because you'll be busy with party stuff.'

I know he's right, but I still feel slightly aggrieved.

'No worries. I've got these to finish,' I say, indicating the remaining blooms on the draining board, 'and Bax needs a walk.

Will you be able to take him later? I don't expect I'll have much time to get ready for tonight once I get home from setting the room up, and I'd like to look good for Ruby.'

'Of course, I'll take him later,' Steve says, ruffling the fur on top of Baxter's head as he makes his way over to me. 'Not that you need much time to get ready, you always look perfect to me. Love you,' he adds. He kisses me on the lips, making me wonder if I should just tell him about my alternative plans for the morning. 'I always have, and I always will. And you will be the best-looking woman in the room tonight – with the possible exception of our daughter.'

I must take too long wallowing in his compliments because, before I can speak, he is out in the hallway and the moment is gone.

TWENTY-SIX

SADIE

23 June 2023 – Ruby's birthday

Sadie takes a sip of her coffee, watching Steve over the rim of her cup as he strides purposefully across the highly patterned lounge carpet of the Highbourne House Hotel towards her. His expression is a mix of concern and annoyance as he covers the short distance in a matter of seconds and plonks himself down on the generously stuffed leather chair on the opposite side of a small round table.

'What's this all about?' he demands.

'And good morning to you too, Steve,' Sadie says, lowering her cup back onto its saucer. 'Can I pour you a coffee?' she asks, reaching for the silver pot from the tray on the table between them.

'I haven't got long. There are plenty of other things I'd much rather be doing on my daughter's eighteenth birthday than meeting up with you in secret.'

They lock eyes, both acutely aware that it isn't the first time.

'Well, at least you came,' Sadie says, pouring coffee into the other cup despite Steve not confirming whether he wanted one. 'Trust me when I say that it was a sensible decision. Remind me how you take your coffee,' she adds.

'Milk no sugar,' Steve says through gritted teeth before accepting the proffered cup. 'Well, go on then. What do we "need" to talk about?'

'This is difficult for me too, Steve, because I don't know how much Mel has told you about me going to live in New York.'

'Just that you had a great job offer and although it meant leaving your best friend at a really difficult time in her life, you accepted it,' Steve replies, taking a sip of his coffee.

'So, she didn't tell you about the baby then?'

Steve appears to choke on the mouthful of coffee he has just taken.

'I'll take that as a no then,' Sadie says, noticing his eyes widen with shock. 'I was pregnant, eight weeks to be precise, when I received the job opportunity of a lifetime. As you know, I'm not the maternal type and was not in a position to raise a child on my own. I did consider having an abortion, but having seen all that you and Mel had gone through in your efforts to have a baby, I simply couldn't go through with it,' she says, eyes trained on Steve, watching for a reaction. He's motionless and speechless, so Sadie continues. 'I even made the suggestion that you and she should adopt it, but as you clearly didn't know anything about the baby, I'm guessing that was never mentioned to you.'

'Hold on. You actually told my wife, who you knew was desperate to become a mother, that you'd fallen pregnant after having casual sex?' Steve says with incredulity. 'Call yourself her friend? She really doesn't know the real you, does she?'

'There's a saying about pots and kettles that I can't quite bring to mind, Steve, but I'm sure you know what I'm getting at.'

They both fall silent, Sadie deliberately giving Steve a

moment to remember the night he had turned up at her West Kensington flat. He'd poured his heart out to her, telling her that he and Melissa were probably at the lowest point in their marriage. They had tried everything to get pregnant and nothing had worked. Charts with best days of the month, even best times of those days, thermometers and lying still after making love... Nothing had worked. He'd tried to tell his wife that he couldn't do it anymore because it was coming between them, but Melissa was relentless in pursuit of something she believed would complete them. The drink had flowed, and he'd completely opened up about how his inability to get his wife pregnant made him feel less of a man.

'Did you set out to get me drunk that night?' Steve asks after a few moments.

'Don't flatter yourself. You above everyone know that I was having a pretty rough time myself.'

Steve gives a derisory laugh. 'A rough time of your own making. People get married because they love each other. What do you think gives you the right to hit on someone else's husband?'

'You know that's not how it happened. And keep your voice down,' Sadie hisses. 'You're drawing attention to us and that's the last thing either of us wants,' she adds, glancing around the lounge area. Only a few of the tables are occupied, but all eyes are trained on them.

'Well?' he says in a much-reduced volume, seeming to heed the warning. 'According to my wife, you're still doing it.'

'You are so self-righteous,' Sadie says, shaking her head. 'You're not exactly squeaky clean yourself. I suppose it never crossed your mind that the reason for me not wanting to get into a relationship with anyone was because the love of my life, the person I desperately wanted to be with, the father of my unborn child, dumped me.'

'He was married, Sadie. You knew that from the outset.'

'We don't choose who we fall in love with, Steve,' she responds sadly. 'And forgive me, but you have to take some responsibility here.'

'I know. If I could go back and change things, I would, but that's not possible. So, I'm going to ask you again, Sadie: why am I here?'

'Don't you want to know what happened to my baby after I couldn't go through with the termination?' she asks. 'I told Mel I'd had a miscarriage, but it was a lie. I went through with the pregnancy and gave birth to a little girl.'

Steve gasps.

'It nearly broke my heart giving her up for adoption,' Sadie says, the uncharacteristic wobble in her voice betraying her emotion. She gives a light shake of her head, trying to erase the memory of one of the worst moments of her life. 'But I knew it was the best thing for her to have two parents who would cherish her and raise her as a rounded human being rather than me solo parenting when I was so bitter and broken.'

'Mel and I would have been there for you,' Steve says.

'Would you though? When you were pouring your heart out to me at my flat, telling me how all the baby stuff was coming between you and Mel, you were totally honest and said you didn't know if your marriage would survive having a child in it because Mel had become so obsessed. You were afraid you would be replaced in her heart.'

'I was drunk, Sadie. I didn't know what I was saying or doing for that matter. I told you yesterday, that night was the worst night of my life, betraying Mel's trust, and with her best friend of all people.'

Sadie can still visualise Steve's mouth closing on hers. She'd made no attempt to stop him. 'Get a grip, Steve. Stuff like that happens all the time, as I know better than most. The point is your marriage has survived and you were eventually blessed with Ruby.'

'But last night you made it sound as though you're going to tell Mel about everything. Why would you do that after all this time?' Steve asks. 'That's the part I don't understand.'

'She came looking for me and found me,' Sadie says.

'Who did?' Steve asks.

'My daughter.'

Steve's face turns as white as the pristine jacquard tablecloth. 'How did she find you?'

Sadie gives a light shrug. 'Does it matter?'

'But you live in New York,' Steve says. 'Did she just turn up on your doorstep?'

'I haven't actually met her yet,' Sadie replies. 'The only contact I've had with her so far has been via mobile phone.'

'Not that it's my business, but how was she with you? Does she want to meet up?'

'Well, to answer the first part of your question, quite rightly, she hates me for abandoning her, as she puts it. Her primary objective is to punish me, and she's made a good start on that already by destroying my business in New York.'

'How could an eighteen-year-old possibly destroy your business?' Steve asks, frowning.

'I gave her a huge helping hand to be honest, but that's for another time,' Sadie replies, wafting her hand dismissively. 'To answer the second part of your question…' She pauses to take a deep breath, closes her eyes momentarily, then opens them to look Steve directly in the eye. 'The reason I had to meet with you so urgently is because my daughter wants to meet up on Sunday morning. She wants to know who and where her father is.'

She watches Steve run his hands through his hair. His face is ashen.

'And you're going to tell her?' he says.

'I've had time to think it over and, despite the circumstances, I think every child – or adult as she is now – has a right to know who their parents are. I don't have a choice really. I'm sorry, Steve.'

'But it could destroy lives...' Steve starts to say.

Sadie interrupts. 'You forget. Mine is already destroyed and I'd rather not destroy yours.'

'But you will, if I don't put you in touch with Luke. You'll tell Mel about a drunken kiss and cuddle, when I was in the depths of hell, if I don't divulge where Luke and his family are living now?'

'Like I said, I'm sorry. You couldn't have known how far it would all go after you passed on Luke's phone number at that party, although I've often wondered if you knew he was married,' Sadie probes.

Steve doesn't answer, instead closing his eyes, an expression of pure agony on his face.

'I truly loved him, you know, Steve. He was my "one", just like Mel always says you are hers. I'd never felt a connection like that with anyone before him,' Sadie says, her voice full of sadness.

Her hand trembles slightly as she reaches for her cup to take another sip of coffee. How many times has she wished that she hadn't agreed to go to Steve's company's Christmas do as a favour to Melissa. But Mel had been persuasive, saying she didn't know many of his employees particularly well and it would give her someone to talk to. Sadie had been between boyfriends at the time and the two of them had joked about her getting dolled up to attract an eligible bachelor. The red dress she had worn had been tight-fitting and low cut and had certainly caught Luke's attention. She'd made eye contact with him over the top of her champagne flute and felt her stomach lurch. The attraction had clearly been mutual. She'd watched Steve take a slip of paper from Luke before he'd left the party, which he'd passed on to her, saying, 'Don't shoot me, I'm just the messenger.' The note said simply, 'You're beautiful. Call me,' followed by his mobile number. She'd called him the next day.

Luke had eventually told her he was married when they had been seeing each other for several months, but, like a lot of men who cheat on their wives, he'd said that he was waiting for the right time to tell her he wanted a divorce. Sadie was already too deeply in love with him to stop seeing him, so chose to believe his lies.

He'd eventually ended things on Valentine's Day when they'd been seeing each other for over a year, telling her that his wife was pregnant again. She'd been totally devastated and that was before she discovered that she was also carrying his child.

'I guess for him I was just some good sex when his wife was too tired from looking after their kids,' Sadie continues. 'I don't know if they're still together and frankly I don't really care.'

Even as the words leave her lips, Sadie realises that they aren't entirely true. What if Luke's wife had discovered their affair and thrown him out? *Would I take him back?* she wonders.

After a few more moments with Steve making no attempt to speak, Sadie says, 'He should know he has another daughter. Surely, as a father yourself, you can see that.'

'Sadie, there is no way for me to tell you this without hurting you,' Steve says, his voice taking on a gentler tone.

'What?'

'I heard other rumours about Luke after you'd left for America. It would seem that you weren't his only affair.'

The revelation lands with as much force as a physical punch in the stomach. Any lingering hope that she had been 'his one' who he had simply met too late evaporates with Steve's words. She battles the tears pricking the backs of her eyes as Steve continues.

'I hear what you're saying about him having the right to know that he has another daughter, but have you considered what her existence might mean for his marriage and his other children?'

'You don't owe him anything,' Sadie says, recovering her composure. 'He used to laugh at you trying to stop him from seeing me once you'd realised the hurt that could be caused. I'm sorry it's falling at your door to decide whose lives should be destroyed, but I don't have any other options. Just ask yourself if he's worth protecting if it could mean losing Mel's trust?'

Steve nods slowly. 'Leave it with me, Sadie, and I'll see if I can track him down. Just promise me that you won't do anything to jeopardise Ruby's birthday. You above anyone know just how much effort has gone into the party and the enormity of her agreeing to it after all these years of refusing to have one.'

Sadie gives him a disdainful look. 'Whatever you think of me, Steve, you must know that I would never do anything to hurt Ruby. Watching her grow, albeit from afar, is probably what saved me from self-harming with alcohol or drugs. Her and Mel's visits to New York have honestly been some of my best highlights from the past eighteen years. So, no, I won't do anything that would ruin Ruby's day. You have my word. But I need to know where Luke is by Sunday morning at the latest. You'll do that for me, won't you?'

'I'll try,' Steve says, getting to his feet. 'For what it's worth, Sadie, I'm truly sorry that I hooked you two up and that you fell in love with him. He didn't deserve you and I should have known better.'

Sadie watches Steve retrace his steps across the highly patterned carpet and out into the reception area of the hotel. If there was another way of getting Luke's details in the short amount of time available without having to blackmail Steve, she would have done it. But there isn't. She doesn't even know Luke's last name. It would be virtually impossible to trace him without Steve's help, but she needs to use the threat of revealing their drunken kiss to impress on him the sense of urgency. Sadie is clinging on to a faint hope that if she is able to provide her daughter with what she has asked for when they meet on Sunday morning, it could be a tiny first step in them trying to build some kind of relationship.

TWENTY-SEVEN

RUBY

23 June 2023

'Favourite bit so far?' Megan asks, climbing onto the warm sculpted bed and relaxing back.

She and Ruby are in the quiet room of the spa, where it is respectfully requested that patrons do not talk, but as they are the only two in there, they don't imagine that the rule still applies.

'Hmmmm, difficult to choose,' Ruby replies. 'I loved the facial and the body massage, but not quite so keen on the ice plunge bath. Just remind me of the point of it, apart from literally freezing your tits off!'

The two girls laugh. Neither has spent a day at a spa previously, so they had no idea what to expect when they arrived at Southdowns Manor at 10 a.m. Megan had needed to book proper appointment slots for the facial and the body massage, but those aside, the time was their own.

They'd started with a swim in the outdoor pool, followed by a Jacuzzi, then back in the pool for another swim before showering and heading to their booked appointments. The facials had been in separate treatment rooms, but for the body massage they were in the same room, lying on tables that were a couple of feet apart. They'd been allowed to choose the music and the aroma of the massage oils used and had left the room after forty-five minutes feeling totally relaxed.

Lunch was next. Ruby stuck with a healthy salad with slices of grilled halloumi as an add-on, while Megan went for the 'dirty' burger with fries, which she insisted Ruby should share. It was washed down with a glass of pink prosecco, Ruby celebrating the fact that she was drinking alcohol in a public place legally for the first time.

Neither of them felt like going in the gym straight after lunch, which had originally been their intention, instead opting for an hour on a sun lounger next to the pool in the beautifully manicured gardens. The fabulous weather that England had been basking in was apparently set to change soon, but there was certainly no sign of it yet.

The ice bath plunge was Megan's idea because she was hot from sitting outside in the sunshine. It was more usual to go directly in from the sauna or the steam room, but the girls had almost every area of the spa to themselves, so they were able to make up their own rules. Standing on the third rung of the ladder with only her feet covered in the icy water, Ruby's teeth began chattering.

'It's my birthday. Why are you torturing me?' she said.

'You don't have to do it,' Megan replied, making the sound of a chicken before bursting into laughter.

In the end, both girls did the ice plunge twice, each time staying submerged up to their chins for thirty seconds. After the first time, they went into the sauna, which Megan wasn't too keen on as she said it made the inside of her nose hurt because of the dryness of the heat. They opted for the steam room after the second plunge before showering and heading into the relaxation room to completely unwind on the heated stone beds. The time had seemed to go much faster than either of them expected and both were keen to pack in as much as they could before they had to think about heading home.

'Thanks for today, Megan,' Ruby says, reaching her hand across the gap between the beds and giving her arm a gentle squeeze. 'I've really enjoyed my first spa day. We'll have to do it again. Maybe for your birthday in September?'

'If you're still around, Ruby,' Megan says with a hint of sadness in her voice. 'It'll be weird being apart from each other after all these years. Have you decided whether it will be uni or full-time theatre school yet?'

'It kind of depends if I get my straight As,' Ruby says. 'If I do, then I'll have to decide; if I don't, then the decision is made for me. Cambridge is the only uni that could tear me away from Laines.'

'It's not all punting around on the river in a floaty dress and a wide-brimmed hat, you know.'

'Course I know. There's the Cambridge Footlights too in my final year,' Ruby says.

'Oh, you're so funny, you're bound to get into that,' Megan says, her reply laced with sarcasm. 'What does Kyle think about it all?'

'As in?'

'As in, how does he feel about you going away?'

'That's a tricky one,' Ruby says cautiously. 'Obviously, we've talked about it a bit, but if I'm honest, he's not really that keen on the idea.'

'But you're still keen on him?' Megan asks.

'Oh yes,' Ruby replies enthusiastically. 'I know I'm inexperienced, but we've been seeing each other for five months now and I think he might be my "one".'

A silence falls between the girls, interrupted only by the distant hiss of water being ladled onto the coals in the sauna room across the corridor. Although they settled their differences months ago, Ruby sometimes gets the feeling that Megan still holds a candle for her boyfriend.

Eventually, the silence is broken by Megan.

'I know I asked you before when you first told me about you and Kyle, but have you and he... you know?'

Ruby turns her head to look at her friend. She's trying to decide whether or not to tell her that she's been thinking about it as her eighteenth birthday approached. The trouble is, she's scared in case it's not as magical as she hopes. She's had sleepless nights worrying that sex might be the one thing that she doesn't excel at. Even her generic 'how will I know when I'm ready to have sex' conversation with her Auntie Sadie without revealing that she was in a steady relationship a couple of weeks previously, after she'd bottled asking her during their call in March, hadn't elicited a particularly helpful response. 'You'll just know' was all Sadie had offered, although, to be fair, she had sounded a little distracted and anxious to get off the phone.

'Actually, Meg, I'm a bit nervous about it,' Ruby eventually admits, her face flushing.

Megan doesn't turn to face Ruby, but instead glances at her friend from the corner of her eye.

Ruby smiles unthinkingly, reminded of how Baxter gives the side-eye when he's been naughty.

'It's not all it's cracked up to be,' Megan says.

Other than the hiss of water hitting hot coals and the distant squeals of the ice plunge participants, the room is completely silent.

'What? Who?' Ruby stammers as the realisation of what Megan has just admitted dawns on her.

Megan lifts her shoulders in a shrug. 'Just a lad at a party that you didn't come to because you were with Kyle. I'd had a bit to drink and so had he. It was all over in a flash, but I can't say it lit up my world. Be certain you want to go there with Kyle because it should be special and it wasn't for me,' she says, regret evident in her voice.

Ruby sits up and swings her legs off the stone bed towards the floor so that she can properly face her friend for what she is about to say. 'I'm sorry. I feel like it's my fault somehow.'

'Well, it's not,' Megan replies. 'If I'm going to have a perfect friend, I have to accept that things in her life are probably going to run a little more smoothly than they do in mine. I made the decision to go with that boy because I didn't want to be second to you in every respect. It was the wrong reason and so had the wrong result. But, hey, at least I'm in the club now. No, not *that* club,' Megan says, reacting to Ruby's horrified expression. 'We had the good sense to use protection, and whenever you decide to take that extra step with Kyle, I'd suggest you do the same.'

'Don't worry, we would. I'm well aware of the consequences an unplanned pregnancy can have. My mum has told me often enough that she was always made to feel as though her arrival ruined my nana and grandpa's life.'

'Your grandpa died when your mum was young, didn't he?' Megan asks.

'She was eleven, so not that young really,' Ruby replies. 'But, to be honest, I don't think Mum's home life had been particularly happy before Grandpa had the accident. She always says that one of the reasons she and Dad rarely argue in front of me is because her own parents' arguments made her feel guilty for something that wasn't her fault.'

'It was even closer to home for me,' Megan says, sitting up and dangling her legs over the side of the bed. 'Like your nana and grandpa, my mum and dad were probably too young when they got together. They didn't give themselves enough time to get to know one another before they got engaged and then married. Adopting me when they couldn't have kids of their own was supposed to save their marriage, but you already know that wasn't what happened.'

Ruby shakes her head sadly in acknowledgement.

'Another overheard gem from Anna on the night I discovered that I was adopted was, "If it wasn't for her, we could have gone our separate ways years ago, instead of being stuck in a loveless marriage." That didn't make me feel like a burden to them at all,' Megan says sarcastically. 'I'm pretty sure they both started seeing other people soon after we moved here from Brighton, if I'm honest.'

'That's awful. Why not just own up that you've made a mistake and get divorced rather than cheat on the vows you've taken.'

'That's the world we live in, unfortunately,' Megan says. 'It just seems to be the accepted norm these days. They felt compelled to stay together because of me and yet it would have been better for all of us if they'd been brave enough to call it a day. Imagine how wanted it makes me feel to be rejected by two different mothers.'

Ruby can't imagine. All she has ever known throughout her entire life is the devoted love of both her parents. She experiences a pang of guilt that she still hasn't told them about her relationship with Kyle, particularly as she has no justifiable reason.

She moves over to where Megan is sitting and slips her arm around her. 'We don't choose our families, and you've been especially unlucky in that department. But we do choose our friends and you're one in a million,' Ruby says, dropping her head down onto Megan's shoulder.

'And our boyfriends,' Megan says, releasing herself from Ruby's embrace and lifting her friend's chin to make eye contact. 'We choose our boyfriends too. Kyle might turn out to be your perfect match and you could end up living a long and happy life together. But' – Megan pauses briefly – 'he's your first boyfriend, so at the moment you have no one to compare him to. Things could change dramatically when you get to university.'

Ruby is about to say that she doesn't believe moving away to university will change the way she feels. But it takes two people to make a relationship work and she and Kyle have already had one major disagreement over it, so she remains quiet.

'Don't get me wrong, Ruby,' Megan says, 'I hope he is your one. But think about what your future together might look like before you make any big decisions. Promise me?'

'Okay,' Ruby agrees, trying to squash the niggling doubt that Megan might not entirely have her best interests at heart.

TWENTY-EIGHT

MELISSA

25 June 2023 – two days after the party

Ruby's first words to me when I picked her up outside Mum's this morning made no reference to our argument the previous day. Instead, she asked me what time I would be back from taking Sadie to the airport. I was a little economical with the truth, telling her that Sadie had decided to stay on in England for a while. I want to be able to sit down and tell Ruby about Sadie's reasons for leaving New York when I have more time to explain it properly, not as she sat beside me in the car on the way to a dancing competition with a slightly tense atmosphere between us.

Her next question had come as a surprise. Would it be okay to invite her nana for dinner tonight? I could hardly argue about having Mum over to dinner. Ruby had turned up unannounced and Mum had done a good job of playing along with the cold caller routine when I'd rung to check on her. The least I can do is make her a nice dinner. The question I refrained from asking Ruby after I'd said 'of course' was why? Why did she want her nana to come for dinner tonight? She visits our house so rarely and she stayed over with us for the first time ever after Ruby's party. Was it an attempt by Ruby to have her nana more closely involved in our family, or was there a specific reason for the request?

My mind had been racing from one possibility to another as we drove along in near silence. Was my mum sick? Had she confided in Ruby last night and my daughter had insisted that she tell me? Or was this something to do with the note left within the pages of the speech? Maybe Mum does know something about Ruby and has persuaded her to tell me. I guess I'll find out over dinner later.

If I'm honest, I could have done with a quiet night in front of the television after the drama of the past few days, which clearly isn't over yet.

Judging by Sadie's parting remark that there is 'more to the story', I'd begun to wonder on my way home in the taxi last night if the note might be referring to Sadie. I can honestly say that, as secrets go, her revelation was huge. Could someone have found out about Sadie's daughter and left the note as a prompt for her to tell me about it? 'She's not who you think she is' would certainly have a ring of truth if that was the case.

I'd been tempted to wake Steve to talk it over with him when I got home last night but thought better of it as we're still not really on speaking terms after the disagreement over the way I approached things regarding the note with Ruby. Having slept on it, I'm glad I decided to keep it to myself until after my meeting with Sadie. She'd told me her secret, but that could have been in a moment of weakness. Maybe she doesn't want anyone else to know.

I'd dropped Ruby at the community centre earlier and then popped into the supermarket to buy some stuff for dinner. I'm sure Steve would probably have offered to do another barbecue, but Mum's not keen and I want the evening to be as painless as possible. I occasionally take cold homemade quiche around for her if we have any left over from dinner the night before and she's always complimentary about it, so I'm going to make one for her to eat warm with new potatoes and mixed vegetables. I'm assuming she won't be staying over again, so one of us will have to stay off the drink completely to drive her home. Unsurprisingly she's of the opinion that one drink is one too many if you're driving after what happened with my dad.

While I was waiting in the queue at the checkout with my basket of shopping, I had an overwhelming desire to watch my daughter perform. When she was younger, I would stay at the competitions all day, helping her to change from one costume to another, putting her hair in different styles for the various routines and making sure she had lunch and snacks. I'm not sure whether it was her suggestion or mine, but over the past couple of years, I've only stayed to watch at the Nationals and the Worlds. At the smaller competitions, I just drop the girls off and pick them up.

Today is a first for Ruby though. Since starting work in the coffee shop, Megan sometimes gets asked if she would like to work overtime, which apparently is what happened yesterday. She rang Ruby last night to say she wouldn't be able to go to the competition as she was working. Part of me wonders if Megan will give up dancing completely when Ruby goes off to college.

Either it was the thought that the competition today is very likely the last one that Ruby would take part in, or I was still feeling guilty that there might be an element of truth in her angry words yesterday. Whichever, by the time I tapped my credit card against the cashier's machine, my mind was made up. There was nothing that would spoil from sitting in the boot of my car for an hour, so instead of driving home, I headed back to the community centre where I'd dropped Ruby an hour previously.

Today's competition is a local festival that the academy enters to show support for the organisers. Most of the smaller local dancing schools don't travel all over the country and abroad, as we had done recently for the World Dance Championship in Lisbon, so having the support from a big school like Milsom Radcliffe is a must in terms of entrance fees to make the festival viable. It also gives their pupils a chance to enjoy performing on a stage in front of an audience.

Ruby had asked Miss Grace to only enter her in two solo classes and a duet with Megan at today's event, although now that Megan is working, she will only be performing in her solo dances. Ruby claimed it was because she would still be shattered after her party, but I like to think it is my daughter being kind and giving others the opportunity to go home with a gold medal or trophy.

I pay my spectator fee and wait by the entrance door for the current performer to finish. A quick glance at the printed programme has Ruby listed as number eight – the final performer in the Song and Dance class, which has just got underway. Under the applause for competitor number one, I slip into the back row of seats in the darkened auditorium.

The standard is surprisingly high for a local competition, but as Ruby takes her place on stage, a hush of expectation falls. I feel goosebumps as my daughter's clear voice fills the hall, controlled at first but gradually building with the emotion of the song before ending in a near whisper. There is a moment of silence before the applause rings out and the crowd en masse get to their feet.

I duck out of the hall before the lights go up for the adjudication, brushing the tears from my cheeks, my heart bursting with pride.

I've only just pulled up on our drive when Ruby calls to tell me that she has won first place in her song and dance routine. I don't tell her that I knew she would because I had been there to witness her captivating performance. She truly is an extraordinarily gifted performer and I feel quite certain that she could make it in the entertainment industry, but talent alone is no guarantee of success. You must want it with every fibre in your body and have total self-belief. There is also a small matter of 'who you know' and nepotism. I could possibly open a few minor doors for our daughter if she chooses to go into radio, but apart from that, my network of contacts would be pretty useless to her.

Ruby also says that I'm not to worry about picking her up as she'll be fine getting the bus. I'm about to argue when I remember Mum's comment from yesterday. I must accept that Ruby is now a young adult and should be given a certain level of independence.

I didn't have a similar problem with my mum. I was walking to and from school alone in the dark in the winter months when I started senior school at the age of eleven until Sadie and I became friends. Even then, the start and end of my journey was alone. I'd been nervous at first, of course, but once I'd stopped jumping at every shadow and footfall behind me, I became more and more confident. There is a school of thought about victims of crime giving off an air of 'being a victim', so maybe my mum's tough love has stood me in good stead. Ruby doesn't have an issue when it comes to confidence, she has it in abundance, so I'm pretty sure she'll be fine travelling home on her own.

I'm just putting the quiche in the oven when I hear Ruby's key in the lock. I've done a mushroom, cheddar and tomato version of one of our family's summer favourites today.

'In the kitchen, Ruby,' I call out to her.

'Something smells good,' she says, dropping her striped bag in the hall and coming into the kitchen.

'It's only just gone in, so you're probably smelling the softened onions,' I say, gathering together the remnants of the shortcrust pastry leftover from lining the quiche dish.

'Can you leave that for a minute, Mum?' Ruby asks.

'Of course,' I say, recognising by the tone of her voice that she has something important she wants to say. I rinse my hands under the tap and dry them on the tea towel before turning to face my daughter. 'You now have my undivided attention.'

There have been times over the past few months when Ruby might have misinterpreted my words and replied with a sarcastic remark, but not today.

'I-I just want to apologise for shouting at you yesterday. I said some pretty unkind things, which you didn't deserve, and I had no right to say.'

There's no denying that some of the things Ruby said about me always being too busy to spend time with her had felt like low blows and had left me reeling. I spent most of my soggy walk with Baxter questioning whether I've been quite as good a mother as I've always believed myself to be.

'It's all right, darling...' I start, but she interrupts.

'No, Mum, it's not all right. It was completely out of order, especially the day after you and Dad gave me my best birthday ever. I behaved like a spoilt brat rather than the adult I'm now supposed to be,' she says, shaking her head as though finding it difficult to comprehend her own actions.

'Okay, I admit you said some hurtful things but not without reason. It can't have been very nice for you to experience such a lack of trust from your own mother, but that honestly wasn't my intention. I just wanted you to know that you could talk openly to me if you were having problems, and that I would try to help,' I say, remembering radio interviews I've hosted with parents who were unaware that their child was going through hell until it was too late. 'I couldn't bear the thought of you being in a dark place feeling alone and with no way out,' I add, battling to speak through the wobble of emotion in my voice.

'Oh Mum,' Ruby says, crossing the kitchen in three steps and throwing her arms around me. 'If I'd been a proper adult, I'd have stuck around and we could have talked it through, but instead I went all dramatic on you. Maybe I should take up my place at Laines Academy without waiting for my A level results after that performance,' she adds, her voice a little muffled as she talks into my shoulder.

'I think you probably should,' I say. I want to tell her that I watched her today and that she should have more belief in her own ability, but that it must come from within if she's going to make it in such a tough industry. Besides, being completely selfish, I want to keep the memory of watching my beautiful girl all to myself.

'Really?' she asks, pulling away from our embrace to study my face.

'Really,' I confirm. 'Now, I need to get on with rolling out the rest of the dough,' I say, turning back to the worktop and dusting it lightly with flour. I have a thing about not wasting the spare pastry when I make a quiche and can usually stretch to a dozen jam tarts.

'Do you want the jam out of the fridge?' Ruby asks, knowing the routine.

'Yes please. It'll save me getting my floury hands all over the handle,' I reply, swiftly flattening the ball of pastry with the rolling pin.

'Where's Dad?' she asks, handing me the glass jar which has already started forming a mist of condensation because of the heat in the kitchen after the cold of the fridge.

'Having a shower after an afternoon gardening,' I reply, taking the pastry cutter and expertly gauging where to position it to make the best use of the rolled-out dough. 'He scrubbed the potatoes before he went up though,' I add.

'Erm... there might be someone extra coming for dinner tonight,' she says.

I stop pressing the cutter into the pastry and turn my head to examine Ruby's face. I know my daughter well enough to say with some certainty that there will be an extra guest for dinner. She looks nervous.

'Who?' I ask, trying to keep my voice light.

'A friend of mine,' she replies. 'I wasn't going to say anything until he gets here with Nana, but it's been on my mind all day and I don't think that's very fair on him.'

And there it is. *Him*. A three-letter word that confirms Sadie's suspicion that my daughter most likely has a boyfriend. Ruby lives under our roof and I haven't noticed anything different about her; Sadie sees her for a few hours and guessed there was something going on between her and the Freddie Mercury boy.

Then it occurs to me. The boy is arriving with my mum. Did she already know about him when she gave me the talk about Ruby not being a child anymore?

She's not who you think she is.

Maybe my earlier suspicions were accurate and it was Mum who left the note because she thought I should know, but she didn't want to betray Ruby's trust.

'I take it your nana has known about your friendship with this boy for a while?' I say, trying not to sound accusatory.

I turn back to the pastry and finish cutting out the fluted edged rounds. There are eight and if I gather the pastry together and roll it again, I should be able to make it up to the dozen. I try to focus on this task I've performed thousands of times previously to stop my mind from taking me to somewhere I can't yet contemplate. When Mum said 'she's not a little girl anymore' was she trying to tell me that Ruby is already in a sexual relationship with this boy?

'Yes,' Ruby replies. 'She's been on at me to tell you and Dad for ages, but I didn't know how you two would react.'

'React to what, Ruby?' Steve says, coming into the kitchen

and making me jump almost out of my skin. Fortunately, I wasn't using the pastry cutter, or I might have lost the end of a finger.

I can see Ruby's scared expression. She's like a deer in the headlights of an approaching car, knowing that it's going to hit her, and yet so paralysed with fear, she is unable to move.

'Ruby wants to introduce us to someone,' I say, sounding a lot calmer than I feel. 'Mum and I thought it would be a good opportunity to meet him over dinner, so he's coming tonight as well as Mum.' I throw Ruby a look that I hope conveys 'don't argue with my explanation'.

Steve's reaction takes us both by surprise. 'I wish you'd mentioned it earlier, Mel. I'd have done a few more potatoes if I'd known we had an extra guest.'

I exchange a look with Ruby. We're clearly both thinking the same thing. Has Steve not realised that we're talking about him meeting his daughter's boyfriend for the first time?

Before either of us can speak, the doorbell rings.

'I'll go,' Ruby says, pushing past her dad to get to the door before he can.

I give Steve a questioning look.

He shrugs. 'She's eighteen and gorgeous, Mel. It had to happen sometime.'

TWENTY-NINE

SADIE

25 June 2023 – two days after the party

Despite feeling nervous at the mere thought of laying eyes on her daughter for the first time since she handed her over shortly after her birth, Sadie can't help making the comparison between Sarabeth's, her favourite café in New York, and Miss Daisy's, which she is currently observing from the pavement opposite. The High Street, which she has walked the length of twice since her taxi dropped her at 9.30 a.m., is quiet, with none of the shops opening until ten on a Sunday morning. She arrived early to make sure she located the right coffee shop, but she needn't have worried, as Miss Daisy's is the only one in Brockledean.

Sadie glances at her phone again checking that her daughter hasn't messaged to cancel before deciding to go into the café to get a table. From the outside, Miss Daisy's appeared to be busy, but on pushing the door open accompanied by the quaint tinkle of a bell, Sadie realises that the café is not as full as it had seemed. It's a ploy used by most cafés and restaurants. Seating customers at window tables creates the impression that the establishment is popular, which it's hoped will encourage more people to give it a try.

To the left of the doorway is a glass counter displaying cakes and scones and pastries, all of which look delicious, but Sadie's stomach is churning too much to consider indulging.

Behind the counter, humming softly to herself as she froths up milk in a stainless-steel jug, is the only member of staff.

'I'll be with you in a moment,' the girl says, still with her back to Sadie as she pours the frothed milk into the waiting coffee cups and adds a dusting of chocolate sprinkles.

Sadie checks her phone again. It's 9.50 and there is still no message cancelling her rendezvous. She slides her phone back into a pocket inside her bag, too nervous to hold it, for fear of it slipping from her sweaty palms.

'Can I get you anything else?' the waitress asks, placing one of the hot drinks in front of a young woman, who Sadie notices is heavily pregnant.

The woman rests her hands on her baby bump and says with a smile, 'No thanks, I've already been doing a little too much eating for two.'

'Ignore her,' the man with her says, reaching for his partner's hand, his eyes filled with adoration. 'She's only put on ten kilograms in weight and we're due next week.'

Sadie swallows down the lump forming in her throat. It had been very different for her in the final stages of her pregnancy, afraid to leave the women's hostel for fear of bumping into someone she knew, despite it being on the other side of Brighton. She'd had no one to share the initial excitement of the first contractions signifying that her baby was on its way, nor anyone to mop her brow with a cool cloth in the latter stages of delivery. There's little wonder that she's tried to bury the memory for so many years.

Seeming to take it as an invitation to engage in a little more conversation, the waitress asks, 'Do you know what you're having?'

'A baby,' the woman says.

The laughter that results from their joke is interrupted by the tinkle of the bell as the door to the café opens. A woman who Sadie guesses to be around twenty enters holding the hand of a toddler. Her pulse rate starts to quicken. Could this be her daughter? She's never given any thought to the possibility that she might already be a grandmother.

The waitress excuses herself from the expectant couple, saying, 'Do let me or my manageress know if you change your mind. The pains au chocolat are to die for. Sorry to keep you waiting,' the waitress says, turning to address Sadie and the young woman. 'I'm on my own until my manageress gets here at ten.'

Catching sight of the waitress's face for the first time since entering the café, Sadie realises that they've met before.

'You're Ruby's friend,' she says. 'Megan, isn't it? We were sat at the same table at her party on Friday, but we didn't really get a chance to talk.'

'Of course,' Megan replies. 'I didn't recognise you when you first came in. You're Ruby's Auntie Sadie from New York.'

'You probably didn't recognise me with this much hair,' Sadie says, shaking her glossy mane.

'Yes. You look quite different from the other night,' Megan agrees. 'Did you want a takeaway or are you sitting in?'

'A nice quiet table please. I'm meeting someone,' Sadie says, casting a glance at the woman with the toddler, 'but I'm a few minutes early.'

'There are a couple of booths at the back. Would you like one of those?' Megan asks.

'Thanks. That would be perfect.'

'I'll be with you in a moment,' Megan says to the young woman with the toddler before leading Sadie to the booth right at the back of the café. 'Can I get you anything while you're waiting?' she asks.

Sadie starts to decline, then has second thoughts. 'A black coffee would be perfect please, Megan. I didn't get much sleep last night,' she admits, as though confiding in a long-lost friend. 'Maybe a coffee will wake me up a bit.'

'I'll be back in a couple of minutes,' Megan says as the bell signifying another new arrival to the café tinkles.

It's a little over ten minutes before Megan returns to Sadie's table carrying a mug in each hand.

'Sorry,' she says, placing one of the mugs on the table in front of Sadie. 'It suddenly got very busy with customers arriving and others wanting their bills. But my manageress is here now, so I get a short break,' she says as though to explain the mug in her right hand.

'No worries,' Sadie says, tapping the screen on her phone to check the time. It's now five past ten and there is no sign of her daughter. She is starting to wonder whether she has been stood up when she becomes aware of Megan sliding onto the bench seat opposite her. 'I'd love to chat, but like I said, I'm meeting someone.'

'Yes, you are,' Megan replies, fixing Sadie with a steady gaze.

The sounds of the café fade into the background and everything seems to move in slow motion as the impact of Megan's words hit Sadie and realisation dawns that she is staring into the eyes of the daughter who she'd thought she would never see again. The deep brown eyes are a mirror of her own, framed by eyebrows with a similar arch, and the hair swept up in a ponytail is the same colour as hers, but the nose and mouth bear a closer resemblance to her father. Her lips are set in a hard straight line, an expression Sadie remembers well from the day when Luke had ended everything, telling her it had all been a terrible mistake. She swallows hard trying to forget the devastation she felt when he left her so that she can fully concentrate on her feelings towards the daughter she doesn't know.

'Hello, Mother,' Megan says with heavy emphasis and a hint of sarcasm on the second word.

Sadie's pulse is racing. She can feel her heart thumping hard against her ribs. What are the odds that she would travel from New York and come face to face with the daughter she gave away at birth, who happens to be friends with her best friend's daughter, in a café in a small village in East Sussex?

'I-I don't understand,' Sadie starts to say in a state of confusion. And then suddenly, she does understand. The pieces of a complicated jigsaw begin to slot into place. 'You used Ruby to find me.'

'It's a bit harsh to claim that I "used" Ruby,' Megan says. 'We've been friends since she was five and I was six. We've grown up together and shared secrets with neither of us having the slightest idea that the biggest secret of all was right under our noses.'

* * *

It had been an almost unbelievable coincidence, but once Megan found out her birth mother's name and the fact that she had moved to New York, she had begun to suspect that Ruby's godmother and her birth mother were the same person. Little details such as where Melissa had gone to school had been easy to find out from Ruby, and once Megan had checked that Sadie Appleton had also been a pupil at the same school at the same time and that the two of them had gone on to Royal Holloway University together, she was certain she had stumbled across her birth mother's identity with minimal effort.

Details about where Sadie lived in New York were shared during conversations that Megan guided without Ruby having the slightest inkling that she was being pumped for information.

No information from Ruby was needed, though, about Sadie's job and the project she had been working on. Sadie had been very keen to post pictures on her Instagram account of the renovation of the Hammers' brownstone. That was where Megan had seen a picture of Alec with his wife.

It could have been tricky explaining her week-long absence from college shortly after her eighteenth birthday. That was when she'd finally got access to the ISA account that her adoptive parents had generously set up for her when she was a baby, before they'd decided that adopting her was a mistake. In the end, she decided that feigning illness would be her best bet. Before she left for America, she made a phone call to the college secretary pretending to be her 'mother' and when she went back to college, she was armed with a letter from her 'mother' that she had faked.

Her adoptive parents had been even easier to fool as they were completely disinterested in her. She told them she was on a college residential trip, the same story she had given Ruby, and that she'd paid for it herself out of the ISA money. They'd accepted it without question. It was true that she had used some of her ISA money to pay for a trip, just not the one she'd described.

Her biggest piece of good fortune had come on her second day in New York. While she'd been following Sadie after an onsite visit to Tonya and Alec's house, a flashy black limo had pulled up at the side of Sadie as she'd rounded a corner. After a few moments and a lot of furtive looking around, Sadie had got into the limo. Megan had experienced a feeling of exhilaration in hailing a yellow cab and uttering the immortal words, 'Follow that car.' And follow the limo they had, to Sarabeth's café opposite Central Park.

It had been the most expensive coffee and cake Megan had ever had, but it had been worth the money to watch the interaction between Sadie and Alec and to brazenly take the photo of them kissing outside while pretending to take a selfie. That had been the defining moment for Megan. She'd started to formulate a plan to punish her mother instead of trying to get to know her.

And now her plan was almost complete.

* * *

'I haven't said anything to Ruby about you being my birth mother,' Megan says. 'She seems to think you're wonderful. If I tried to tell her otherwise, I'd run the risk of losing her as a friend. That's not a risk I'm willing to take.'

'But she will find out eventually. Don't you think she'd be better hearing it from you?' Sadie says. She is struggling to deal with the situation herself and can only imagine the impact it would have on Ruby if she discovered the truth rather than being told.

'What makes you think she'll find out? We could just agree to keep it as our secret.'

'Secrets have a habit of coming to light, and besides...' Sadie takes a deep breath, unsure whether or not to tell Megan that Melissa already knows everything, apart from her baby's identity.

'Besides what? If you've got some weird idea that I want you in my life, you can think again,' Megan says spitefully. 'You offloaded me because I wasn't going to fit in with your lifestyle without giving a second thought as to whether I would be happy.'

'That's not how it happened, Megan, I promise you,' Sadie says in a faltering voice. 'I-I thought I was doing the best for you. The agency that handled your adoption told me they'd found a couple that would give you a stable and loving home. I trusted them and I'm so sad to hear it didn't work out that way.'

'And you expect me to believe that?' Megan scoffs. 'You've

already told me I was a mistake. Well, I happen to think that people should be accountable for their mistakes.'

Sadie takes a sip of her coffee to give herself a moment to think. There is so much hate being directed across the table at her, and she must concede that some of it is justified. But her intention had genuinely been to give her daughter a better start in life than she could offer at the time. *Why couldn't she have sought me out in New York to hear my side of the story?* she wonders.

'Did you never consider giving us a chance to get to know one another?' Sadie says, searching Megan's eyes for the merest hint of a softening in her attitude.

Megan holds her gaze but doesn't respond.

'I guess I'm just struggling to understand why you needed to be so vindictive without hearing from me how things actually happened,' Sadie adds.

'If that's meant to make me feel bad, don't bother because I don't,' Megan says without emotion. 'I flew out to New York with every intention of trying to make up for lost time and to try to build a relationship with you. But then I discovered that you were having an affair with your client's husband. I don't know the circumstances of how you became pregnant with me, and I was prepared to give you the benefit of the doubt that some guy had just left you in the lurch, but seeing you kiss Alec Hammer so openly changed my mind. You can't be allowed to go around wrecking lives. I saw a way to stop you and to punish you for abandoning me.'

'I didn't abandon—' Sadie starts to say, but Megan interrupts.

'Abandoned, gave up for adoption; they amount to the same thing really. You didn't want me because I would get in the way of your sordid lifestyle.'

Sadie is shaking her head to rebuff the accusation, but Megan either doesn't notice or isn't prepared to listen to a different version of events from what she has decided is the truth.

'You know, Alec Hammer was surprisingly gullible when I approached him and told him that I was gathering evidence against you on behalf of a former client. I mean, what kind of idiot would believe that an eighteen-year-old English girl was working for a New York investigator?' Megan gives a light shrug of the shoulders before continuing. 'I told him to take you to places where he would be recognised so that if his wife ever found out, he could claim that you'd initiated everything. After all, why would he risk his marriage and reputation for someone like you?' Megan spits, the pent-up anger that has built up over the preceding months pouring out of her.

'And I suppose you told him that you wouldn't go to his wife if he played along,' Sadie says.

'Yes, and the sucker fell for it. He sent me pictures of you and him at all the fancy restaurants and hotels he took you to.'

'And then you sent them on to Tonya,' Sadie concludes.

'I didn't need to. You two had been so visible that word had got back to her, so she hired her own private detective to follow you. I never broke my word to Alec, which I'm quite glad about because he seems quite a nice chap, apart from cheating on his wife, of course.'

'So, Tonya was telling the truth about the private investigator?'

'Why wouldn't she have been? You and Alec were the only ones lying. Look, much as I'm enjoying our chat,' she says, her voice laced with sarcasm and giving a quick glance beyond Sadie towards the clock over the front door of the café, 'I only get a fifteen-minute break and I don't want to upset Suzanne by taking liberties. My time's almost up and I haven't got what I invited you here for yet. I take it you have got it?' Megan demands.

Sadie reaches into the handbag next to her on the bench

seat and removes an envelope bearing the crest of the Highbourne House Hotel. She slides it across the table towards Megan, her eyes never leaving her daughter's face. 'It came as a bit of a shock to me,' Sadie says.

'Please tell me you don't mean that you didn't even know my father's name,' Megan says, taking a butter knife from the side plate, slipping it under the flap of the envelope and cutting cleanly along the fold.

'What I mean is,' Sadie says, ignoring the fact that she hadn't ever known his surname despite their relationship lasting for over a year, 'I knew him as Luke. I had no idea he was Polish.'

Megan is looking down at the writing on the single sheet of paper. The name written is Lukas Frackiewicz, followed by a phone number and the words 'Returned to Pruszkow, near Warsaw after Brexit. No contact since.'

'Did you try the number?' Megan asks.

'Yes. It's not in use, but I thought it might help us to trace him.'

'*Us?*' Megan says incredulously. 'I don't need your help. And besides,' she says, moving sideways along the bench seat and getting to her feet, 'if you'd wanted to find my father, you'd have done it a long time ago. I'm going for a pee before I need to get back to work. Don't be here when I come out,' she adds, pushing through a grey swing door with the words 'Staff Only' embossed on a wooden plaque.

The sound of the door swinging back and forth accompanies Sadie gathering her things and trying to do the same with her thoughts. The meeting hasn't gone as well as she'd dared to hope. At no point during their conversation did Megan show any sign that she was prepared to listen to any kind of explanation, let alone try to understand it. Sadie had known that meeting her daughter would be difficult, but she hadn't been prepared to be so totally shunned. Her heart is heavy as she heads towards the front of the café to pay.

She offers over her credit card, but the woman behind the counter dismisses it with a waft of her hand saying, 'On the house for a friend of my best waitress.'

The word 'friend' only adds to Sadie's pain as she stumbles out into the bright sunshine with tears pricking the back of her eyes. She knows it couldn't be further from the truth.

THIRTY

MELISSA

25 June 2023 – two days after the party

It's unusual for me to be sat on my mum's couch sipping tea, but virtually unheard of for it to be as a result of her going out of her way to invite me in. She clearly has something on her mind. Maybe she wants to apologise for not telling me and Steve about Ruby and Kyle. If it had happened a few years ago when Ruby was too young to have a boyfriend, I might have made more of an issue of it, but, as everyone has been at pains to point out over the last few days, Ruby is now officially a young woman. Truth be told, she could marry Kyle without requiring permission from me and Steve, so the fact that we are being allowed into that part of her life without requesting it should be accepted as a bonus.

Kyle seems a personable young man. He'd been completely at ease accepting a lift home from his girlfriend's mother who he'd only been properly introduced to for the first time a few hours previously. I suppose that comes with him being a couple of years older than Ruby and probably working in the industry that he does. You need a certain amount of self-confidence to be able to stand in front of a room of people and put them through their paces, but even more so for one-to-one personal training sessions. Whatever eventually happens with him and Ruby, I'm glad that her first experience of having a boyfriend is with someone like him.

Mum seems to be taking an inordinately long time preparing her own hot drink, so I decide to start the conversation while she is still in the kitchen with her back to me.

'Kyle seems very nice,' I offer as an opening gambit, working on the assumption that he and Ruby are to be the topic of conversation.

'Yes,' my mum replies, finally picking up her mug and carrying it through to join me in the lounge. 'I've been encouraging Ruby to tell you about him for ages, but she wasn't sure how the two of you would react.'

'When you say "ages", Mum, how long have the two of them been dating?' It's a question I hadn't felt comfortable asking at the dinner table. We all knew that the situation had been going on behind our backs, but there didn't seem much point in drawing attention to it and making it awkward for everybody, particularly as Steve, the person who we all assumed would be the most difficult, was handling it surprisingly well.

'They first met for a coffee back in January.'

I raise my eyebrows in surprise. Judging by how comfortable they had been around each other tonight, it was obvious that they'd been dating for a little while, but I wasn't expecting it to be as much as five months. 'A bigger secret than I thought,' I say, trying not to sound too annoyed. It's not my mum's fault that Ruby chose to share her private life with her grandmother rather than her parents.

'I know what you must be thinking,' Mum says. 'For what it's worth, I'm pretty sure Ruby wouldn't have told me about it either if it hadn't been for the falling out with Megan.' Mum reacts to my puzzled expression. 'You remember, Melissa? Back in January, Megan went home from a dancing competition early and you were worried because you were supposed to be giving her a lift.'

'Oh yes, I remember,' I reply. 'So, it was a falling out over Kyle. Did Megan like him too, then?'

'Apparently, she'd had a crush on him for a long time and Ruby knew about it. I told Ruby that it wasn't her fault if Kyle preferred her. That was the right advice to give, wasn't it?'

I suppress a smile. My relationship with my mum never ceases to amaze me. She spends most of the time criticising me for the things I do, and the way Steve and I have raised our daughter, and yet here she is checking that I'm okay with the advice she gave to Ruby. Maybe it's just her way of acknowledging that when I'd reached out to her as a teenager, she was either totally disinterested or too drunk for me to make sense of.

'It's what I'd have said, Mum,' I reply.

Mum takes a sip of her decaf coffee, then says something that brings a lump to my throat. 'I wish I could have my time with you again.'

I can barely believe what I'm hearing. Mum has never shown me much affection and yet, if I'm interpreting her words correctly, she has regrets that we don't have a better relationship.

'I haven't been very nice to you, have I, Melissa?' she adds.

I want to contradict her and say that I've always felt loved, but it would be pointless because we both know that's a lie. Instead, I say, 'You had your reasons. It was hard for you after Dad died.'

'It wasn't only after your dad's accident. I'm talking about your entire childhood. The sad thing is that I wanted to show you how much I loved you, right from when you were a tiny baby, but I couldn't seem to do it.'

The lump in my throat is now so huge, I can barely breathe. I can't remember my mum ever saying that she loved me and yet here she is claiming that she did. She's been looking down into her mug as though she might find the answers in the murky brown liquid, but now she lifts her eyes to look directly at me.

'Seeing you and Steve with Ruby tonight underlined that a child can love both of their parents equally, even if they show it in different ways. You always had the biggest smile for your dad and I'm ashamed to say that made me feel jealous. And it wasn't just that you might have liked him more than you liked me but also that he might have liked you more than he liked me too. I was so damn insecure,' she says, giving a slight shake of the head.

'All parents feel like that, Mum. When Ruby was little, I used to stand at the kitchen window watching her playing in the garden with Steve and feeling exactly what you are describing. Steve would lift her above his head and tickle her mercilessly until she was shrieking with laughter. She never did that with me. At bedtime though, after I'd read her a story, she'd whisper that I did all the voices much better than Daddy. We were a team. Team Ruby.'

'And we weren't,' Mum admits. 'The truth is, your dad and I were only kids ourselves. We were too young to be parents, but we wouldn't be told. If we hadn't been so headstrong and run away to get married, our relationship would have had the chance to blossom and grow with just the two of us. We could have learned from the things we disagreed about and tried to see the other person's point of view.'

The disagreement with Steve over my mishandling of the note springs to mind. Although we've been okay with each other, neither of us has actually apologised for the things we said. I intend to put that right when I get home.

'Instead, we wore blinkers,' Mum continues. 'When you came along and joint decisions should have been made which were in your best interest, neither your dad nor I would budge from what we thought was right for you. It felt as though we were constantly battling each other, each needing to win and score points, rather than calling a truce and working things out. We failed you, Melissa, both of us, and I'm so, so sorry that it's taken me such a very long time to be able to speak these words out loud, but they've always been in my heart.'

I'm really struggling not to get emotional. Mum is very pragmatic and doesn't react well to people bursting into tears at the drop of a hat, but what she is telling me is huge. I've never believed that she loves me like a mother should love her daughter, so to hear her talking like this is a bit overwhelming.

I take another sip of my tea and swallow it along with the tears that are threatening to fall. I can't look at Mum because I know she is watching me and if we make eye contact, it might just push me over the edge.

'If only I'd worked harder at creating a special bond for the two of us,' she says after a couple moments, 'instead of being jealous of the one Dave had with you. Things might have been very different. He might have lived into old age to see his daughter grow up to be the success she is.'

Mum has never opened up to me like this before. It's difficult connecting the childhood memories I have of voices raised in arguments and doors slamming when one or other of my parents would storm out of a room with what Mum has just said. I had no idea that the reason she struggled to show me affection was because she simply didn't know how to. Some daughters would be able to pat the space on the sofa beside them and within moments be enveloped in an embrace, but that's not the relationship Mum and I share. Instead, I pick up on her last sentence.

'I didn't know you viewed me as successful, Mum,' I say.

'Just because I don't tell you doesn't mean I'm not proud of you,' she says, lifting her chin slightly. 'People don't know what you had to deal with as a teenager. The times you came home to a mother who was too drunk to make you dinner and had to take it upon yourself to make beans on toast for us both or use money from your piggy bank to go to the chippie. I knew I was hurting you, but I couldn't, or wouldn't, stop.'

My eyes are properly watering now, but I refuse to cry in front of Mum. 'I never really understood why you started drinking, if I'm honest,' I manage to say. 'It was what killed Dad. I would have thought that would have been the last thing you would want to have done?' I say, voicing a question that has niggled at me since I was eleven years old.

'I blamed myself for his death,' Mum says. She doesn't sound emotional because that's not her personality, but she does sound incredibly sad. 'The truth is, he started drinking to dull the pain of an unsatisfactory life. He was a clever man, you know. We were both clever, to be fair. We should have taken our A levels, gone to university and got our degrees and been set up for life in fabulous careers, but we chose a different option and ended up resenting each other. He spent a lot of his life on the road, parking up at night in laybys or lorry parks, sharing toilet block facilities and eating in transport cafés. He had nothing in common with many of the other drivers, so he kept himself to himself and gradually he made a new friend, presumably to mask the feelings of loneliness. It was quite heartbreaking to see the change in him, particularly the way he was with you. If you knew he was expected home, you would set up your little chair at the end of the hallway opposite the front door. You'd rush to greet him the moment the door opened, and he'd drop his work bag and swing you around in the air.'

Now that Mum mentions it, I have a vague recollection of it. I was usually in my pyjamas and slippers and would have to go to bed soon after he got home, but for those few moments, I was in a happy place with my dad.

'I should have realised something was wrong when he stopped being so engaged with you. You were his one ray of sunshine in an otherwise grey existence and when your love for him could no longer lift him out of his depression, he relied more and more heavily on the drink. Even so, I wasn't aware of how dependent on alcohol he'd become until I started finding it hidden in places it shouldn't have been. One morning, I confronted him with the evidence of a dozen or more bottles lined up on the kitchen table. I accused him of loving the drink more than he loved you, in the hope that it would force him into a reality check. The sad thing is, I believe that is exactly what happened.' She pauses. 'We hadn't been particularly loving towards one another for a long time, but that morning he held me in an embrace so strong that I thought my ribs might crack and he told me that he loved me more than life itself. They were his last words to me, Melissa,' she says, her voice little more than a whisper. 'Later that day, I got the news that his lorry had crashed through a safety barrier and plunged off a cliff. At first, they said it was a tragic accident. Maybe he'd lost control after blacking out at the wheel. But I knew, even before they completed the post-mortem examination, that they would find huge amounts of alcohol in his blood.'

'What are you saying, Mum?' I ask, almost afraid of her response.

An eerie silence falls between us.

Eventually she breaks it. 'I'm saying that I think he crashed deliberately after I accused him of being an alcoholic. I was responsible for his death,' she adds, her shoulders slumping forward.

Her words are hard for me to hear, so I can only imagine how incredibly difficult it must be for her to speak them.

'I'd never been a big drinker myself, but after you'd gone to bed that night, I made a start on the bottles I'd confronted him with earlier in the day. That was the start of it, Melissa,' she says. 'Senseless as it might sound, I took a drink to numb the pain of losing your dad and just didn't stop. Whisky, vodka, brandy or whatever happened to be cheap at the off-licence, I just wanted to drown my sorrows. You see, despite all our arguing, losing him made me realise that he was my one true love.'

The pain is still so obviously raw after all these years. It's no surprise that she's never attempted to have another relationship. What she had was special and could never be matched.

'Oh, Mum,' I say, putting my mug down on the low table next to me. I want to go and hug her, but I'm still afraid of being rebuffed. 'I wish you'd been able to tell me this years ago. It feels as though we've wasted so much precious time.'

'I know.' She nods. 'But it was the guilt, Melissa. What I gave no thought to at the time was that in punishing myself by drinking to oblivion, I was also punishing you. I haven't been the mother you deserve and yet you've never given up trying to make things better between us. I don't expect you to forgive me, but I do want you to know that I'm truly sorry.'

I move across the small space between us at lightning speed and throw my arms around her neck. She doesn't attempt to pull away from me, instead relaxing into my embrace in a way she has never previously done. Mum has a relationship with Ruby that I could only have dreamt of having with my mother. But tonight has given me hope. Mum has opened her heart to me in a way I wouldn't have thought possible and although it might take time and patience, I'm prepared to try, if she is.

THIRTY-ONE

MELISSA

25 June 2023 – two days after the party

It's after midnight and the front of the house is in darkness, as I'd expected it would be given the lateness of the hour, by the time I finally pull the Toyota onto our driveway. For a few minutes, I sit with my head resting on my hands, which are holding the top of the steering wheel. I'm feeling utterly emotionally drained after Mum's revelations surrounding my dad's death and I need to gather my thoughts in case either Ruby or Steve has decided to wait up for me.

I've always known that Dad died when the lorry he was driving crashed through a barrier on a sharp bend in the road in the Lake District. I'd also heard rumours that he was under the influence of drink, which may have affected his judgement. But until tonight, suicide has never been mentioned. I'm finding it hard to accept that my dad would have willingly taken his own life, but now I've heard Mum's account of what happened between the two of them a few hours before the crash, I can see why she believes his actions were intentional. How desperate must someone be to even contemplate suicide, let alone carry it through, especially when they have a child that loves them as much as I loved my dad. It's beyond my ability to imagine what might drive me to deliberately leave Ruby alone in this world and I know Steve would feel exactly the same.

So much of my mum's behaviour towards me following my dad's death has been explained tonight. Although she claims she blames herself, I think she's finally recognised that it was me who she was blaming, and that she's been punishing me for something over which I had no influence or control.

I don't know if our relationship will ever truly recover, but we've both resolved to try. We've also agreed to keep it between the two of us because no one will benefit from knowing what she shared with me tonight. There is no definitive proof that my dad took his own life and there never will be.

I let myself into the house and head towards the kitchen. Steve may have taken a glass of water up for me, but I'm not taking any chances and I'll need to take a couple of paraceta-mols as I can feel a headache coming on. I flick the light on, and over on his dog bed next to the back door, Baxter lifts his chin and blinks rapidly in the bright light.

'Sorry, Bax,' I say softly.

He gives a small sigh and settles himself down again to sleep, unconcerned now that he knows it's only me.

I also emit a sigh. Mine is of satisfaction. The kitchen looks as clean as a new pin, with all the work surfaces clear and nothing left in the sink to soak. I get myself a glass from the cupboard and fill it with chilled filtered water from the fridge. As I flick the light off and close the door behind me, I hear the dishwasher beeping to signal that it has finished the wash cycle, which tells me that Ruby and Steve probably went up to bed about an hour ago.

The calm of the house right now mirrors Steve's reaction on discovering that his precious daughter has a boyfriend and has been secretly dating him for months. You could have knocked me over with a feather earlier not only over his initial response but also at the welcome Kyle received from my husband. There was no awkwardness between them at all, something which both amazed and delighted me. He was barely through the kitchen door before Steve was offering him a beer and bemoaning the fact that he hadn't done a barbecue, saying he was sure he would have preferred it to a quiche. Kyle had been quick to respond that although he liked barbecues, it was nice to have something home-cooked from scratch as he rarely bothered for himself.

The most awkward person in the room was Ruby, but that only lasted around ten minutes. Once she'd realised that her dad wasn't going to grill Kyle about his intentions towards his daughter and his future prospects, she relaxed. Of course, Steve did ask what Kyle did for a living, as any caring father would, and ended up getting tips on specific exercises to help with his golf swing. It really couldn't have gone much better.

We all had a thoroughly enjoyable time, and I was quite sad when the evening came to a somewhat premature end. Mum said she would get a taxi home because she was still tired after all the excitement of Ruby's party. Obviously, I couldn't let that happen as I'd specifically not been drinking for that very purpose. I insisted on driving her and offered to take Kyle too as we would virtually drive past his flat on the way to Mum's. I would have been back a couple of hours ago if Mum hadn't surprised me by asking me in. Despite everything I've learnt tonight, I'm so glad I accepted the invitation. Maybe, just maybe, this will be the first step in a much closer relationship between me and Mum, which is really all I ever wanted.

I go up the stairs, carefully avoiding the creaky step in the turn of the staircase, and am surprised to see a flickering light from beneath our bedroom door. I assumed that Steve would be fast asleep and probably snoring, which could still be the case, I think, twisting the doorknob as noiselessly as I can.

He's sitting up in bed flicking through the channels on the TV which is mounted on the wall above the cast-iron Victorian fireplace opposite our bed.

'You were a long time,' he says, leaving the TV on so that I can see without the need for putting the bedside lamp on but turning it to mute.

'Yes, sorry. Mum wanted to talk, so I went in for a cuppa. You don't mind, do you?'

'Of course not,' he replies. 'Linda was on good form tonight.'

'How was Ruby after we left?' I ask, crossing the room to our en suite and reaching into the mirrored cabinet for my toothbrush and toothpaste.

'She was good,' Steve says. 'I think she wants to talk to you about the whole Kyle thing tomorrow. I can't believe she's been keeping their relationship secret for five months,' he adds. 'I've never thought of us as that scary.'

I rinse my toothbrush under the running tap and stand it back on its shelf in the cupboard.

'Not scary,' I say, tipping some micellar water onto a cotton pad and wiping it swiftly over my face in preference to my normal more thorough routine. 'But introducing your first boyfriend to your parents is always going to be a bit daunting, especially for an only child.'

'I don't recall you having a problem with it,' Steve says, pulling back the lightweight quilt on my side of the bed while I slip out of my dress and underwear before getting in next to him.

'Maybe it's because I didn't have a dad,' I say. 'I think dads are always more protective of their daughters,' I add, kissing my husband gently on the lips and starting to roll over to go to sleep. The last few days have been emotionally exhausting anyway without the heart-to-heart I've just had with my mum, so the conversation I planned to have with my husband, apologising for not dealing with the 'Ruby and the note' situation better, will have to wait until tomorrow.

Steve takes hold of my bare shoulder and pulls me back over to face him. I still love him very much, but tonight I don't think I can muster the energy for lovemaking.

'I'm sorry, Steve...' I start to say, but he holds his fingers up to my lips to stop me talking.

'No, not that,' he says, 'although you did look very sexy just now slipping out of your clothes. I... I just need to tell you something before you hear it from anyone else.'

I'm struggling to stay awake. What on earth could he possibly need to tell me in the middle of the night when I'm absolutely shattered that can't wait until the morning?

'Unless someone is hiding under the bed, Steve, I'm not likely to hear whatever you're desperate to tell me from anyone else, am I? Are you sure it can't wait until the morning?'

'You're seeing Sadie in the morning, aren't you?'

'Yes,' I reply. 'But not until eleven. You can tell me over breakfast if you're not going at the crack of dawn. Hold on,' I say, suddenly picking up on the inference that the 'anyone' he referred to could be my best friend. 'Do you mean you need to tell me something before Sadie does?' I can't imagine what it could be, but now he's got me worried. 'Is she sick?' I ask, feeling panicky. My husband always has my best interests at heart. Maybe he wants to be the one to tell me to prevent me from getting too upset.

'No, nothing like that. It's kind of to do with her daughter,' he says.

'How do you know about her daughter?' I ask. He now has my full attention. When I was with Sadie last night, she asked me if I'd told Steve about her pregnancy, and I told her I hadn't. So how come he knows? I'm starting to get an uneasy feeling in the pit of my stomach. Steve has been home for the entire day, so unless Sadie came to our house this morning while I was out dropping Ruby at the dance festival and popping to the supermarket, he couldn't have seen her for her to tell him. And if she did come to our house, why didn't he tell me? 'What's going on, Steve?'

'Oh God, Mel, I don't know where to start,' he says, sitting up in bed and running his fingers through his hair like he does when he's feeling nervous. 'I've been keeping a secret from you for years because I was afraid of what you might do if you knew. I'm so sorry, Mel.' He twists his torso so that he can look at me. 'I never meant to do it, but I was drunk, and you and I were in such a bad place at the time.'

The words tumble out of his mouth in a rush, and it takes me a moment to register them. When I do start putting two and two together, I'm arriving at a completely unthinkable answer.

'Please tell me that what I'm thinking isn't true, Steve,' I say. 'Please tell me that you're not the married man that Sadie had an affair with? The one that she claims was the love of her life and is the father of her child?'

I've pulled myself into an upright position in our bed and I'm clutching at the duvet both to cover my nudity and to provide a barrier between us.

He's staring at me with an expression of horror on his face. The flickering lights from the television are reflected in his eyes and are adding to the effect. 'How could you even think that, Mel?' he asks. 'I've never and would never be unfaithful to you in that way.'

'Then what?' I demand, aware that the volume of my voice is increasing and could potentially disturb Ruby who is sleeping in the next room, and yet I'm unable to control it. It feels as though my normally dependable husband is about to tell me something that I don't want to hear, but now he's set the wheels in motion, he can't simply apply the brakes.

'It was in a moment of madness, Mel. Sadie is good-looking but I've never looked at her in that way, I swear to you. I'd called her because I didn't know what else to do. The whole baby thing was driving a wedge between us. We were arguing over tiny, irrelevant things like not replacing empty toilet rolls and leaving milk on the work surface instead of putting it back in the fridge. We were at breaking point. Our once perfect marriage was becoming a nightmare and I know you felt it too.'

I shudder, remembering how awful those years were for us both.

'I was terrified that it might eventually split us in two. I couldn't bear the thought of that,' he continues, 'so I reached out to your best friend in the hope that she would be able to make you see what it was doing to our marriage. I was pretty upset on the phone, so she invited me round to her place to calm down. She wanted to prevent me from saying or doing anything that would be the final straw that broke the camel's back. We were drinking, and to be honest I got the sense that she was feeling pretty low too. I guess the relief of unloading all my fears, combined with the alcohol, relaxed me too much and before I knew it, we were kissing. I'm so sorry, Mel. Truly I am. I never meant for it to happen. Can you forgive me?'

I've been listening to the words pouring from my husband's lips, sensing his relief that he's finally unburdened himself.

'Is that it?' I ask.

He nods.

'That's the big secret that you've been keeping from me and getting yourself so worked up about telling me?'

He nods again.

'Do you really think that I didn't already know?' I ask.

He's staring at me, his face filled with confusion. 'Did she tell you recently?' he asks.

'No. I've known for years. My obsession with getting pregnant was driving our marriage onto the rocks. Sadie telling me about the kiss was the wake-up call I needed.'

What I don't add is the circumstances surrounding the

hysterical call I had made to Sadie the evening of Steve's company barbecue in September 2004. That call will be forever etched in my memory.

Steve is staring at me open-mouthed.

'What?' I ask.

'She told me you didn't know about the kiss,' he says. 'She used it to blackmail me into giving her the contact details for the married man she was having the affair with.' He clearly notices my puzzled expression because he adds, 'You know, the father of her child.'

'How bizarre that she would claim I didn't know about the kiss,' I say, 'And why on earth would she want to contact this man now, after all these years?'

'It's not her, Mel. It's the daughter. And, in fairness, she has a right to know who her biological father is.'

'What? Wait a minute. Sadie has been in touch with her daughter?' I say, thinking that must be the rest of the story that she is planning to divulge tomorrow.

'Yes. That's why she needed me to find out where he went after he stopped working for me.'

'Wow! That's a tricky situation. We know he was married, so in part it will serve him right if his daughter turns up unannounced on his doorstep. But I'm pretty sure I remember Sadie saying he has children of his own? It could destroy their lives if it causes the breakdown of his marriage.'

'I don't think she'll be turning up on his doorstep any time soon. When I started asking around to try to get his details for Sadie, it turns out he's no longer in the UK,' Steve says. 'I could be underestimating her, though. After all, she tracked Sadie down in New York, so she must be pretty tenacious.'

'I guess we all would be if we'd discovered we're not who we thought we were. I know I'd want to find my birth parents. Wouldn't you?'

'I suppose. You know, I never realised he wasn't British. He didn't have a foreign accent and he always used the anglicised version of his name. Then Brexit happened. He was one of the tens of thousands of Europeans who felt as though they weren't welcome here. Apparently, Luke, or should I say Lukas, upped sticks and went back to live in Poland with his wife and five kids.'

My heart starts thumping and I can feel the blood pulsing through my veins. It's all I can do to prevent myself from gasping, such is the shock I'm feeling. The man who inadvertently shaped Sadie's whole life has also played his part in shaping mine. It's too much of a coincidence for two Polish men named Lukas with a wife and five children to be working for my husband's company at the same time. My emotions are running riot, but I can't let Steve see that.

'How did Sadie react when you told her?' I manage to ask.

'It was over the phone this morning while you were out, so I didn't see her face, but she seemed surprisingly unmoved. Maybe it was because she was about to meet her daughter in person for the first time,' Steve says.

Steve must be mistaken. Last night, Sadie said she couldn't see me today because she was going to London for a meeting with a potential work contact. Unless she was lying. It has me wondering all over again about the note left at Ruby's party. 'She's not who you think she is' is ringing more and more true, but the only person who could know all these things about Sadie is Steve and he flatly denies leaving the note. She must have her reasons for not being honest with me, but I'm hardly in a position to judge when I've withheld the sordid details of what I did for years. One thing is certain: I can never tell her now.

'I'll ask her when I see her tomorrow,' I say, deliberately making my voice sound sleepier than I'm feeling. 'Do you want to turn that off?' I nod towards the television. 'I'm shattered.'

He clicks the red button on the remote control and our

room is plunged into darkness. 'Am I forgiven?' he asks, kissing the nape of my neck as he cuddles into the curve of my back.

'You already were,' I reply, reaching over my shoulder to touch the side of his cheek.

'No more secrets between us ever again. Agreed?' he says.

'From this moment on, we tell each other everything,' I reply.

He doesn't respond but kisses my neck again before rolling onto his other side. After a few moments, I hear his soft rhythmic snoring, but I'm still wide awake. Steve and I have agreed that there will be no more secrets between us from now on, but I'm still carrying my guilty secret. Should I tell him so that we can start with a completely clean slate? But if I do, can our lives ever be the same?

THIRTY-TWO

MELISSA

26 June 2023 – three days after the party

Steve has already left for work by the time I finally surface just before nine o'clock. I've taken the whole of this week off as I know from experience that I just keep on pushing and pushing and then crash and burn for a few days.

Although Ruby's party wasn't quite the same as a work deadline, so much organising had gone into it, plus the worry of things not going to plan and the excitement of having Sadie back in the UK meant that I knew it would have a similar effect on my mind and body. And that's without taking into consideration the huge revelations of the previous few days.

All the stuff with Sadie and her daughter, the remaining part of which I have yet to find out about this morning, Ruby admitting she's had a secret boyfriend for the past five months, Steve finally confessing to the kiss with my best friend almost two decades ago, and Mum opening her heart to me for the first time ever. It's little wonder that I was tired and have overslept, but I also still have the headache I went to bed with because I forgot to take the paracetamol last night.

I'm just helping myself to a glass of water to take the pills with when Ruby walks into the kitchen. My daughter usually has a pretty sunny disposition, but the expression on her face could be described as sulky.

'Everything okay, Ruby?' I ask, placing both tablets on my tongue and knocking them back with a huge swig of water. Steve doesn't understand how I can do this. He hates swallowing tablets and it drives me mad when he grinds them between his teeth, all the time shuddering because they taste so disgusting.

'Oh sorry, Mum,' she says, instantly brighter. 'I didn't see you there. Have you only just got up?'

'Guilty as charged,' I say, sitting down at the kitchen table to allow the tablets to kick in before attempting a slice of toast for breakfast. The thought of the crunching is more than I can bear until the hammering in my head has lessened a bit. 'What was the face about?' I ask.

'You don't miss a thing, do you?' she says. 'It's nothing really. It's just Megan and I were supposed to be going out for the day and she messaged to cancel me for the second day running.'

'Is she working again?' I ask.

'She didn't say. She just said something had come up and she couldn't see me today. What are you up to, Mum?' she asks hopefully.

'I'm meeting up with Sadie,' I say. If it wasn't for the fact that she still has the final part of her story to divulge, I would have said that Ruby could come with me. I pre-empt her before she can suggest it. 'If you take Baxter out for one of your famously long walks, you can join us for lunch at the hotel. How does that sound?'

'Pretty cool, actually. But how will I get there?'

'That, my darling, is why your dad is so keen for you to learn to drive,' I say, raising my eyebrows at her. 'But, for today, I will leave you my card and you can book a taxi to pick you up. How does 12.30 sound?'

'Perfect,' she says. 'Come on, Bax, we'd better get going.'

Baxter wags his tail enthusiastically and if I had one, I'd be doing the same. The dog needs a walk and I'm so late up that I wouldn't have had time before going off to meet Sadie. More importantly, if things are a bit scratchy between Sadie and me after I question her reasons for lying to me about meeting up with her daughter, Ruby will relieve any tension.

Mind you, I'm hardly one to be judgemental about keeping secrets. In the heat of the moment last night and following on from the relief of his big confession about kissing my best friend, I'd been on the point of telling my husband what had happened at the barbecue in September 2004 but, in the cold light of day this morning, I'm so glad I didn't. As close and strong as our marriage is, I'm not sure it would survive such a shocking confession.

Sadie had already gone to live in New York, or so I believed at the time. I was alone at the gathering, which was at Steve's business premises rather than our house, but he was still very much in charge of flipping the burgers and sausages. He was in his element, but it was not so much fun for me. The summer barbecues were always more family orientated than the Christmas parties. Most people were there with their spouse and children, but I got talking to a man who was also on his own.

Lukas was Polish, although his English was perfect, and he had no accent that would have indicated his heritage. He told me that he was married with five children and when I asked why he hadn't brought them, he said they were in Poland visiting his wife's family because it was her mother's fiftieth birthday on the same day as the barbecue which he felt obliged to attend. They were due back the next day.

I'll never know if it was the heat of the Indian summer we

were enduring in the UK or the wine going straight to my head as I'd stopped drinking alcohol completely two years previously in the hope that it would increase my chances of becoming pregnant. Maybe it was a combination of the two. He was paying me attention and refilling my wine glass. He made me feel desirable in a way that my husband hadn't since we'd become bogged down in trying for a baby. I knew I was mid-cycle because of all the charts I was keeping. I was in the middle of the few days that would give me the optimum chance of conceiving. Steve and I had been there many times before and all to no avail. But if I were to have sex with a man who had already fathered five children, surely that would increase my chances. Steve would never need to know. It would be his child as much as mine and it would complete us as a family.

Lukas had not needed much encouragement. He probably couldn't believe his luck that someone would come onto him and offer him sex with no strings attached. He told me where his office was and to meet him there in ten minutes before going over to where the drinks were laid out to get himself another bottle of beer.

I could have changed my mind, but I was a woman possessed. I could only think of one thing, and this was my chance to have it.

Merely the thought of it now brings a flush to my cheeks that has nothing to do with my menopause. I still can't believe that I broke my wedding vows, such was my desperation to become a mother. There was no foreplay. No kissing, no touching, just the act of penetration that was over in a matter of minutes. He left his office immediately afterwards. The moment the door was closed, I broke down and sobbed because I was so disgusted and horrified with myself.

I left the barbecue early, feigning a headache. I needed to speak to my best friend and for once Sadie responded quickly to my almost incoherent voice message and called me straight back. I began to pour my heart out, trying to justify what I was about to tell her, but I couldn't find the words to admit to what I'd actually done because it was so abhorrent, and I didn't want her to hate me. That's when she'd told me about the kiss and said Steve and I needed to get our act together. I'd sometimes wondered whether she made the story up just to shock me into taking action to save our marriage before it was too late, particularly as Steve chose not to tell me about it. It now seems it was the truth after all but any feelings of betrayal towards either of them have long since passed.

Exactly as I told Steve last night, it was the wake-up call I needed, but it had come too late for me. I'd been unfaithful and six weeks later I discovered I was pregnant.

My joy at finally seeing the confirmation that I was pregnant after doing a test when my period was late was tempered with both guilt and confusion. I had no way of knowing for sure who the father of the child I was carrying was and, if I'm honest, I'm not sure I wanted to know at first. I was going to be a mum and Steve was going to be a dad. Nothing else mattered. It was years before I finally felt brave enough to send off a DNA test.

Watching Ruby reach for Baxter's lead and attach it to his collar, I can't imagine what my life would have been like without my beautiful girl in it.

'Just a short one today, Bax, cos I'll need a bit of time to get ready for my posh lunch,' Ruby says, opening the back door. 'See you later, Mum,' she adds with a carefree wave and without a backward glance as she sets off down our garden path.

The symbolism isn't lost on me. Soon she will be heading out into the world on her own and she will need to set about that journey without a backward glance too.

THIRTY-THREE

MELISSA

26 June 2023 – three days after the party

Thankfully, the tablets have kicked in by the time I'm walking across the car park of the Highbourne House Hotel and up the front steps less than an hour later. Before I ask the receptionist to ring up to Sadie's room to tell her I'm here, I book a table for three for lunch in the restaurant at 12.30.

'You can go up,' the receptionist says. 'First floor, turn left at the top of the stairs and it's on the right after the fire door.'

'Thank you,' I say, resisting the urge to tell her that I already know where room 7 is. She's being helpful, which makes a pleasant change in today's world.

As I arrive upstairs, Sadie is waiting at her door and I can tell from the expression on her face that something monumental has happened since I last saw her. I wonder how the reunion with her daughter went, but experience a pang of guilt that I already know about it without her telling me.

'Hey,' I say, giving her a brief hug and following her into her room. Nothing has changed in the thirty-six hours since I was last here except for Sadie. 'How did your meeting go?' I ask, willing her to be immediately honest with me.

'Meeting?' she asks, looking startled as though I've caught her off guard.

'Yes. You said you had a meeting with a former colleague about some potential work,' I clarify, sitting down in one of the chairs next to the window.

'Erm, actually, Mel, that wasn't entirely true,' she says.

Relief floods through me. I hate the fact that Sadie has been keeping her daughter's existence secret for all these years. Now that she's told me about her, I'd like to think that we can be totally honest with each other about everything moving forward.

'No. I know,' I say, carrying out my side of being honest.

'Steve told you then?' She sounds defeated.

'Yes,' I admit. 'I take it things didn't go too well.'

She shakes her head and sits down on the chair opposite me. 'She hates me, Mel. I thought no one could make me feel as loathed as Tonya did when she confronted me about sleeping with her husband, but I was wrong. My own flesh and blood despises me so much that she set about destroying everything I've worked so hard to achieve in New York.'

'Hold on,' I say. 'What do you mean? What has your daughter got to do with Tonya destroying your business?'

'She came to New York looking for me and happened to see me with Tonya's husband, Alec. That's when she decided I needed to be taught a lesson.'

'So, your daughter was the whistle-blower on your affair with Alec?'

'Yes. Rather than meeting me to find out why I'd given her up for adoption, which she claims was her original intention, she just saw red when it seemed to her as though history was repeating itself. In her eyes, it's payback for the unhappy childhood she endured at the hands of her adoptive parents, who I honestly believed would give her a better life than I could have done.'

'You couldn't have known they wouldn't!' I blurt out.

'That doesn't seem to matter to her. How could I have got it all so wrong?' she asks, misery etched across her still beautiful features. 'It was obvious when we met in Daisy's café yesterday that she has nothing but contempt for me. I feel as though my whole existence is pointless. I want to go to sleep and never wake up,' she says, her voice faltering.

Her words hit home harder than they might have had Mum not told me her belief about my dad's death. 'Oh Sadie,' I say, going over to crouch by her chair and taking her hands in mine. 'You don't really mean that. We all make mistakes, it's just that some carry more consequences than others,' I add, trying to reassure her. 'There isn't a blueprint for life for us all to follow, so sometimes we make the wrong decision. She'll come round eventually and realise that you did what you did because you thought it would give her a better chance in life.'

'You're wrong. She doesn't want to listen to my reasons.'

I can hear that Sadie is still talking, but I'm only half listening. My words that were intended to comfort my friend have highlighted yet again that I'm still living with the consequences of my own guilty secret. For years, I was too afraid to send away a strand of Ruby's hair or some saliva to a DNA testing centre for fear of what the result might be. I couldn't bear the thought that the daughter Steve doted on might not be his biological child. When I finally plucked up the courage, I waited anxiously to see what the results might uncover.

Because of my wandering thoughts, I only fully tune in to the end of Sadie's sentence. '...because she was on her break, but all she really wanted was the details for her father.'

'Sorry,' I say, wondering if I've misheard because I wasn't paying full attention. 'Did you say she was on her break? Does your daughter work in Daisy's? She must know Ruby's friend, Megan, then.'

Sadie has an odd expression on her face. 'She doesn't know Megan, she is Megan,' she says slowly and clearly as though talking to a small child.

I can hardly believe what I'm hearing. Sadie must have got it wrong. But as I look into her chocolate-brown eyes, currently red-rimmed from crying, I see the ghost of a resemblance to Ruby's best friend, and they have the same mane of copper-coloured hair. Why have I never noticed the similarity before? Probably because I wasn't expecting to see it.

'Let me get this straight. Megan is adopted, and she is the baby you gave birth to,' I say, struggling to comprehend how it could be possible.

'Yes. I was wondering how my daughter could possibly have known that I was back in England and where I was staying when she called me a few minutes after I checked in. Now I know. She was getting all her information from Ruby.'

'From Ruby? Does she know that you're Megan's mum?' I ask, an awful thought occurring to me. 'You don't think it was one of them who left that note for me to find, do you?' I add, allowing my imagination to run riot.

'I'm pretty sure that Ruby doesn't know,' Sadie says, shaking her head. 'Megan told me that Ruby had no idea she was spoon-feeding her all the information she needed, including the address of my apartment in New York. She was simply answering her unassuming questions.'

'Megan then?' I persist.

'It could have been. I suppose she might have been trying to warn you and Steve that you have a monster among your close family friends?'

'But we know that's not true, and once she starts to see things from your point of view, she'll realise it too.'

'That's never going to happen. Megan doesn't want

anything to do with me; she made that clear yesterday. She's convinced herself that I'm wicked and has punished me by wrecking my life in New York. Her sole purpose for meeting me was to get information about her father. Well, she's got that now,' Sadie says, giving a heavy sigh of defeat. 'Although what good it will do her, I don't know. The number Steve gave me was discontinued and even if she can trace him, Luke – or should I say Lukas – probably won't accept that he is Megan's father. It's all such a mess.'

Despite my decision last night and the impact it could potentially have on our friendship, I'm now wavering. Maybe Sadie should know that Lukas was not a very nice man. If I'm going to tell her about my association with him, now is the moment. She has always believed he was the love of her life, the soulmate that she has been denied for the past twenty years, whereas in my mind he is nothing more than a serial womaniser. Sadie needs to know the truth so that she won't spend another minute thinking about what might have been if he'd left his wife for her, because that was never going to happen.

'I-I know how in love with Lukas you thought you were, and one day it will be important for Megan to know that, on your part at least, she was conceived with love,' I start to say in a faltering voice.

Sadie interrupts me. 'I didn't just *think* I was in love with him, Mel. It was the real thing,' she says, her voice filled with emotion. 'I've never felt like that about another man in my whole life.'

'Even Alec?' I venture.

'Yes,' she replies, 'even Alec. True, I was developing feelings for him but it wasn't the same. Lukas was my one, but sadly I wasn't his. I should have been strong enough to resist my feelings the moment I found out he was married, but I just...' She pauses. 'I just couldn't.'

In that moment, my decision is made. I can't see what

would be gained by her discovering that she was not his only affair, particularly as she is already so devastated by the way she has been treated by both Alec and Megan. 'Okay,' I say gently. 'But surely you can see that you've been a prisoner of your past, Sadie? Maybe all this was meant to happen because it's time to move on with your future.'

'What future? My daughter has made sure I don't have one.'

'I disagree. You've had a harsh life lesson, but it doesn't have to be a life sentence,' I say. 'You're so talented, you'll be able to start over and you may learn to love living back here in England. There might even be an opportunity for you to develop a relationship with Megan.'

Sadie looks sceptical and seems about to speak when there is a frantic hammering on the door. For a moment, I wonder if it is a member of staff. And then we hear the desperate shriek, 'MUM!'

I'm up out of my chair and across the room before the word has even registered with Sadie. I fling the door open, expecting to see my beautiful Ruby, but instead I'm met with the sight of Megan, bent almost double as though in agonising pain.

'Megan?' I say, instantly putting my arm around her and pulling her into Sadie's room. 'Whatever is the matter?'

'He's dead,' she wails, clinging on to me as if her life depends on it.

I've taken care of Megan's various scrapes and falls over the years when she's stayed overnight at ours or come on holiday with us, but this is different. She hasn't turned up on my doorstep, she's come to her mother's hotel room. It's not me she needs in this moment, it's her mother.

I motion for Sadie to come over and between us we guide Megan towards the bed, while she sobs uncontrollably.

Eventually, as her heaving sobs start to subside, I ask, 'Who's dead, Megan?'

'Lukas,' she replies.

Sadie's hand flies to her mouth as though to capture her agonising pain rather than allowing it to escape in a scream.

Above Megan's head, I manage to make eye contact with my friend. I have no way of knowing what is going through Sadie's mind, but one thing is now certain. After all the years of loving him, even after the way that he ended things, he will never be a part of her happy ever after. It's so final. And I feel so sad for her.

Such is her shock, Sadie probably didn't notice the thing that resonated the most with me. Megan referring to him as Lukas rather than 'my dad' might be hugely significant when she starts to process her grief.

'Do you want to tell me about it?' Sadie asks.

Megan takes the tissue that Sadie is offering her and nods her head. Weird as it seems, considering I've known Megan for twelve years and Sadie has only just entered her life, I feel like the outsider.

I pick up my bag, signal my intention to Sadie and leave the two of them to comfort each other.

It doesn't feel right for Ruby and me to have lunch at the hotel, knowing what is unfolding on the floor above, so I cancel the reservation and wait for her on a bench outside, feeling the warmth of the sun on my skin as I think over what has happened. Lukas had his faults, but it still chilled me to the bone to find out that he was dead. No doubt I'll hear all about the circumstances from Sadie when she feels able.

Ruby's taxi arrives and my breath catches at the back of my throat as she climbs out. She looks stunning, the sun shining on her hair as it cascades down over her shoulders in a golden halo. Ruby is still my angel, my beautiful girl, but the last few days have taught me that she's not perfect. Nobody's perfect. I have no intention of disappointing her after promising to take her to lunch.

'Change of plan,' I say brightly. 'Sadie isn't feeling too good, so it's just us two for lunch. I thought La Conservatoire might be nice as it's your favourite.'

If she's disappointed, she doesn't let it show. My girl is definitely growing up.

THIRTY-FOUR

MELISSA

28 June 2023 – five days after the party

'What time is Megan coming round?' I ask, taking the plate from Ruby's hand and turning towards the sink to rinse the toast crumbs off it before loading it into the dishwasher.

'I told her your hairdresser appointment was at ten, so she said she'd get here for quarter past,' Ruby replies. 'Thanks for arranging to go out, Mum. I don't think Megan is up to facing anybody apart from me and her mum just yet.'

It feels strange to hear Ruby refer to Sadie as Megan's mum, particularly as she has only known about it for less than twenty-four hours.

Much as I wanted to, given my desire for there to be no more secrets between Steve, Ruby and me, I decided not to mention anything to Ruby about the situation with Megan and Sadie during our lunch at La Conservatoire on Monday. Firstly, I didn't think it was my news to tell. Ruby is very close to them both. Not only did I feel that it would be better for her to hear it directly from them, but I also thought they would want to tell her. Secondly, and rather more selfishly, I didn't want to spoil our lunch as we do it so rarely and there won't be many more opportunities before she goes off to college. Even so, I struggled to finish my salade Nicoise, an absolute favourite of mine, but if she noticed, she didn't comment.

I was on tenterhooks for the remainder of Monday afternoon, wondering whether she would receive a call, so it was a relief when she stuck her head around the kitchen door while I was preparing dinner and asked if it would be okay for her to go round to Kyle's to watch something on Netflix.

I'd heard nothing from Sadie since I left the two of them in her hotel room, which I was hopeful meant that she and Megan had been doing some serious talking, trying to understand each other's actions and comforting each other too. It won't be an easy road ahead, but every journey starts with a first step.

Although it didn't feel right to tell Ruby about Megan being Sadie's daughter, I did tell Steve as he already knew so much of the story. To say he was shocked is an understatement, but he did say he was pleased that we had taken her into the heart of our family and looked after her like a second daughter. I also told him that Lukas was dead, but I couldn't fill in any further details as I didn't know them.

The call to Ruby had finally come yesterday morning. She was up in her room sorting through some clothes to donate to the charity shop when I heard the distinctive ringtone. She has her phone set up with different tones for different people, so she knows who is on the other end of the call without looking at the screen. It was Megan.

I made sure I was in the house in case she needed me but gave her the space to take the call without me listening in. It was a full hour before she appeared at the kitchen door looking slightly dazed. That's when she asked if it would be okay for Megan to come round to our house today. I figured it would be better for the girls if I wasn't around and, fortunately, Debbie was able to fit me in for a wash and blow dry this morning.

'Right, I'll just go up and brush my teeth and then I'll be off,' I say. 'You know where I am if you need me,' I add.

I want to offer my advice to my daughter on how she should handle the situation, but something tells me it would be unwelcome. There is a saying about parenting that I've always admired. There are two gifts we should give our children: one is roots and the other is wings. I think Steve and I have done a pretty good job in giving Ruby a safe, secure upbringing. Now we have to trust her to fly.

THIRTY-FIVE

RUBY

28 June 2023 – five days after the party

Ruby decides that Megan would feel most comfortable talking in her bedroom even though there is no one else in the house. It was something familiar that the girls had done from a young age. In the early days, Melissa would bring up milk and biscuits for the girls to snack on while they played with Ruby's dolls or colourful plastic ponies. In their teenage years, when the girls did their homework together, the snack would either be tea and toast or fruit, depending on which phase the girls were going through. The four walls of Ruby's bedroom had been privy to some secrets over the years, but nothing came close to the revelations of the phone call yesterday.

Ruby gives Megan the top end of her bed so she's propped against her pillows and arranges some colourful cushions against the metallic foot of the bed frame so that the two girls can face each other. Ruby has even allowed Megan to cuddle her teddy – something she has previously never permitted in all the years they have been friends.

'I'm only just coming to terms with it all,' Ruby says, 'so I can't imagine how you must be feeling.'

'Surprisingly okay,' Megan replies. 'I feel pretty bad about wrecking Sadie... I mean Mum's business after she worked so hard to build it up, but she kind of brushed it off and said it was probably the right time for her to come home.'

'So, you two are getting on all right?' Ruby asks. There's a hint of anxiety in her voice. Megan and Sadie are two of her favourite people and she would have hated to have been forced to choose between them.

'We're actually quite alike really,' Megan says. 'You know that whole "nature or nurture" thing that people go on about? Well, in our case it's definitely nature. We even look alike.'

'Funnily enough, Mum and I were saying that now we know you're related, the family resemblance is obvious,' Ruby agrees.

'Apart from the mouth,' Megan says. 'That's definitely more like my dad's.'

'Had Sadie kept a photograph of him then?' Ruby asks.

'No. There was one in the online news report. Do you want to see it?' Megan asks, tapping the screen on her phone and handing it to Ruby.

Ruby can immediately see what Megan means as she casts her eyes over the photograph, underneath which is the headline:

HERO RESCUES CHILDREN FROM BURNING BUILDING

Father of eight, 49-year-old Lukas Frackiewicz, a construction worker, died yesterday, two days after being admitted to a Pruszkow hospital suffering from third-degree burns. He had repeatedly gone back into the burning building to rescue his five younger children who still lived in the family home and were sleeping on the upper level when the fire broke out.

All five children and their mother escaped serious injury thanks to his bravery.

While hailing Frackiewicz a hero, the fire department chief, Jarek Kaminski, emphasised that it is better for members of the public to wait for the fire crews to arrive rather than taking matters into their own hands.

Frackiewicz was being successfully treated for the life-changing burns but is believed to have died from extensive damage to his lungs caused by smoke inhalation.

The cause of the fire is still unknown.

Ruby raises her eyes to look at Megan. 'I'm so sorry,' she says. 'However badly he treated Sadie, he didn't deserve this.'

Megan gives a small shrug of the shoulders.

'When was this?' Ruby asks, handing the phone back to Megan.

'2017. The year after the Brexit vote. He won't have been the only foreign worker to return to his home country because he didn't feel welcome here anymore.'

'And if he hadn't, this would never have happened,' Ruby says, shaking her head sadly.

'At least I won't have to decide whether to explode the myth that he was a hero and devoted family man,' she says.

'Well, he was most definitely a hero,' Ruby says. 'It must have taken a tremendous amount of courage to keep braving that raging inferno to rescue his children.'

'Yes, I can see that. His wife and kids have already suffered enough. There's no point in tarnishing the good memories they have of him.'

'But what about you? You have eight half-siblings. Don't you want to meet them?' Ruby asks.

'Not really,' Megan says with a slight shake of her head. 'They would hate me for being a product of their father's infidelity and for ruining their memories of him. I can do without the guilt of destroying their lives. Remember, I know what it feels like to be part of a dysfunctional family.' She pauses to take a deep breath. 'That's why I did what I did.'

'I'm sure Sadie understands and will be able to forgive you eventually,' Ruby says. She'd been stunned into silence throughout most of the telephone conversation the previous day when Megan had told her about going off to New York to track her mum down, before proceeding to destroy her business when she didn't like what she found.

'That's not what I meant. I... I need to tell you something and you're probably going to hate me.' Megan drops her gaze to avoiding looking directly at Ruby. 'The thing is, it was me who left that note for your dad to find.'

'*You* did?' Ruby says, a shockwave running through her.

'Yes,' Megan says, lifting her eyes to connect with Ruby's.

'I don't understand,' Ruby says. 'We're supposed to be best friends. Why would you do something like that, not just to me but also to my parents after all they've done for you? It doesn't make any sense.'

'I did it *for* your parents, Ruby,' Megan says. 'I already knew that my adoptive parents viewed me as a mistake, and I'd found out that my birth mother had given me away without even considering changing her lifestyle to include me in it. You've got the perfect parents and yet you thought it was okay to keep them in the dark about Kyle. I also felt sorry for him. He's such a kind person.'

Ruby searches her best friend's face for signs that she may still have feelings for him, but all she can see is desperation.

'He deserved better than to be kept secret, as if you were somehow ashamed of him,' Megan continues. 'I think the final straw was when you told me he was going to be sat on a table with his sister rather than at our table where he should rightly have been. All just to preserve this image that you're their perfect little girl. It's not healthy, Ruby. I'm sorry, something in me just snapped. I wrote the note and slipped it between the pages when no one was looking because I thought you should start your adult life by behaving like an adult.'

Megan has barely paused for breath, her anxious confession spilling out of her.

'Do you hate me, Ruby?' she whispers. 'I can see now that it wasn't my call to make. It could have gone disastrously wrong if the whole thing with Kyle had come out at the party.'

'I could never hate you, Megan,' Ruby says. 'I'm not going to lie. The note caused a massive blow-up between me and Mum, and my parents had a big argument over it too, but what it achieved is exactly what you set out for it to achieve. My parents know about Kyle and really like him, and he's going to start looking for gyms in Epsom in readiness for me starting at Laines Theatre Arts in September. So, although your method was questionable,' she says, stretching out her right leg to jab Megan's knee with her big toe, 'you got the result you were after.'

'You're definitely going to Laines?' Megan asks.

'Yes. I talked it over with Mum and Dad last night. We reached a joint decision that life's too short to not follow your dream.'

EPILOGUE

MELISSA

17 August 2023

'It's time to go, you two,' I call up the stairs. 'It doesn't matter how long you delay; the results will be what they are.'

It's A level results day and although Ruby and Megan were both up bright and early for breakfast, they disappeared back up to their respective rooms an hour ago and neither has yet re-emerged.

Ruby is driving, going first to Megan's college and then to her school to collect their results in her little Ford KA sporting her L plates, with Kyle in the passenger seat as her supervising qualified driver. He's already been out with her a couple of times for practice sessions since he turned twenty-one at the end of July. Ruby has had half a dozen driving lessons so far and her instructor thinks she's progressing quickly enough to book her test as there is quite a wait at our local test centre. He added the caveat that she needs a bit more practice on her parallel parking, which Steve has volunteered to help with. My parking has always been a bit hit-and-miss.

Sadie and Megan have both been living with us since a

couple of days after the dramatic discovery of Lukas's passing. In some respects, the courageous action that resulted in his death made the loss more bearable. It had still been awful for Megan, of course. She had found out who her father was and within twenty-four hours had the chance of ever meeting him face to face snatched away from under her nose. I have sometimes wondered whether she would have risked ruining his marriage by confronting him and telling him who she was, or if getting into a casual conversation with him while waiting at a bus stop or to be served in a shop would have been enough to satisfy her need to look into her father's eyes. None of us will ever know the answer to that, including, I suspect, Megan herself. There is a small part of me that thinks that for everyone other than the man himself it was the best possible outcome.

The relationship between Megan and Sadie is progressing much faster than I could ever have imagined and I wonder if in part it is something to do with an observation Ruby made on the day that Megan came to our house to confess that she had left the note for Steve to find.

'I told Megan that I think what Sadie did in giving her up for adoption was actually very brave,' Ruby had said when we were in the kitchen together after Megan had left.

Until she said that, my thoughts were more aligned with Megan's. A baby didn't fit into Sadie's lifestyle so she'd acted selfishly. But viewed from a different perspective, I could understand what Ruby meant. It is brave to hand over a living, breathing entity who has been part of you and reliant on you for nine months, knowing that you will probably never see them again.

'That's a very generous thing to say, Ruby,' I'd replied.

'Not really, Mum. We both know the real Auntie Sadie. Her biggest mistake was falling in love with the wrong person. She probably regrets all the time she and Megan have lost, but hopefully they'll be able to make up for it.'

Her words had particularly resonated with me as Mum and I find ourselves in a similar situation albeit down to vastly different circumstances.

Even Ruby has been amazed by how close Megan and Sadie have become in such a short space of time, although they are both mindful not to exclude Ruby. Knowing what we do now, I suspect that Sadie's relationship with Ruby may have been strengthened by a subconscious desire to make it up to the daughter she had felt forced to part with.

As for Megan and Ruby, they have become even more like sisters since they started living under the same roof, an irony which is not lost on me. I had no idea that the married man who I'd cheated on my husband with on the most shameful day of my life was the same man Sadie had been so besotted with. I also wasn't aware that she had given birth to a daughter who could quite easily have turned out to be Ruby's half-sister.

For Sadie, discovering what had happened to the man that she had loved so deeply and for so long was utterly devastating. It's probably why she agreed to move in with us for a while, despite Steve's reservations about it. I knew my husband would understand that she needed the support of people who loved her to help her past the initial trauma because that is the kind considerate person he is. He did, however, struggle to comprehend the depth of her grief.

For the first couple of weeks of her living in our house, we would often hear her crying at night in the next room as we lay in bed.

'I don't understand why she is grieving so deeply for someone she lost a long time ago, and arguably was never hers in the first place,' I remember Steve whispering.

What he hadn't considered was that while Lukas was alive, Sadie probably clung on to the faint hope that there was a chance, however miniscule, of him one day reappearing in her life and admitting that he'd made a big mistake in ending their affair. Hope can be cruel, but when all hope is gone, there is nothing left but emptiness and despair.

Just like Ruby being there for Megan, I've played a similar role for Sadie. If she's wanted to talk, I've listened, and if she's asked for my opinion, I've given it. That's how the decision was reached for her and Megan to visit Lukas's grave in Poland. The online newspaper that had run the story about his death had also run a follow-up story about his funeral, giving details of where he was being buried. I expressed the view that it might help her to draw a line under that part of her life if she saw his place of rest. Apparently, Ruby had said something similar to Megan, which is how it came about that the two of them are flying out tomorrow to pay their final respects. I honestly believe it will allow them both to move on with the next phase of their lives.

Sadie starts a new job on Monday, back in her former role of set designing for theatre productions. It isn't attached to one specific theatre and a lot of it will be working from home, so wherever Megan goes to university she can rent a home nearby and continue to build their relationship. Grieving for a man that neither of them truly knew has also strengthened the developing bond between them which, in my opinion, is the best thing to come out of all of this.

Upstairs, I hear a door slam and Ruby's voice.

'Come on, Megan, we need to go. Kyle's got a client at eleven,' she says.

'Coming,' is the response, followed moments later by another door slamming and two pairs of feet thundering down the stairs.

'Where's Dad?' Ruby asks, taking her keys from the row of hooks next to the front door.

'Outside talking to Kyle,' I say as the girls spill through the front door. 'Good luck,' I add.

'It's a bit late for luck, Mum,' Ruby laughs, going around to the driver's side of the car. 'Like you just said, the results will be what they are.'

I remember being really nervous on exam results day, but Ruby and Megan don't seem to have a care in the world. In a way, their results are not as crucial as mine were. Ruby has her confirmed place at Laine Theatre Arts. If Megan doesn't get the grades she needs for university this year, which is possible with all the distractions she's had, she seems fine with the prospect of resitting in January for a university start next September.

As Ruby reverses out of our driveway, Steve comes to join me in the doorway.

'I don't know where the last eighteen years have gone,' he says, draping his arm across my shoulders and waving in the direction of the silver Ford KA as it does a couple of bunny hops before moving off. 'It doesn't seem that long ago that we brought our miracle baby home from hospital.'

I tilt my head to look up at my husband. The DNA test result letter that I'd opened with shaking hands having finally plucked up the courage to learn the truth had confirmed that Ruby was indeed 'our' miracle baby. Although I'll never fully be able to forgive myself for my actions on that summer day, I truly believe that the hurt it would cause Steve to clear my conscience is too big a price to pay. Some secrets are better left untold and this one I will carry to my grave to protect those I love.

'She's worth everything we went through to get her, isn't she?' I ask, searching my husband's eyes for validation.

'Everything and more,' he replies, dropping a kiss onto my lips. 'You were right. Ruby completed our family, but we'll soon be back to just the two of us.'

'You say that, but I expect we'll be seeing a lot more of Mum once her tenancy agreement is up at the end of the month,' I say.

Mum has finally agreed to leave the maisonette on the

outskirts of Brighton that she shared with Dad and me when I was growing up to move to Brockledean and be closer to us. Maybe opening her heart and sharing her feelings with me has released her from her past, just as Lukas's death seems to have done for Sadie. She refused the offer of actually moving in with us though when Ruby goes off to dance college, which I'm secretly relieved about. There's still some work to do on our relationship, but we're already in a much better place.

'Is it bad to say I'm glad she refused the offer to move in with us?' Steve says, almost as though he has been reading my mind.

'Will it help if I say it too?' I reply, smiling knowingly at him.

'We'll be okay. Won't we?'

A shiny wet nose, followed by a black furry head, forces its way between us at knee height and Baxter whines softly, his huge doleful eyes going from one to the other of us.

'I think you're forgetting someone,' I say, reaching down to fuss Baxter and receiving grateful licks in return.

'Make that the three of us,' Steve smiles. 'We've got this.'

A LETTER FROM JULIA

Thank you so much for choosing to read *My Daughter's Lies*. If you enjoyed it and want to keep up to date with all my latest releases, please sign up at the following link. Your email address will never be shared and you can unsubscribe at any time.

www.bookouture.com/julia-roberts

As authors, we're often asked where we get the ideas for our books. *My Daughter's Lies* was actually inspired by an Instagram post from a friend of mine whose daughter is very talented in the world of theatre and also academically. To all intents and purposes, she is the perfect daughter but as we all know, nobody's perfect and in fact, that was my working title. The line 'She's not who you think she is' sprang into my head almost immediately after seeing the Instagram post and it was then just a case of developing the idea.

I played around with various scenarios of how Ruby might be less than perfect, but I didn't want to make her into a villain, just a girl who is about to become an adult and is unsure how 'adulting' works. I wanted the focus to be on Ruby's relationship with her mum, Melissa, which has always been very close and how it will inevitably change as she prepares to fly from the nest.

I was also keen to highlight the very different relationship that Melissa has with her own mum, Linda. The chapter where the two 'reconcile' had me in tears at every stage of the editing process and has made me appreciate even more the fantastic relationship that I have with my own mum who is ninety-seven years young.

And then there is Sadie, Melissa's best friend and Ruby's godmother. I loved writing Sadie because in some ways she's the most flawed of all the characters. Funnily enough, she was originally called by a different name which I kept meaning to change because I'd decided it didn't suit her. On the day I finished the line edit, I got the news that my best friend from dancing school's mum, who my mum still regularly wrote to, had passed away a couple of weeks short of her ninety-ninth birthday. Her name was Sadie and not only did it suit my character, it felt like the perfect tribute to Teresa's mum.

I know I shouldn't have favourite chapters in a book, a bit like we shouldn't have a favourite child, if we have more than one, but I must admit that I absolutely loved the Tonya confrontation chapter... did you have a favourite?

I hope you loved *My Daughter's Lies*. If you did, I'd be most grateful if you would take a few minutes to write a short review or leave a star rating. Not only is your feedback important to me, it can make a real difference in helping new readers discover an author for the first time.

I love hearing from my readers – you can get in touch on my Facebook page, through Twitter, Instagram, Goodreads or my website where you can also sign up to receive my newsletters should you choose to. I send them out periodically when I have some exciting book-related news to share or when I want to alert people to the competitions/giveaways that I run.

Again, thank you for choosing to read *My Daughter's Lies*,

Julia Roberts

KEEP IN TOUCH WITH JULIA

www.juliarobertsauthor.com

facebook.com/JuliaRobertsTV

x.com/JuliaRobertsTV

instagram.com/juliagroberts

ACKNOWLEDGEMENTS

This is where I say a huge thank you to all the members of 'Team Julia' for their work on *My Daughter's Lies*.

I have worked with a new editor for this book, Ruth Jones and I don't know who found the prospect most daunting at the outset. The relationship with your editor grows closer with every book you work on together as you each start to understand the other person's idiosyncrasies. I worked on five Bookouture titles with my previous editor (who was also a Ruth), so we'd ironed out a lot of the creases. I'll be honest and say I was a little nervous, just as we all are at the start of something new... a new job, a new relationship, even moving home to a new area. I needn't have worried. From the very first conversation with my new Ruth, I knew we were going to get along just fine.

It hasn't been the easiest book to write as I felt a little rusty having had a year away from writing due to personal issues, but Ruth has been patient, encouraging and persistent for us to make *My Daughter's Lies* the best it can be. I feel fortunate to have her as my new editor and hope we will have a long and productive relationship.

I'd also like to say a big thank you to my copy editor, Jade Craddock. It's so interesting when someone other than your editor sees the book for the first time and makes suggestions for small changes or notices something that requires more explanation. A book is definitely a team effort and I'm lucky to have both Jade and Ruth on Team Julia.

Thanks to my cover designer Alice Moore for agreeing to change the colour of what the mum on the cover is wearing – I love the magenta shade and feel it really pops from the background. And also for the team decision on the title which has intrigued people when I've mentioned it to them.

All the PR, publicity and marketing team members have my eternal thanks as I understand so little of what goes on behind the scenes to help my books to fly – just know that you are all so appreciated, but a special mention to Sarah Hardy for the work she puts in to organising blog tours and making suggestions on how best to spread the word prior to and post publication.

I always thank my family for the part they play in each new book, although to be fair, these days it is only my husband, Chris who bears the brunt of the long hours I spend tapping away on the computer. I'm very lucky that he is so amenable to bringing me drinks and snacks throughout the days at my writing desk and he's actually become a pretty good cook, making lots of delicious dinners from scratch – needs must, I guess!

I'm not sure he deserves thanks, but Wilfie the cat is an almost constant at my side while I'm writing, which is fine until he decides to add a few words of his own as he traverses the keyboard! Hopefully I edited them all out.

I must give a special shout out to my daughter's stepdaughter, Amber who is the same age as Ruby in the book and has been invaluable in checking the language that eighteen-year-olds use. And I must also thank my mum for her unwavering, 'Is that book finished yet?' question. Both she and Chris's mum, Audrey who sadly we lost shortly before publication of my previous book, *The Dilemma* read all my books and I'm pleased to say gave me very favourable feedback.

Which leads me to my final thank you, and it is to you for choosing to read *My Daughter's Lies*. What started out from a single line that sprang into my head, 'She's not who you think she is', has blossomed into a full-length novel which I truly hope you've enjoyed reading.

PUBLISHING TEAM

Turning a manuscript into a book requires the efforts of many people. The publishing team at Bookouture would like to acknowledge everyone who contributed to this publication.

Audio
Alba Proko
Melissa Tran
Sinead O'Connor

Commercial
Lauren Morrissette
Hannah Richmond
Imogen Allport

Cover design
Alice Moore

Data and analysis
Mark Alder
Mohamed Bussuri

Editorial
Ruth Jones
Melissa Tran

Copyeditor
Jade Craddock

Proofreader
Jennifer Davies

Marketing
Alex Crow
Melanie Price
Occy Carr
Cíara Rosney
Martyna Młynarska

Operations and distribution
Marina Valles
Stephanie Straub

Production
Hannah Snetsinger
Mandy Kullar
Jen Shannon

Publicity
Kim Nash
Noelle Holten
Jess Readett
Sarah Hardy

Rights and contracts
Peta Nightingale
Richard King
Saidah Graham

Made in the USA
Monee, IL
07 June 2024